Scotland or No

Peter Burnett

THIRSTY BOOKS
EDINBURGH

First published by Argyll Publishing under the imprint Thirsty Books in 2014.

Registered Office 1 Rutland Court, Edinburgh

© Peter Burnett

The moral rights of the authors have been asserted.

A catalogue record of this book is available from the British Library

ISBN 978-1-908931559

to Seán, or no

*'Through the mists beyond our watershed,
I hope that what I think I can glimpse might
actually emerge – a nation without the
disastrous paraphernalia of a nation state.'*

Angus Calder

1. The referendum vote is coming. It's what they want

I knew my father only through Twitter. That was the story of my twenty first year, a twenty first century story, and not having seen my dad for six years, however strange it seemed, I could at least observe him on social media.

Dad had once been a journalist and despite the ridicule he suffered since his sacking, he had taken to publishing conspiracy stories online. Every month he appeared with a new story about secret internet agencies and armies of online fakes, never backing up his claims, and perpetually pointing to evidence that he argued he could not reveal because it had been obtained by hacking, or by anonymous leaks. Once upon a time he had gone to press conferences and collaborated with other journalists crushed in the corners of Edinburgh's city bars, but now he worked alone and published through a blog, in which with the moral passion of a modern day prophet, and much like the other frothing bigots who blogged about Scottish politics, he styled all of Scotland's politicians, law lords and corporations as a criminal cabal, intent on enslaving the public.

I was fifteen years old the last time I'd seen my dad, it was the same time that he'd been sacked from *The Scotsman* newspaper. Now, other than his online writings, all that was known of him was one photograph, the same one which graced his social media profile. In this tiny image, a tousle-headed Dad leaned towards the viewer with a knowing smile. There was no address for him and no email and no phone numbers and sometimes people asked if he were even real, or whether he wasn't an online fake. Mum and I knew he was real, and although Mum spent every waking moment online she would have nothing to do with him. What a family business; he was a blogger, Mum was a social media addict. My aunt was a spammer, but that's another story. Mum had a couple of photos of Dad from the 1980s, but after that there was nothing, so all I had of my dad by the time I was twenty one was that one public profile photo and the same access as everyone else to the many web pages upon which he conducted his monstrous online battles.

Online, Dad ignored the rising claims of national feeling, and meticulously argued that armies of bullies were being employed to disrupt every democratic process in the land, and although he could barely prove any of this, he maintained that he had infiltrated the mechanisms of political power and that his big scoop was coming — although it never did. In his writing Dad came across as compulsive, edgy and not very bright, and mostly he talked about his belief that secret groups had been creating mass amounts of fake online personalities. Journalists and politicians were also frequent targets, particularly those in the employ of big media, but any public figure was fair game and overall Dad's blog gave the impression of a living room wall mapped in newspaper clipping push pins and balls of string — the classic conspiracy theorist.

It was a great surprise then in August of 2014 to spot him in Edinburgh. It was one month before Scotland went to the polls to vote YES or NO to the historic question: DO YOU THINK SCOTLAND SHOULD BE AN INDEPENDENT COUNTRY? and I had arrived back in the city after attending another dud job interview in London.

I was standing near Waverley train station, caught in a daydream below the arches of the North Bridge. The Edinburgh Festival was in full parade and backpackers, clowns and tourists clustered wherever I looked. There was something extra in the air in 2014, as the whole fell and bloody debate about the future of Scotland was nearing its highest point. Edinburgh was the centre of attention, you need not have doubted that, and it appeared that all the world had stopped to look at us. I had never seen so many tourists on our streets, and the competing British and Scottish flags and the political canvassers made an odd addition to the public fray.

It was at this spot and while I was rapt in meditation, that I saw Dad emerging from the gloomful doorway of one of the narrow closes near the Edinburgh Dungeon tourist haunt, and I watched as he disappeared again up one of the many stone passageways that climb the sloping tail of rock that makes up the city's Old Town. I was stunned for a moment, and asked myself how did I know that the man I had just seen was my dad?

It was a good question. It may have been uncomfortable for me to attribute a form of instinctive recognition to my thinking, but nonetheless as I crossed the road to follow him I knew it could not have been anyone else. I stepped into Carrubbers Close in time to see Dad moving with purpose up the pend and I made after him, arriving on the High Street where I circled the Festival crowd, fearing I had lost him. Dad had taken refuge in one of the other narrow alleys and when I had made my way after him and peered down Dickson's Close, I saw his back bustling quickly down there. Without any delay I ran after him and once I was in the shade and away from the noise of the High Street I shouted: 'Hey Dad!' at him.

The old man certainly missed a step when he heard the word 'Dad', but he didn't turn, and so I shouted again and stumbled after him with my heavy bag, determined not to let him escape. It was only when we reached the veiled stone overhangs near the foot of Dickson's Close that I obliged him to stop and face me and when he did we gazed at each other like strangers. Close up Dad looked scared and his eyes darted to and fro. Then he moved me by the shoulders into a doorway saying: 'Alan we have to get off the street.'

I looked up the close, a sombrous array of dirty back doors and bins, but there was nobody else to be seen. Dad glanced about and said: 'Are you alone?' and 'Where did you come from?' Then I noticed that he was frisking me, and checking my pockets. 'Give me your phone,' he said although he already had it and was giving it the once over. Then: 'What's in the bag?'

'My clothes,' I said. 'I've just been to London.'

With a small tool not unlike a paperclip Dad took the battery out of my phone and then he opened my bag and rifled through it before suddenly looking sheepish.

'Have you followed me?' he asked, and he produced his own phone and snapped a picture of me.

'I follow your blog,' I said and although this was just for something to say the truth was that nobody could follow Dad's blog. Surprisingly, the idea that I had read his work made Dad more nervous still.

'Not everybody is who they say they are,' he said.

Now that I was close to him, Dad was not the man I remembered. In my imagination there had been more to him than this, but here was a small, piercing-eyed man, his face lean and his whole demeanour closed and furtive. Somehow when I had thought of him in the past I had imagined conversations, laughs and gifts, cycle rides and holidays and a world of affection that belonged to another universe. Dad perhaps felt the same thing. Here he was as plain as print, as if all of those walks in the hills and birthday presents had really happened, as if they were memories and not fantasies. In that second there seemed no difference.

'What are you up to?' I asked and Dad's brow creased.

'Occasionally I need to see stuff for myself,' he said. 'I need to see if certain people are real and not just the invention of Sandy Steward.'

'Who's Sandy Steward?' I asked and Dad's eyes snapped back to fix me with a most intense stare.

'That's a very Sandy Steward question to ask,' he said. 'You say you read my blog but if you did you'd know that Sandy Steward is the one taking this independence referendum apart.'

Dad looked up the empty close to the High Street. He pulled some scraps of paper from his pocket.

'I've been smeared for years and not just by Steward,' he said. 'Just don't believe what you read about me online Alan. I have to go now.'

Dad let go of me but it was like being dropped in a hole. He stepped out of the doorway and checked his phone, his jacket matching the blotted out murk of the wall. As he turned to say goodbye to me he must have sensed my disappointment.

'Sorry,' he said, 'but this is a bad time. If you can't silence someone then you can at least persuade the world that person is mad. The referendum vote is coming. It's what they want,' he said, ' — and take this,' and with that he gave me the following print out which had nine names on it — a seemingly normal enough list. 'These people are trolls and they've all written their own smear articles about Scottish politicians,' he said, 'but they are all one person and that person is Sandy Steward.'

I looked at the list:

NAME	ALIAS	ADDRESS	TOWN
Stuart B Strathie	weementalstuarty	12 Pennan Road	Bankfoot
Mary Rintoul	bogsider	16 Mayfield Road	Methven
Charles Fraser	lion1961	18 Mayfield Road	Methven
Anne Courser	anonymous	10 Union Court	Blackness
Billie Chisholm	hairytoes	18 Union Court	Blackness
Gerry Macdonald	antlers	34 Elgin Road	Blackness
Lars Olsen	problembear	4 Teal Street	Memsie
Brian Thill	anonymous	12 Hyndford's Close	Edinburgh
Andrea Killen	jako	5 Sanquhar Court	Blackness

'Believe it,' he said. 'They are all Sandy. He has hundreds of these accounts.'

Dad was mantled in the darkness of the doorway and gazed at me in defiance. It had been six years since I'd seen him. Back then he had been one of the boys, just another boisterous hack, and it had been fun to see him in those newspaper offices where he seemed to me to be a most important person. Now he was more like a tramp.

'Go,' he said, and I backed towards the High Street.

'Could I at least have your phone number?' I asked.

'Leave messages for me at my blog,' he said. 'I won't reply, but I will get them.'

The thought of my polite enquiries for Dad displayed on his blog, along with the many crude effusions of the enormous army of his abusers, did not inspire me. It was hard to see what Dad was scared of, and sad. It was sad that he was the victim of his own energy and fervour and just my bad luck, I thought, that I might not now see him again for another six years.

When I reached the top of the close I could still see him and he waved. Then he swung around and was gone into the sheer crowds of Edinburgh, off back to the computer screens of spleen from where he tweeted his thoughts to the world.

That was when an unfamiliar anger hit me as if I really had missed out on something from having this absent wanderer as a father and I wondered if having laid hold of him this once, I might never have the chance again.

2. Many members of the public are not even real

I returned to my flat in Forrest Road, thinking about my dad and Twitter. My route took me through the packed Old Town where tourists were serenaded by buskers and regaled by actors dressed as warriors and crones, while above them the splendour of the skies lay unveiled. Visitors young and old stared in open-mouthed awe at the ancient facades and overhanging tenements of Edinburgh, even though for myself it had become exhausting and finally commonplace. Having been brought up in various small flats and caravans in the Borders, it was pleasant to be in the centre of Edinburgh, but the entire square mile was changed beyond recognition, captioned with signs pointing to fake histories and shops selling off our nation, one tartan tammy at a time.

Arriving at my door, which was at the base of a tenement upon which were ornately carved the words Oddfellows Hall, I pulled out my phone and checked Dad's Twitter and saw that he was active. He was fighting with someone, and there was no mention of his meeting his long-missed son.

I was no stranger to Twitter and although I didn't use it for personal business having nothing to say and not wishing to say it, I still managed several hundred accounts. This business of having multiple social media accounts had begun one year before when I'd answered an advert looking for a flatmate. That was when I met Edinburgh's resident self-styled 'psychogeographer' Iain Inglis, and within ten minutes of my knocking on his door I had moved in and established that we both loved computers. By the end of that day Iain and I were in business together, and had started a company called Friendly Social Media.

This had come about when Iain had agreed to acquire Facebook LIKES for a friend, and we had achieved this at first through a number of hacks, until finally we found it was quicker and safer setting up our own false Facebook accounts. Both Iain and I shared a competitive attitude to these false accounts and within a month we had 600 Facebook profiles between us. This grew over the first year of my unemployment in Edinburgh until we had created several thousand Twitter accounts as well as any amount of accounts with other social media sites. Some of our account creation was automated, as was much of the activity of our sock puppet accounts, but the more companies and websites our fictional personae endorsed, the more real our fakes became.

Our only expense in this process was the purchase of

proxy internet addresses through which we routed our activity. A proxy is an address on the internet that you use instead of your own, because if you are running thousands of social media accounts it is best if they don't appear to all come from the same house. Iain and I were busy and happy however because what we did was in huge demand as everybody wanted to display that their company was LIKED by thousands of people, and even if they were not real people it did not matter, as most internet users would judge a business on that figure alone. None of what Iain and I did was illegal but our sock puppets did have blogs, photos, backstories and plentiful friends. Having looked at Dad's list of suspected fake accounts I hadn't been surprised. I was presiding over something similar, a digital army that myself and Iain employed for a few quid a time. With this army we made just below minimum wage, because as hard as we worked, what we hadn't considered at the outset was that in reality, LIKEs are cheap.

Like myself, Iain had graduated in computer science although his real passion was his psychogeography. What psychogeography meant as far as I could ascertain was an intense personal topography which often found Iain travelling the city on foot, examining street signs and photographing street furniture. From this, he drew charts showing ancient paths, marking the dead spaces between building projects and other developments. For Iain this was the antidote to the virtual services we provided and an alternative way of exploring the city's history, both of which were important, because we found that spending so much time online somewhat distanced us from life.

Virtual services. I'm not sure whether the meeting with

Dad had soured me, but something about this term struck me as deadly as myself and my shoulder bag apologised our way through the crowds to my front door. The world was busy. A squat red mail van loaded up outside the post office watched by the smokers who gathered at Sandy Bell's World Renowned Folk Bar. A group of pony-tailed technicians bantered at the back door of the Bedlam Theatre while the tourists on the pavement interlocked, taking photographs. Nearby and in the face of the sun a larger group of tourists gathered at Edinburgh's most despised historic remnant, the statue of Greyfriars Bobby. Year round people gathered at this midgetous effigy and photographed it although they knew not why. Iain and I could see the wee dog's statue from our window and longed to tell the visitors that Bobby was created by Disney. That whole concoction of Bobby was then somehow grafted to this junction near our door, and the statue was considered one of Edinburgh's most important artefacts.

I climbed the stairs still thinking about Dad. When I got into the flat Iain was working with sheets of paper many of which he'd sellotaped to the wall, the centrepiece, a diagram of a human arm with electrodes attached to the hand and shoulder.

'Hello Alan,' he said. His dark hair and eyes displayed an intensity that made me realise that I had come in during one of his brainstorms. Glancing between myself and the diagram, Iain assumed that I was keen to know immediately what he'd discovered, and so he continued with a lazy matter-of-factness. 'Skin is an amazing conductor of broadband,' he said. 'Very low frequency signals can stream a movie faster along your skin than our home set-up, and completely safely, and with less interference. Uses 90% less power than Bluetooth too. That must have applications?'

Rudimentary as the drawings were I could see that Iain had been thinking about health apps for phones, another dire money earner, got bored, and ended up designing something that looked like a cross between a Dalek and Google. In the frame was a person with a headset, a phone, and other devices like remote controls attached to them.

'It's just an idea,' said Iain. 'Practically anything conducts broadband better than wireless. Salt is good. And the earth. The earth is very good.'

This happened time and again. Iain's ideas ran off with him, but, with flair and flawed logic, he found no difficulty in seeing each one of them to the end.

'What is it?' he asked looking at me. 'Did you get the job?'

'No, it's not that,' I said, and I realised I was still carrying my bag. I dropped it and told him: 'I've just seen my dad.'

Iain's eyes widened. 'The troll?' he said.

'He's obsessed with this guy called Sandy Steward,' I said. 'He kept going on about him.'

'I know that person,' said Iain. 'He writes a hill-walking blog. He's the guy your dad accuses of running everything. Your dad hates him, that's all I know.'

'What does he do?' I asked.

Iain bid me follow him, and led me to the overburdened in-tray which lay in his window recess.

'Nothing suspicious,' he said, digging. 'There are rumours about Steward but most of them derive from your old man I'm afraid. Your dad says that Steward uses persona management software to interfere with politics. Your dad wrote a bunch of articles saying that Sandy Steward is part of a group called No Scotland.'

I knew what persona management was because it was in its most basic form how I earned my living. Our own persona management software allowed Iain and myself to monitor several thousand accounts but it would never make them seem real in regards of any official scrutiny. Iain found the sheet of paper he'd been looking for.

'Your dad hates this dude,' he said. 'Ranald Stewart says and I quote that Sandy Steward has groups of 100 fake personas per user, assigned to he doesn't know how many users, and each persona has a complete background, complete history with supporting details that are, and I quote again, technically, culturally and geographically consistent. This all happens from one workstation and personas can appear to originate in any part of the world and can interact through conventional online services and social media platforms. Then it goes on about powerful deniability, which you can imagine has your dad accusing this Sandy guy of leaving false trails also.'

Iain paused. 'Your dad has proved nothing though. All he has are accusations. He says that Steward is running these fake accounts for political ends. He says he's using them to attack journalists and independence campaigners, but when you look up Sandy Steward, all you see apart from your dad's smears and accusations is the guy's hillwalking blog. It's all quite innocent.'

I stared at the sheets that described the sort of software my dad had been speculating about. I thought I had been pretty sharp creating all those false Twitter accounts but my users didn't have home addresses, and nor did they have National Insurance numbers. I went to the window and looked towards the bustling Old Town.

'It's the Independence Referendum next month,' said Iain. 'At least after that they'll give it a rest and the battle will be over for a while. Now tell me again did you have a nice trip?'

'Yes,' I said, 'but I fluffed the interview. They kept looking at me strange. I think they found out about my hacking charges.'

'Those were dropped,' said Iain and I nodded.

'Stuff sticks,' I said. 'They can dig up anything. They may have heard about my aunt and her spam farm.'

'Your family sound nuts,' said Iain. 'Are they all cyber criminals?'

'How did we do while I was away?' I asked.

Iain's eyes darted to our pile of mail. 'I haven't opened a single letter in a week,' he said. 'There's no money in LIKEs so I'm trying to figure out something new for us to do. Worse than that there's some competition on the block.'

I turned from the window but I did so with a double take. I thought I'd seen my dad down there slipping into the penumbral slope of Candlemaker Row, a tiny Edinburgh street that led from Greyfriars Bobby's sanctimonious wee perch to the drunken darks of the Cowgate. It hadn't been Dad however but merely another shabby guy in a coat. I blinked and wondered once again if he really did stay nearby.

'Look at these names,' said Iain. 'They were all signatories to what they call the National Convention. It's a bullshit kind of statement to the effect that Scotland should remain within the United Kingdom, a campaign that you click to support.

Your dad thinks this is all a part of this group called No Scotland. I mean: No Scotland? Sounds like a basic epistemological denial of a place that is definitely there. The declaration says: We the undersigned stand against the idea that Scotland should separate from the United Kingdom. And this is fine except that I noticed that the signatories aren't real. Look at the website.'

National Convention is a non-party movement founded with the aims of purging Scotland of apathy by registering every young person to vote.

We hope to reach every Scottish city town and community and aim for a 100% turn-out in every current and future election.

In 2014 donations have allowed us to register 1000s of young people for voting in local and national elections as well as the Independence Referendum.

Fraser Evans	**5 Balvenie Wynd**	**Blackness**
Pascal Farrington	**7 Balvenie Wynd**	**Blackness**
Jane Rodger	**9 Balvenie Wynd**	**Blackness**
Musheer Anand	**11 Balvenie Wynd**	**Blackness**
Christina Renton	**13 Balvenie Wynd**	**Blackness**

'Socks,' said Iain proudly. 'This is exactly the sort of pathetic thing your old man was going on about. But look, they all live in the same street. It's changed now, but the first hundred people to sign this declaration were almost consecutive neighbours.'

By socks Iain meant sock puppets, which was another name for fake profiles like the ones we used for our company, good old Friendly Social Media. I looked at the screen. If you were going to create online identities and use them for campaigning, you would have been better advised not to have your fabricated people all living in the same street.

Delving into my back pocket I found the piece of paper from Dad and I showed it to Iain who searched Google maps for the town of Blackness which was about fifteen miles from Edinburgh up the coast towards the petrochemical refineries at Grangemouth.

'Is that where all these people live?'' I asked.

Iain showed me his Google maps reference. 'Yep,' he said. 'They're all there. Blackness is a town of 9,000 people, mostly new build houses, but there's a school and swimming pool and an old castle.'

I looked at the maps but that didn't tell me much. Iain selected STREET VIEW and we took one of those virtual walks around Blackness, waiting only to refresh the screen to see the next portion of the street, the next scrubbed out human face.

Funny,' I said. 'I'd never thought of using our socks for political ends but I suppose it could be done.'

'Barely,' said Iain. 'There must be real people in those houses so I don't quite get what's going on.'

For several minutes we continued that virtual tour of Blackness eventually scrolling to the water's edge where a row of boats were prettily moored on the Firth of Forth.

'I'm guessing,' said Iain, 'that someone has added a layer of reality to these personas by giving them real addresses but they've done it clumsily, because the consecutive addresses obviously makes them look fake.'

I held Dad's scrap of paper in my hand. The paper was

now my sole memento of his minimal role in my life. I scrolled the maps application out so that I was able to see the entire town of Blackness with its neat rows of houses nestled comfortably amid the fields of West Lothian.

'Whatever it is,' said Iain with a smirk, 'I'm going to track it down. It intrigues me and we may learn something or even hook up with some of these virtual people. It could be fun.'

We checked the details of the National Convention, which seemed to be a properly funded group in service of the NO vote, talking about encouraging young people to vote, to register to vote, and to make the most use of their freedom of speech.

This is National Convention. Write for us, share our content, participate in our projects, and add yourself to the growing resource pool.

'Who makes this up?' Iain asked.

'My dad says this is Sandy Steward's group,' I said. 'The deeper you go, the murkier the waters, the murkier the waters, the harder it is to see who anyone is. But Dad definitely thinks that National Convention is a part of it. Everything's part of it.'

'Part of what?' Iain asked.

'A good question,' I said. 'I think he would describe it as an underground political attempt at mass influence through relentless use of social media. All these writers and artists have signed up to it, and the public will too — although comparing these two lists it looks like many members of the public are not even real.'

I glanced across the lists and then put them down, and Iain and I stared at each other with a good moment's pause for thought. Something of dad's keenness had infiltrated the room, and I remembered again my astonishment at seeing him, and my anger that he had left so quickly. Now I wanted more than ever to speak to him.

3. There's no Ran Stewart, and you certainly can't be his son

It had been two weeks since I'd bumped into Dad and although I found myself reading his blog every day, the actual evidence he had for his theories was barely measurable. I was even taking an interest in the referendum itself, although Dad's blog wasn't a good place to start.

His blog didn't so much discuss actual political issues, as reiterate the dirty tricks he accused Sandy Steward of master-minding, and the wickedness of the NO campaign. Despite the lack of moderation and journalistic etiquette however, Dad's blog did at least present a full-throated articulation of how the NO side were cheating the public process. Conspiracy theories always lead upwards and generally in the direction of billionaire tycoons, and Dad's work was typical in that respect. Donald Phiggs, the untouchable controller at the zenith of Dad's pyramid of paranoia was an American business magnate and the president of Phiggs Entertainment Resorts, which owned the occasional golf course in Scotland. Phiggs was one of the wealthiest entrepreneurs in the world, in fact, and with his twin passions for Scotland, he said, and democracy, he was the perfect target for Dad, because no link could be proved between Phiggs and No Scotland, except that Phiggs was supposed to have donated to The National Convention. Even that was something that Dad could ill prove on his blog, but all day long Dad sent Phiggs and his associates menacing tweets, messaging like fury, demanding that Phiggs respond to his allegations, in short doing everything he could to stress a link between Phiggs and NO.

Every message that Dad sent online was tagged #indyref. That was the common hashtag for the discussion of Scottish independence in 2014, although in the final few months leading up to the vote, the subject came to encompass a whole lot more. What had started as a political attempt to separate Scotland from the United Kingdom became something more vital, a conversation about the inefficiency of British party politics and a persistent debate among the people regarding inequalities — at least that was what I was discovering. This was movement politics, as opposed to professional politics, and it was something that everybody, even myself could be involved with. I hadn't seen the likes of that since the Occupy movement, but more than Occupy, the debate for Scottish independence swept us all up and promised something for everybody.

Where I worked, on the internet, #indyref was a war of

words, a battle that raged between two legions of political writers and the sputtering clicks of bloggers that had mobilised to attack this subject head on. But among the people a spark was lit, and although it might not have been directly related to independence, people found themselves discussing health, wealth, poverty, law and sovereignty in a way they never had before — all because of #indyref. In its initial appearance, this was a final chance for Scotland to leave the United Kingdom and become a small country in its own right, often like Norway they said, perhaps like Denmark they said, a small country and not part of a larger united entity such as Britain, they said. In the final run up however everybody was talking politics, and wherever I went discussion was inevitable. That was a good thing for people like me who avoided talking politics, and the end consensus was that regardless of the vote, the previously unengaged mob to which I belonged had begun to care more carefully about the social order. It was 2014 and the vote was coming any day now, and people asked each other all day how they were going to vote.

I had no evidence to go on but I had selected a couple of places where I was sure Dad might have lived, and I began to search for him. One of these places was James Court which is the largest of all the Old Town squares and home to the Jolly Judge pub, and once home to many historic luminaries such as David Hume and James Boswell, you can look them up, I had to. There was no reason for me to assume that Dad stayed in James Court other than it fitted a romantic notion that I'd secured myself, something to do with my fondness for the ten storey tenements which teetered over the sloping street. I imagined the shabby figure of my father turning the corner to slip into one of this place's many tiny doors, and so I went to James Court one evening to look for him. I'd searched for him online but all I could ever find were the same smears and chatlogs. He didn't reply to messages and he didn't leave any clues. That didn't stop others having a go at him, and there seemed to be a barrage of offensive posts for and about my father, like:

@ranstew is not well and yanking his chain isn't funny

and

@ranstew I'd like to staple the truth to your chest ya numpty

So it was that I walked to James Court one evening and began to wait in the hope that I might see him. The nearby Royal Mile was dying of tourists, but there were still one or two, enough to justify that the show continue. At the side of the road were at least two kilted figures with swords and Braveheart face make-up, the pair of them silently draped in Saltires, which is the famous blue and white Scottish flag. A stall that had been selling Celtic jewellery daily since May looked ragged and exhausted, and the sellers ready to go home. I waited in James Court looking around me and watching the doorways until nine in the evening when I turned for home. It was then that I was hailed by someone as I gave up my lonely station.

'Young man,' said a gruff voice and I looked up from my phone to see that I was being addressed by a smartly dressed man of middle age. He was smoking a cigar.

'For whom do you look?' asked the stranger. His smile was crooked, probably due to alcohol, and although it may have been a genuine attempt at kindness I found his leer sinister.

'Why do you ask?' I said.

'My boy,' said the stranger in the cigar smoke, 'you look forlornly at these tenements and then at your phone and you wander around the square like a lost dog. I know most of the people here so I'm asking in case I can help.'

I looked at this man and I admitted that I had seen his type before, an establishment individual who probably, I thought, worked at the nearby courtrooms. The man was not deterred by my silence and gazed hard at me with his head cocked, so as to mentally repeat his question. I glanced above me to the hundreds of windows that overlooked James Court and wondered again if Dad was in there somewhere. About a quarter of the windows were lit demonstrating some meagre occupancy and I focused on these, aware that if my guesses ever proved correct Dad could be watching me right now.

'I'm looking for my father,' I said to the man. 'I think he lives round here.'

The man whom I decided must have been a lawyer smiled softly and nodded, sympathetic to this case and pleased to have his curiosity satisfied so far as to have extracted from me an answer.

'What's his name?' asked the man. 'I'm an old QC and I get around these parts. I've lived here 35 years just in this very court.'

'He used to be a journalist,' I said. 'His name is Ranald Stewart.'

I suspect that the choking noise that this cigar-smoking Queen's Counsel made arose in an effort to stifle his laughter because his face became redder yet, and even though he wiped his eyes there still remained a smile on his face and a spluttering confusion in his voice.

'You are joking?' he managed speaking into his handkerchief. 'That's very funny,' he added, wiping his brow.

'Not funny,' I said angrily, 'but true. So tell me, does he live here?'

The stranger took several small puffs on his cigar, composed himself and said: 'I don't know what you're researching and it's probably quite innocent but Ranald Stewart doesn't have any children and he certainly doesn't live around here.'

My phone buzzed and I saw that Dad had tweeted once more. Each waking hour of the day Dad tweeted and so there were always a steady stream. I held the phone up so that its blue electric glow reflected in the twin screens of this man's spectacles and I showed him the picture of Dad. Stepping closer to the man, and near enough to smell the aroma of the pub that clung to his suit, I showed him the picture. He waved it away.

'I've seen that,' he said, 'and I've no desire to see it again. I'm surprised at you but since you're young I'll give you some advice for free. Take it from me and I know this. Just because somebody has a Twitter account it doesn't mean they are a real person.'

I gathered myself enough to respond. 'I told you he's my father. His name is Ranald Stewart and he used to work at *The Scotsman*. He runs his own blog.'

But the smoking stranger shook his head. 'It's a nice story,' he said, 'but Ranald Stewart does not exist. He's an agit-prop social media account created by nationalists to discredit politicians, spread smears and release so-called leaks, most of which are fake anyway. I work in the law and I see it all the time.'

'Why would anyone do that?' I asked, shocked.

He spoke more quietly: 'As an example, one might use a Ranald Stewart to prejudice a legal case by releasing information that's prohibited by law. That's just one possibility of many, but I'm telling you this because even if yours is a mission of innocent curiosity, you would be better going home. There's no Ran Stewart, and you certainly can't be his son, so I would give up on that lie before these people come after you. They've ruined lives before.'

I pocketed my phone. The man of law smoked and he said no more. I backed away willing myself to thank him for the advice but unable to do so, and so I nodded and left the scene.

On the way home I flicked to read Dad's live tweets, they were the same old.

> **RAN — I can give you scoops. I've been handing them out like candy to the press just to have the press ignore them.**

> **USER — The press ignore you cause you're a whackadoo.**

> **RAN — Sandy Steward has tried to press charges against me because I wrote articles about him. Articles got shut down.**

> **USER — But Steward wasn't doing anything wrong.**

> **RAN — Sandy Steward is a vindictive extremist paid to create hundreds of profiles. He has been harassing me for years with those profiles.**

> **USER — Listen to yourself.**

RAN — Look at all those accounts that troll me. They are all Sandy Steward.

USER — They are people who think you are a freak.

RAN — I have e-mails to prove it some of which I'm still going through. I made the first round of e-mails available for download but they were taken down. They all get taken down.

I reached our front door and climbed the steps. Perhaps, I thought, I will leave this alone. It might, I thought, be easier to find Dad online and trace him that way.

'What is it?' asked Iain when I mooched in.

'It's Dad,' I said. 'I just met someone who said my dad wasn't real and that he is in fact a made-up political tool.'

'He's real enough on Twitter,' said Iain.

'I know, I've just been reading it,' I said. 'They're saying this is all a sideshow, though, for misleading the public.'

Iain shrugged, and although I sat down at the computer and began my social media effort as I did each evening, my heart was not in the process. I was thinking of Dad and the temptation to flick over to his blog was awful. Dad was out there somewhere, inveighing against the elite who were now manipulating opinion by flooding the internet with fake profiles, and even though his writing never led to a conclusion, I still wanted to read it, like it were a soap opera which drove from episode to episode, promising resolution in increasingly larger circles. That resolution however was not to be found, and although Dad left clues, such as tweets, emails and chat-logs posted by people he said didn't even exist, I wasted hours in reaching infuriating dead ends.

That night, like others, I found myself staring at Dad's profile picture, and I trembled at the prospect that I might meet him again. I had at my disposal several details about him I could claim as true, including that picture, but my information was somehow out of focus. I knew some of the facts, but I had no idea of the reality of Dad, and it appeared that the only reliable way to get any information about him was from the most unfailing source on the internet, which was gossip. Dad was real enough on Twitter, I would have agreed with that, but the idea that he was an invention, or a smear artist, made me long to know him, and find out what he really knew. He was a man yes, but a man whose substance was elusive, and I thought again of that creepy QC and wondered what he and others like him could gain from persuading me that Dad was not, and never had been, real.

4. Fake smoke and dirty mirrors

Edinburgh's Old Town is such a formidable tourist destination that all things Scots are arranged on every wall and window display, and they stay there even when the weather is turning poor. I say this because it happened that on my next trip along the Royal Mile that I stopped thinking about Dad and started thinking about politics, a field in which he professed to operate, when I came face to face with my destiny, scripted in curls and tails on the street wall of the embarrassingly named Robert Burns Tavern. The rain was beginning to fall, and I found myself staring at these lines, which I must have passed a hundred times without reading:

> *O wad some Power the giftie gie us*
> *To see oursels as ithers see us!*

It was September and the vote was nearly upon us, and although the city's festivals were over, some hardy visitors persisted. What floored me concerning the tackily printed lines of Robert Burns' poem *To a Louse* was the nature of the Scots language and a peculiar revulsion took over me concerning my place in this scheme of things.

To be precise it was the word *giftie* that bugged me so. Was this a trick of the Scots language? Not only did the extending of the word *gift* to *giftie* allow the couplet to scan, but it gave the verse a quaint flavour as parochial and crudely expressed as the painted picture of Burns himself that decorated the wall. The poet had performed a cheap trick to wow the Edinburgh ladies and after a couple of centuries the owner of the Robert Burns Tavern had performed an equally crass miracle by painting a shitty Burns-like face on the exterior of their premises and finishing it off with this famous quote. Tourists were drawn towards this verse, suckered by the quaint gravity of the lines, but to simply misspell English, I thought, did not make Scots. Is this how *would* became *wad* and *give* became *gie*? Rooted to the spot I wondered if there was even such a thing as Scots?

'What's the problem?' somebody asked. There was a woman in an apron straight ahead of me and I hadn't even seen her. She was resting on the wall of the Robert Burns Tavern.

'Nothing,' I said. 'I've just never read that before.'

The woman wiped her hands on her apron and turned to face the words I'd been reading.

'Plain enough shite,' she said. 'We painted that years ago. Believe it or not, it really draws them in.'

'It's a good sentiment,' I said, but she shook her head.

'Try no to buy it,' she answered me. 'Like the independence stuff it sounds good. But it's a trick.'

'I don't know how I'm voting yet,' I pleaded.

She dropped her cigarette on to the cobbles and smudged it extinct while we both watched a brewery lorry pass, followed by a police van. The two vehicles bumped down the uneven road, barrels gently bashing on the truck while the police van seemed tooled to the rafters with aerials, cameras and riot equipment.

'I mean,' said the woman from the Robert Burns, 'what divides people is not their country. The same bastards will always be in charge.'

I nodded that I understood and glanced across the frontage of the Robert Burns Tavern. It had been a narrow escape, but in the course of avoiding the subject of the referendum I had surprised myself. The answer that I didn't know how I was voting had been enough to satisfy her, but it was me that wasn't convinced now.

The woman in the apron smiled and I smiled back, once more reading those crazy lines of Robert Burns.

As I walked slowly up the Royal Mile with these thoughts in mind I was confronted in a sudden swoop by a tall grey man whose face was drawn with blood and whose clothes hung in tatters. The ghoul raised his arms as if to attack me, and he moaned, his eyeballs bulging and a gaping wound in his side revealing a dagger wound. It was Ghost Tour Doug and I smiled as I admired his dramatic get up.

'How's that thin tissue of lies you call a business?' asked Doug and he took my hand leaving a splash of body make-up on my sleeve.

'That tissue of lies got your own business off the ground you cheeky bastard,' I responded, shaking his hand.

Doug smiled, revealing blackened teeth and blood clot. There were at least five ghost tours in Edinburgh's Old Town and Iain and I had boosted Doug's operation and ended up making his one popular for a brief time. That was what you could do with Facebook LIKES back then, merely providing them offered a business a strange credibility.

'So. How's that thin tissue of lies you call a business?' I asked him and he made to hit me.

'Steady!' he said, then he whispered, closing in so that only I would hear what he had to say. 'You know how it goes. People expect a bit of the supernatural. We tell them grue-some tales of auld Edinburgh and everybody's happy.' Doug was correct in that assumption and looking towards the castle I could see another two men in robes regaling a small group of tourists.

'How are you ghosts going to vote in the referendum?' I asked, a question that caused Doug the ghoul to laugh.

He scratched a fake wart. 'The ghosts will be voting YES,' he said and he looked wistfully up the Royal Mile. As far as we could see there were adverts for shows, for drinks and for cinema spectaculars, posted to walls, booths and stands. 'You would hardly know the referendum vote is happening though,' he said. 'Don't you remember when you were wee and there would be an election and every lamppost and railing in the country was covered in cardboard signs? I don't know why they don't do that anymore. I guess it's all online now.'

Seeing that he was needed by a nearby group of tourists, Ghost Tour Doug bowed and departed, smiling evilly at me as he licked his lips in anticipation of the monetary feast he would make of these latest victims. I watched him work for a moment, raising his arms in mock horror and causing many giggles among his audience.

With nothing else to do, I was in no hurry to get home and so I began to wander from shop to shop, thinking about what I'd read on the wall and wondering what would turn my DON'T KNOW regarding the referendum, to a YES.

In one shop I found myself facing the racks of wines, beers and the other concoctions that exist far beyond the potentialities of either, and although it wasn't my habit to drink, this had always been for lack of experimenting and I had had it in the back of my mind that I should like to try it and see what mental revels ensued. Then I'll engage Iain in debate, I thought, and we'll have it out, and sort all our referendum issues in one glorious sitting.

The main choices of drink within this smallest of the small shops were of the cheap and potent kinds that Scots prefer. These were golden tins of cider and bottles of blue carbonated alcohol with suggestive names that in themselves were vaguely frightening when you considered how descriptive they could be ('Reelers', 'Sheet Lightning' and 'Vievely'). These bottles were racked with tightly-packed plastic containers of strong ciders, most of which borrowed their marketing liveries from the world of gambling. The wines looked syrupy and promised realms of darkness behind smoked glass, but all the wines being priced the same, I took the one with the prettiest label and purchased it, and began my walk back home.

Clutching my wine, I resolved that I would turn to thinking

about politics. It occurred to me that Iain was the only person I knew who had not so far expressed an opinion on Scotland's future, or asked me how I was going to vote, and I wondered if it wasn't time to challenge him. It would certainly help my own thinking on the matter, I realised. I passed the statue of the god-awful Greyfriars Bobby which even at 10pm on a September night still had a small crowd of tourists around it, and as if I were already drunk I barged through the tourists, pulling my bottle of wine from its paper bag and reading the label as I walked. I surveyed the bottle, trying to make sense of the image printed on it, that of a man with a red nose, a cartoon image which was charming if crudely expressed. Looking at the bottle as my pace grew slower I wondered if the purchase of the drink was not an answer to Robert Burn's question. Here am I, I thought, mulling as others before me on the possibility of a miraculous power being granted which would bring self-knowledge and the ability to witness myself from an objective viewpoint, and maybe even answer great questions. Perhaps, I thought, drink will bring that power, and maybe the wine will furnish this *giftie* and place everything in perspective.

I was midway through this appealing revelation when the door of Sandy Bell's World Renowned Folk Bar swung open and a tangle of three people tumbled into me, causing my wine to leave my hands and land in the gutter.

The magic potion exploded and a black and bloody splash hit the streets in a mess of broken glass, with myself falling after it. As the wine exploded into a stain, my heart sank, not because the drink had gone but because the moment had been taken. In that bashed up green smash of wine-darkened glass lay revelation. A national expedition of exploration had been cancelled and the outcomes would never be known.

The largest of the three, the one that had knocked the wine from my hand, now grasped my arm and began apologising. He wore an army-green anorak and spoke with the nasal twang of the Edinburgh streets, offering me five pounds, holding the sides of his head and saying: 'Naw!'

While this guy was apologising he was berated by his female companion who kept saying to him 'The offie's shut Barry,' reminding us that since off-sales ceased at ten o'clock my wine couldn't be replaced even if I accepted his money. As I had passed from the sober contemplation of potential drunkenness into the whirl of these people's inebriation I thought it best to just leave them and I made to cross the road but they did not want that to happen.

'Come into the bar,' Barry kept saying, all the while rifling his anorak for money.

'Let us buy you one,' said the lady companion. She was friendly though unsure on her feet and dressed for battle in black leather.

The third of this turbulent hubbub of drinkers was an intellectual type, and although he wore a long coat and didn't seem to be as drunk as the other two, he was not aloof from these invitations and took my arm.

'We're real sorry about that son. One of these awful things but you seem to be taking it well. See if it had been the other way round, Barry'd have battered you. So come on.'

I glanced at the door of Sandy Bell's bar, a frosted glass portal through which I had never passed despite it being opposite my own front door, and strange as it was, I accepted.

Within the bar was a world I didn't know, but my wine was gone and so one way or another, I realised as I was ushered inside, I would be drinking tonight.

The interior of Sandy Bell's pub was warm with many people of a sociable nature lining the walls. In there the trio of Barry, Mhairi and Walfrid — he was the intellectual one — squeezed me in at the end of the bar and delivered me of my first pint. As they resumed their conversation which was of politics, I listened carefully and politely. The bar was all a yatter and whichever way I looked I met a smile. The blether was of course about Scotland's referendum for independence which was now only three days away and it appeared that Barry had been campaigning for a YES vote for years. Indeed, Barry's question to me was not how I would vote, but if I could contain myself for the next few days given the obvious excitement.

'Can you even wait?' he asked, but entertained by my new surroundings and struggling to cope with the sudden loss of what I realised had been my first ever solo bottle of wine, I replied that I would be glad when it was over.

Now Sandy Bell's is as lively as any other bar in Edinburgh and is perhaps more lively than most given that its owners eschew the curse of piped music on their premises. In Sandy's there is always some real music playing courtesy of the local musicians, and by *real* be in no doubt that this means actual instruments played by people, which you do not often see these days in Scotland that is a fact. Still, I don't know how my words came to be heard by the fifty or so people in there but they were. Perhaps it was a latent pub instinct which allowed the collected entity of drinkers that night to assess their new arrival by having an ear ready to hear what I said. But a dip occurred in the din, and there was a breathless instant in those around me as they waited to see what I meant.

'I've been thinking a lot about it today,' I said hastily. 'It's a tough decision and not to be taken lightly. And for my part I would say that there are a couple of good reasons for voting YES.'

'The vote is in three days,' said Barry.

'Three days til destiny,' said Mhairi and she had raised her bottle of cider. When she drank from this bottle it merely seemed to glance off her lips.

'You've obviously not seen my theatre show,' said Barry and he unfolded a flyer from his top pocket and showed me. The show was called '1320 Reasons Why Scotland Should be Independent.'

I shook my head. 'I don't go to the theatre much,' I said but I should have said 'not at all.' In fact I didn't recall ever being in a theatre. 'How long does it take you to list all the reasons?' I asked.

'It's multimedia,' said Barry. 'Lights, images, a projector, film, sound and myself.'

'His fastest was 66 minutes,' said Mhairi. 'That's one reason every 3 seconds so you can imagine him belting them out.'

I surveyed the flier while Barry reeled off a few of his reasons much to the enjoyment of the others in the bar.

'And you say you've only got a couple,' he laughed.

'This is why we ask what your reason is,' said Walfrid when Barry had quietened down. 'This has been coming for so long, decades for some of us. His point is that every single person has a reason to vote YES to Scottish independence and there's a different reason for each person. You take whatever walk of life you're in and then look at how it might be better in a new country. Then you've got your reason to vote YES.'

We knocked glasses and the atmosphere of the bar took over and sounds rose and fell. For a second I found myself engrossed in the two folk musicians at the distant end of the room, a wide-haired wild woman with a guitar and a younger man, drunk in charge of a fiddle. The song the woman sang was unknown to me although somewhere deep within it made a strong impression. It was as if I could understand something beyond the words, which must have been the case, because the words themselves made scant sense to my young intelligence.

When Maclean meets wi's friens in Springburn
Aa thae roses an geans will turn tae blume
An yon black boy frae yont Nyanga
Dings the fell gallows o the burghers doun.

I was about to ask Walfrid if he had any idea about the song, but I noticed that I'd nearly finished my drink. Realising that it was probably my round, I dug my hand into my pocket, but there was nothing there, not even enough to furnish myself with another pint, far less my friends.

Barry was also near the foot of another glass and it appeared that he had ready funds and was tapping the side of my empty. 'Another, good.'

The song was over and although applause was muted, the tune had brought about an immense satisfaction within the bar.

'Did you ever hear of No Scotland?' I asked but Barry shook his head.

'There are a lot of campaign groups but I've not come across that yin,' he said.

Another drink arrived and I thanked Barry but he waved away my words. 'I can't remember how I even met you,' he said. 'Who are you? What are we talking about?'

We laughed and knocked glasses. An effect of the drink yes, but the situation made enormous sense.

'I'll vote YES,' I said and a strange thrill deepened within me as I saw my new friends' faces glow with approval. I continued. 'I mean why not vote YES because what's to lose? My thing used to be the Occupy Movement and I can see what it's inspired and it's people getting together for change.' I was havering and so I drank to collect my thoughts but I saw that I still had their attention. 'They say that Scotland will never manage by itself but I say let's see. You never know what good might come of it. I'm voting YES because there's got to be a better way, and things aren't working the way they are.'

The others nodded. Now I was talking the national talk I was pouring sweet music into their ears. I had no doubt that they spent their days in discussion of economic and social arguments concerning the fate of our country, and yet my basic affirmation seemed to be of the greatest comfort to them as if it helped them look down on the steady bedrock of their thinking, often overlooked and rarely enjoyed. Walfrid stuck a cigarette in his mouth.

'Bravo,' he said before sliding away from us and pushing the door to exit for his smoke. Barry was now holding my head in his hands.

'The boy may look daft,' he said, 'but he's got a brain in there after all. See Scotland wherever you go and everybody is voting YES. No matter what you say there is such a thing as people power and one day it will prevail. That day is Thursday.'

'Sure thing,' I said. I was reeling from excitement and Barry was in my face and excited.

'Your vote is sacred,' he whispered. 'It's as close as we get in this country to a religious act. It's going to be like a national high. That is why you need to vote with all your heart. People will begin to care about their home, and stop coming out with this bullshit that there's nothing they can do to change things.' He tapped me on the shoulder. 'I ken the hallmark of your generation is apathy and defeat and I'm glad you don't suffer from it. What is it you do son?'

At this point Walfrid arrived at our side again still with that same knowing smile. He nodded to a few of the regulars and placed a banknote on the bar for yet more drinks.

'Social media,' I said.

'Web shite?' said Barry, darting his head to the side as if to seek an answer from another quarter.

'You could call it marketing,' I said. 'But it is as you say, internet stuff. People advertising their businesses and projects through social websites. That kind of thing.'

Barry opened his mouth to argue but thought better of it. He placed his glass down and nodded.

'What is your social media then?' he asked steadily. He nodded to Walfrid when another drink arrived and said: 'Last one.'

'Well it probably is quite fatuous,' I said, 'but I get people lots of LIKES on Facebook or improve the way a company ranks in searches and basically promote people's businesses online.'

'My god,' said Barry slurping his drink and laughing when he spilled a little down his front. 'Does that mean you can get me lots of Facebook LIKES?'

'Of course,' I said.

'So let me get it straight,' said Barry. 'You go online and get people to click on my site saying they LIKE it? '

'Effectively yes,' I said.

Barry paused mid-drink and his eyes widened, a result of the dilation of the palpebral fissure, showing the roundness of the eyeballs as the information I'd just delivered filled his mind. He downed the rest of his pint and gripped my arm.

'Can you show me?' he asked.

'Aye of course,' I said. 'I live just across the road.'

'Come on then,' said Barry and he snapped his fingers to hasten the finishing of my own drink before he led myself and the others from Sandy Bell's World Renowned Folk Bar and into the floodlight street where my puddle of wine glistened in the glow of the street lamps creating a mottled and oily effect as if the spill were a mysterious portal to somewhere far beneath.

That first blast of air on exiting inspired us all. It was as if the night acted as a refresher upon the alcohol brightening every sense and intensifying the thoughts, and I felt ready for anything. Most of all however I hoped to show my new friends that I was as socially useful and that the young generation could work miracles with machines, even if it was all fake smoke and dirty mirrors.

I waited while they all lit cigarettes, and as the singing died down within Sandy Bell's, Walfrid tapped my arm.

'There's your country in there,' he said. 'A Highland girl, singing in an Edinburgh bar.'

5. The internet doesn't have a Scottish part

Iain was stretched out on the sofa when we burst into the flat, and he watched our drunken rush for the toilet amused by both myself and Barry pushing our way there only to realise that Mhairi also wished to make way. Mhairi overtook us and Barry and I bowed to one aside where we waited jigging our legs. I made the introductions.

'Barry, Walfrid, this is my business partner Iain Inglis. He helped write the software we'll be using.'

Iain nodded. He had been deep in thought and was browsing a pile of printouts.

'Hello,' said Iain. 'I'd better speak to you Alan. There's been a huge upsurge in activity.'

I assured Iain that I would help him but shoved the idea

to the back of my mind being keen to show Barry the techno-logical toys which would grant him his dreams of social media popularity. I had never been this drunk before and the flat positively spun with new and exciting options. Iain followed us to the front room, and once everyone was relieved I showed them how we could manage all our many social media accounts at the same time.

It didn't seem to interest Barry and he lit a cigarette and began to pace in front of the window.

'We've got a website called Creative Resistance,' he said. 'That's what I need you to promote. I can't get it to anywhere near the following it deserves. It's the NO campaign hate websites. They're filling the internet with garbage, or at least the Scottish part of the internet.'

'The internet doesn't have a Scottish part,' said Iain. He'd been watching us from the door and he should have known better than to gainsay this radical who was now in full flight.

Barry stared at Iain and said 'Of course it does,' and continued his pacing.

'My blog keeps getting trolled,' said Walfrid. He peered into one of our screens as if looking for a clue.

'That's another matter,' I said, 'but an easy one to deal with.'

'Can you get us loads of LIKES?' asked Barry. 'Can you do it? This is war and you are on our side.'

Unengaged as I was from the referendum debate it had been impossible for me to ignore the fact that on the blogs and on the social media sites the independence discussion had been a slanging match that didn't so much rely on informed discussion as out and out spite, replete with insulting profiles, threats and fake accounts purporting to be in favour of a NO vote. I located the website for Creative Resistance and it was pretty hammy and much in keeping with the general over-excited tone of bedroom campaigning.

'That's our site!' said Barry moved by his own work and unable to contain his pride at seeing it writ large on our big screen.

'You want some Facebook LIKES for this?' I queried and he nodded enthusiastically. 'Would 5,000 be a good start?'

'5,000?' asked Barry and he stepped back reeling at the idea. He looked about him. Iain and I kept our flat looking as technologically busy as we could with cables running into odd boxes and various hacked laptops waiting in states of disrepair. Command prompts flickered on screens that we used for nothing at all other than testing because Iain and I had a secondary ambition of reconditioning old computers believing that this would create a little income but all it had created so far was a mess.

'I could get you over 9,000 LIKES in a week,' I said, but Barry stopped me. He lost focus as if the clarity we'd all felt on leaving the pub had collapsed leaving synapses as dusty and confused as the trail of cables under our table.

'I don't get it,' he said. 'Are they going to be real LIKES?'

Iain spoke up. 'Nothing is real in digital terms,' he said. 'You've got to understand that from the off.'

Barry blustered. 'Aye I know, but you know what I'm saying. I'm saying real people making LIKES in as far as they aren't just made up. Or at least LIKES coming from real accounts or from real people interested in ma thing?'

'Nothing is real in digital terms,' repeated Iain. The others were thrilled to notice that Iain had a bottle of wine in his paw. 'Money isn't even real anymore,' he said. 'If Occupy taught us anything it was that.'

'Yes?' said Barry, patronised by Iain's explanation, but keen to get his hands on the wine.

'He was in Occupy,' said Iain indicating me, but the only one of the three who seemed to find this of note was the sagely nodding Walfrid.

'This isnae money though,' said Barry. 'This is just clicks.'

'Those clicks are still a form of currency,' said Iain. 'How many LIKES has your page got?'

'It has 60,' I said having navigated my way through the repeated variations of flags that made up the landing pages of the Creative Resistance website.

'For most people LIKES are a measure of popularity,' said Iain. He screwed open the wine and poured measures into various glasses and goblets. 'So in two days and with no effort on your part we'll increase that number by a few thousand. The question as to the reality of any of it is rather moot.'

Barry stood as straight as the alcohol allowed. He looked suspiciously at Iain and then around him, as if for something foul.

'How are you voting?' he asked Iain — and Iain turned away from him and shrugged. Barry didn't like the shrug. 'How are you voting?' he asked once again and he glanced at Walfrid for support.

'I take the view that there's no point,' said Iain slowly. He addressed Barry directly. 'The debate has been running for years and has co-opted the left. All radicals in fact. So the vote on Scotland becoming an independent country is

manufactured and fake. The powers that be in the world
are not going to let it happen. I don't know who runs
things, but my take is that there's no point getting involved
because whatever it takes, those people are not going to let it
happen.'

I could tell that it was an argument that Barry had not
heard before and he seemed to pause, unsure if this was a case
of YES or a NO.

'Who are you talking about?' asked Walfrid but Iain
shrugged.

'Whoever they are,' said Iain. 'They can do whatever they
like and make anything happen, and they are just not going
to let this go through.'

'This is people power,' muttered Barry. 'If they capitalists
think they can do anything then they were wrong to give us
this vote cause we're going to take it all the way. The polls say
it's going to be YES and the whole internet says the same.
Everyone is saying YES.'

'I hope you're right,' said Iain, killing an awkward pause.

Barry found his way to a computer. 'Can I use this one?'
he asked.

He'd found the most user friendly machine in the room,
one of two desktops on the far wall, both with eminently safe
looking images on their screens and a selection of innocuous
looking icons.

Iain smiled. 'Those are our honeypots,' he said. 'They
won't do you any harm.'

Barry stood poised over the machine with his fingers
inches from the keyboard and a drunken leer on his face. He
looked unsure if it was safe to move a muscle.

'A honeypot?' asked Barry, clearly in some technological rictus.

'It's safe.' I said.

'What is it then?' asked Mhairi, moving closer.

'Those that treat the internet as a battlefield tend to see individual computers as soldiers,' said Iain. 'For example we've twelve computers in here but they do what we order them to do, without leaving a trace. That's not the case with our honeypots.'

'It's moving,' said Barry. He raised a finger to point at the screen. 'It's working by itself,' he said.

'Not quite,' said Iain unscrewing the cap of a bottle of wine.

'Someone else is working that computer,' I said. 'Iain's curious and he just wants to know who it is.'

We all moved in closer to see what was happening on screen. The others were impressed. First the cursor opened a browser and loaded several windows all of which began different operations. A window opened on to an adult site and scrolled through several pages of pornography.

'What's it doing?' asked Barry, transfixed.

'I've never seen it doing that before,' said Iain. 'But I think it's streaming pornography. But where is it sending it?'

'Look,' said Barry. Other routines had started on screen and although Iain and I were familiar with the white on black command interface and a few of the instructions that zipped up the screen it must have looked like gibberish to the others.

'Don't touch it,' said Iain as he moved in, reading everything that transpired.

'The other computer's doing it too,' said Mhairi.

'In the battlefield,' I said, 'the most common soldier you'll find is the zombie computer. These two are zombies. They're controlled by someone else. Hence the honeypot.'

'Amazing,' said Walfrid. 'Are you saying you set these computers up to attract hackers?'

Iain smirked. 'That's why I've made this computer look as if somebody's granny owns it,' he said. 'Most computers in the world are a part of someone else's illegal network. Some of the networks have up to a million computers in them but the average size would be about ten thousand. They use these networks for sending spam or attacking websites or stealing bandwidth. Most home computers in the world are probably infected but every botnet is growing as fast as it is being shrunk. A good bot-herder will have zombies in every time zone in the world so as to always have roughly the same computing power.'

'Where does your granny come in?' asked Mhairi.

Iain's second machine was streaming material that Granny would never approve of.

'Criminals are always looking for the safest machines to infect,' said Iain. 'The most perfect one would be, as in this example, the desktop in your Granny's Highland home. What they want is a computer that's always switched on but doesn't get used much. Then all you have to do is get Granny to infect her machine by clicking on something, and once she's clicked you can install your software on her machine and you've got a computer you can control remotely.'

Iain attached a circuit board to a port on one of the computers as carefully as if he were diffusing a bomb.

'He's so proud,' I said.

'My aim is to catch the bot-herder,' said Iain. 'These two

machines are loaded to appear innocent. Each one has a bunch of letters to the gas company and a few photos of the grandchildren at the zoo or at the park or with Granny on her birthday. I got them from Facebook.' Iain inserted his USB and began typing on his phone. 'I got to find this guy,' he said.

Everyone watched Iain but interest waned quickly. Barry looked around as if he'd forgotten what he was doing and so he had a big drink, as did Walfrid whom I noticed had written a few things down in a black notebook.

'For my blog,' he said.

Mhairi wandered to the window and stared on to Forrest Road, quite lost in a dream. The drink had this effect. It could make the familiar seem quite new. For the first time I sensed something grubby about the flat, perhaps it was the empty bottles and glasses which had materialised from nowhere or maybe the new pall of smoke which Walfrid, Barry and Mhairi had brought with them. The smoke had a strange effect on the atmosphere and loaned our room a seedy haze.

'Do you know who would like all this stuff,' said Mhairi. 'Ranald Stewart.'

Walfrid and Barry smiled.

'You're not wrong there!' said Walfrid. 'This is right up his street, you could hardly ask for a wilder computer set-up.'

'Fuck aye,' said Barry, and then to me: 'Do you know this guy?'

I nodded.

'He attacks my blog,' said Walfrid. 'He attacks everybody's blog. He's the biggest troll in Scotland.'

'He's crazy,' said Mhairi. 'He once accused Walfrid of working for the police.'

'This guy is like a computer himself,' said Walfrid. 'About two years ago I had an exchange with a blogger who was arguing with me about independence. His name was Sandy Steward. Well this guy is the arch enemy of poor Rancid Stewart and he basically linked me to this guy and wouldn't let go.'

'That's how I came to hear about him,' said Mhairi. She produced a flask of whisky and necked a measure. Given the wrenching motion which was working its way up from my gut I decided to swill some of the whisky when it was offered to me. The drink shot down and calmed the butterflies that were winging their way through my arteries and causing me to feel anxious.

'So Rancid used to be a journalist,' said Mhairi. 'But he was crazy and it all went bad. He can't fit in anywhere except the internet. He lost his job but nobody knows why except that if you go on Twitter there are quite a lot of theories, like he was editing *The Scotsman*'s archives, or he was drunk, or one that he hit another journalist. Most of Scotland trolls him for it. He gets so angry and that makes it funny.'

'And he hates Sandy Steward,' said Walfrid, 'though the real joke is that maybe Steward doesn't even exist. Steward might be some composite government troll or better still a figment of Rancid Ranald's own dreams.'

'That'd be likely,' said Barry. He took the flask and knocked back a long one before handing it to Walfrid. 'Who is real on the internet, yous can't tell. One doesn't believe in the other and the only person that believes they both exist is Rancid. But if Rancid doesn't exist, then maybe neither of them do.'

'Well somebody has to be doing all that posting and writing,' I said. 'Ranald Stewart has a blog.'

'And Steward definitely exists,' said Iain.

'I'd hardly call Rancid's site a blog,' said Walfrid. He drank from the flask and coughed. 'It's paranoid ranting about imaginary characters who are hijacking the referendum. And you only ever hear about Sandy Steward through Rancid. There is a real Sandy Steward but he just writes a hillwalking blog. Could be the same guy. Probably isn't.'

'When he got chucked out of *The Scotsman* Rancid went to work in a bar on the Royal Mile,' said Barry. He lowered his voice. 'He got chucked out of that because he was caught smoking crack in the toilets.'

'Where did you hear that?' I asked. I half choked on the sentence unable to bear the thought.

Barry grinned a fat smile, he was now completely drunk. 'Everyone knows that one,' he said. 'It went round like wildfire.'

'Everything is about Sandy Steward,' said Walfrid. 'Stewart versus Steward. Perhaps Rancid is a creation of Steward. Personally I think it could all be one big entertainment laid on by some hackers.'

'Nah,' said Barry. 'The guy is a dick. He's out there somewhere. You can only find one archived article by him at *The Scotsman* from about seven years ago. And the real Sandy Steward the blogger has taken legal action to get him to shut the fuck up. That's why he's hiding. No address no phone and only one picture.'

Iain was watching me closely and I squeezed a smile out to show him that I didn't mind what I was hearing. Some of it I knew from Dad's web presence but hearing it aloud was new.

I had the flask in my hand again and I drank a long draught which brought with it the words of Robert Burns once again. This was life as observed objectively — myself head tilted back while the amber poison inflamed my blood — three older strangers in the house producing more drink and cigarettes from pockets and bags while maintaining several political conversations at once — Iain in habitual pose on the floor quite sober and seeming almost vulnerable in light of the drunkenness around.

Barry took the flask and raised it. 'Independence for Scotland!' he shouted, giving us all a shock. 'The vote is in two days and here's to we five votes for YES. And for other millions that will be voting YES! Here's to them!'

Between them Barry, Mhairi and Walfrid produced a cheer that shook the windows and Barry finished the flask, pouring the last few drops into his throat. When he was done Barry slumped in a chair and lit a cigarette and produced another flask which he shook at me. I passed him an old coffee cup and he gratefully took it as an ashtray and stared at the roof.

'All righty,' I said and I sat down at the largest computer on the table. 'Let's get you your 5,000 Facebook LIKES.'

6. A punk for independence

The month of August showed a sharp spike in voter registrations — 60,000 new registrations to be exact. Figures have been disputed but of the 120,000 16 and 17 year olds eligible to vote in the referendum for Scottish independence 180,000 of them have completed registrations.

I awoke and my friends were gone. My head hurt and I couldn't remember getting to bed but I would never forget hearing those conversations about Dad. Memories after that were blurred, mere impressions, the laughing faces of my friends and my drinking everything they could offer me and everything we could find. At some point my every sense had become subject to that same unseeing place where I could hear muffled laughter and see nothing but feel only rough objects around me and taste nothing I was drinking. When I breathed I smelled so much cigarette smoke that I wondered if I had started smoking myself.

The front room was more than its usual collision of wires boxes and furniture, and there was a hardy fug of smoke in the air and everywhere I looked was a glass a cup a bottle or an improvised ashtray. The computer screens repulsed me as if they had lost their taint of innocence and had become smoky old workhorses to which I was the slave. These were the machines that had processed all of Barry's Facebook LIKES although I now felt embarrassed looking at them. I made to return to bed but changed my mind at the last minute turning instead to lean against the window. I didn't know if I wanted food or coffee or water, and because nothing seemed to satisfy the unpleasant gurgle in my guts I merely looked out of the window feeling sorry. I glanced between this view and the computer and eventually I went to it and searched for Dad like I did each day.

Iain strolled into the living room. He looked well, and he passed the computers on the table in a clockwise motion bending to inspect each screen. He grimaced on finding a pile of cigarette stubs near to his favourite chair.

'How exactly do you register to vote in this referendum?' I asked. The words were the first I'd spoken and they emerged like husks, parts of sounds that had been generated on the dark streets the night before.

'I've been asking the same,' said Iain as he brushed the ash from his desk. 'You enter your postcode on the Scottish Parliament website, then you get a form and that's you registered. For a postal vote you need to enter your date of birth and address on the website, then they send you the form.

All you need to do is sign that form and cast your vote on it, and that's it. It's too late for you to do it now Alan, but your own voting slip is pinned to the wall beside the front door.'

'Oh thanks,' I said. Then, 'Dad might be right about that being open to abuse.'

I began to help Iain with the empty bottles, clinking them in shame to the kitchen dustbin. Next were the ashtrays, but even with them removed I had the feeling that nothing would ever clean our room and that things had been damaged beyond restoration.

'What time did they go?' I asked.

'Four o'clock,' said Iain. 'I see you got that man his Facebook LIKES.'

In that dreary state of mind there was something about this that bothered me. The activist Barry couldn't believe the faked-up army we had made and he wanted a part of it. Our legions of bots and false accounts had come into their own and Barry had been fascinated in the company of these many and unreal personae. I was the opposite and had been happy to find myself in the sudden company of real people with views to discuss.

'Is there any chance we could switch all this off for the day?' I asked. It was a question which caused Iain quite some shock.

'For what?' he said.

'I'm not sure,' I said. 'But I'd like to hear what this room would be like without the hum of these hard drives.'

'You should go back to bed,' said Iain. 'Or go out for a walk.'

I looked at my feet which sported two odd socks. A crumpled seam ran up my trousers and continued through my shirt. I knew that leaving the flat was not an option because of the certainty that I would gravitate towards the Old Town, always in the hope of spotting Dad. I picked up the last empty glass and gazing into it I caught a red wine-stained remnant of the night before, a reminder in vision form of what had passed.

'I'm sorry,' said Iain. 'It just wasn't funny when they started talking about your old man like that.'

I shrugged.

'He deserves it,' I said. 'If he wasn't such a troll then we wouldn't even be talking about him.'

'He did put me on to the town of Blackness,' said Iain. 'Whatever he says about the independence crowd he's on to something there. I can't get this town out of my head.'

Iain produced a sheet of paper on which was a collection of names of some fake internet accounts, all from the town of Blackness.

Bill Partyh	5 Sanquhar Court	Blackness
Wendy James	7 Sanquhar Court	Blackness
Alan Gordon	9 Sanquhar Court	Blackness
Lorna Swanepoel	11 Sanquhar Court	Blackness
Elspeth Kerr	13 Sanquhar Court	Blackness
Natalie Barton	17 Sanquhar Court	Blackness
Gordon McAuley	20 Sanquhar Court	Blackness
Shania Grieve	21 Sanquhar Court	Blackness

'Blackness is an interesting town,' said Iain. 'I'm looking at it online and the population is 9,000. Two primary schools a swimming pool and a newspaper. *The Blackness Advertiser and Farm Journal.*'

'Sounds archaic,' I said.

'It is,' said Iain. 'It's a weekly paper but the archive goes back to 1913. I've got that too. Then there's Blackness Castle. A fifteenth century fort that sticks into the Firth of Forth.'

I had a gander at Blackness Castle, the sight of which sharpened my senses. Even on Iain's screen Blackness Castle was impressive. A large tower behind huge walls and a spur which jutted dramatically into the tidal firth.

'That's not the most interesting bit,' said Iain and he switched to Google street view allowing us to see the entire town nestled between the water and a patchwork of green and brown fields separated by darker green areas of trees and a spider web of small roads. I read the various names attached to the locale: Golf Road, Station Road and Craig's Road. As Iain zoomed in I could see the McDonald Golf Club, the Blackness Dental Clinic and other innocuous markings. In a matter of seconds Iain had zoomed the map's feature in to allow us a virtual street level tour and as a matter of example he took us to Sanquhar Court.

'This is the street I was talking about,' he said. 'It goes Arnage Avenue, Slains Avenue and then Sanquhar Court. So having identified these fake accounts I concentrated on the ones that were in Blackness. Now these are sophisticated fakes because they have addresses and telephone numbers and even mortgage account numbers in some cases. The thing about Sanquhar Court is that there are 12 home owners and according to those on the list your dad gave you, every one of them is under 18 years old. Now I'm not saying that's impossible but it's actually more unlikely than possible. So what I think is that the records have been adjusted. A name and a photo and a date of birth can be faked but a mortgage and an address, no.'

'What about that?' I asked. Cross referencing Dad's list, Iain had turned up some phone numbers. 'Let's call one of them up and see if they sound like they're 17.'

Iain tensed. He was locked in eye contact with the Google street view of Sanquhar Court. The photograph was perfectly sharp. A narrow cul-de-sac made up of a row of slated bunga-lows with gravel drives and neat hedges — a fence of vertical dark boards which curved around the corner and into the next street — a satellite dish and a breeze block wall with a rose garden.

'It could be an error,' said Iain. 'I might have got it wrong, or it could be a wider bug. But as your Dad has highlighted there's something going on here.'

'I say we phone them,' I answered. 'We can't settle this by computer. At some point everyone needs some hard evidence.'

I glanced at my mobile phone. It wasn't the obvious fear of calling strangers for no reason but it was the thought of using my own phone. Wandering back to the window I found some coins and spied Sandy Bell's bar across the road. I knew that there was a payphone in there because I had seen it the night before, and so picking up Iain's piece of paper I nodded gravely and left the room.

I worked my way down the stairs, thinking about Blackness and glancing at the list and trying to calm my thoughts. I thought of Dad again and realised that I was still drunk.

The day was warm and there was a mild buzz in Forrest Road which was as always a bottleneck of vans and lorries making difficult deliveries. That was the fault of the city's 19th century planners who had failed to predict that we people of the future would generate so much road traffic. My immediate duty was to internet traffic which, I reflected, was worse. Somewhere, not far from Edinburgh, there was a wild country with neither type of traffic, perhaps back home in the Borders. At times that was where I wanted to be.

Outside the door of Sandy Bell's bar I glanced up to our flat and saw Iain standing in the window. He waited there perfectly still and I bravely swung open the door. Within Sandy's were a quieter crowd than the night before, but the singer was there with her guitar, and I took a seat at the end of the bar, next to a tall roughly bearded man who was chatting quietly to the barman.

The chunky black handset of the telephone was cold to touch but I pressed it to my ear and looked at my list of numbers and dialled one of them. This number rang out and so did the next two but I worked my way around Sanquhar Court from one number to the next. I plugged numbers into the sticky silver dial on the chipped face of the phone for five minutes, so long in fact that I became engrossed in many other things, including overhearing the conversation next to me.

The tall fellow was a local resident, and his continuous chatter, delivered in an Irish accent, was of localism, community, and of the YES vote he would be making in two day's time. When he caught my eye watching him, and my ear eavesdropping, he stared at me in surprise.

'What is it son,' he asked, but I shook my head. The door to the bar opened and there stood three stout Americans, two women and one man, the three of them pointing cameras into the pub. They paused, unsure if they should enter, although because of their dark glasses, it was impossible to read the entirety of their motives.

'Greyfriars Bobby is that way,' spake the Irishman, and the door was released consigning the trio once more to the unreal world of the tourist trapping city.

The Irishman turned to me and, as if he had forgotten what he was about to say, shook his head. 'Some of us have to live here,' he said.

I was about to respond that I lived here also, but I was taken by surprise. The phone had been ringing in my ear all of this time and I was shocked in that moment to find that someone had picked it up at the other end.

'Hello?'

The voice was male and middle-aged, definitely Scottish.

'Good day,' I said. I ran my finger across the list that Iain had printed. I glanced along the bar, but everyone had returned to their genial mutters, which meant the coast was clear for my deceit. 'Is that Mr Gordon McAuley of Sanquhar Court?' I asked.

'Yes,' said the voice. 'Who's calling?'

'I'm phoning from Forrest Research for a market research survey. If you wouldn't mind.'

I had no idea what I was going to say and my plan had formed in the split second between the telephone being answered and the first word I spoke. I was interrupted.

'Where did you get this number?'

'I apologise sir but this number is on our database,' I said.

'Well remove it,' said the voice.

'Certainly Mr McAuley,' I said.

The voice was certainly not that of a 17 year old but that was only a minor concern. Another concern was that several in the bar had noticed that I was behaving strangely.

'The number is public record,' I said, butching it out. 'We try not to do too many cold calls but this is important research for the Scottish Parliament.'

'This number isn't listed anywhere,' said McAuley. 'This is a new number.'

An ambulance outside Sandy Bell's stuck on its siren in order to move the traffic, and when the noise died the voice was closer and more threatening.

'Who is this? Where are you calling from?'

I ended the phone call with my finger. A pain in my gut rose and I pressed the receiver down and wondered if I would continue. Several eyes were on me now, and so steeling myself I continued to work my way around Sanquhar Court and three numbers later at the address of a Martin Fotheringham I struck lucky once more and another voice responded.

'Hello?'

'Hi,' I said. This time I decided that I would play the harried delivery driver. 'I'm hoping this is Mr Fotheringham of Sanquhar Court, Blackness. I have a delivery for you and I can't find your street. Sat Nav is sending me in the wrong direction.'

'I haven't ordered anything,' came the reply, a steady counterpoint to my performance as the harassed shipping agent.

'Mr Martin Fotheringham?' I asked.

'What are you delivering?' came the voice, slow and mean.

'West Lothian Council,' I said. 'New bins. On my docket it says that you're due one.'

'I have a bin,' said the voice. Then the voice pressed closer to my ear and asked sharply: 'Who is this?'

'These are the red recycling bins,' I said. 'You'll have a green bin and a brown bin and your grey bins are up to date along with the blue bins, but I've got a new red bin here for your green waste, but I can't find your street.'

'What's your name?' asked the voice.

'Jimmy Burns from West Lothian Council,' I said now feeling my hangover. Only a head sair from the bevvy could produce such an awful sounding alias. 'I'm outside the swimming pool and the Sat Nav says that you are up the hill and to the left, though I've driven round there and can't see Sanquhar Court anywhere. What should I look out for?'

'You're outside the swimming pool?' asked the voice. 'Which swimming pool?'

'Blackness Swimming Pool, Schoolhill Road.' I said referring to Iain's printout. Glancing at the map I could see that Sanquhar Court was straight ahead of the swimming pool, but as there is no accounting for the mental workings of delivery drivers I allowed my lie to stand.

There commenced a pause during which I was sure my lies were exposed because anybody with Caller ID affixed to their telephone service would know that I was calling from Edinburgh. Mr Fotheringham returned in anger after a short delay.

'You've got the wrong town mate,' he said venomously. There then followed a second of interference and a cough.

'Blackness,' I said. 'That's where I am looking for.'

'You are not who you say you are,' he said.

'You're not who you say you are either!' I shouted and the

line went dead leaving me with a buzzing tone which seemed in perfect keeping with my frailty.

I gazed at the scrap of a map in my hand, and seeing once again the swimming pool, I thought I would try and call them. The people in the bar were ignoring me once again, and either way I thought, if I get through to the swimming pool, the staff there would be bound to be civil.

The voice that answered from Blackness Swimming Pool was authentic, a woman's voice speaking in a strong Scots accent saying: 'Hello. Welcome to Blackness Swimming Pool. Opening hours for the pool are between 8AM and 8PM Monday to Thursday 8AM to 6PM on Fridays 7AM to 6PM on Saturdays and 9AM to 5PM on Sundays.'

The depressed voice then struggled through a list of children's classes and classes for the aged and classes for special needs and the lunchtime sessions which were available for the holders of West Lothian Leisure Cards. I listened to this with a pain rising behind my eyes which now more than ever wanted to sleep until finally at the end of this three minute announcement, the miserabilist lady announced in her most awful tones that Blackness Pool was closed until September 19th due to essential upgrade work.

I folded the paper into my pocket and looked along the bar. I walked the length of the room, nodding in an embarrassed fashion to the wild-looking lady who had begun to sing with her guitar, and I visited the toilets to wash my face and hands. When I exited the song was in full flow:

The black flag they hoisted, the cruel deed was over,
Gone was a man who loved Ireland so well,

There was many a sad heart in Dublin that morning,
When they murdered James Connolly, the Irish Rebel.

I joined the others transfixed at the bar, and took a part in the muted applause.

'They're singing about an Irishman?' I said to the tall Irish fellow next to me, but he cast me a disdainful look, replete with generations of disappointment.

'James Connolly was a Scotsman,' he said and he made a dismissive noise and returned to face the bar. 'He's from just down there.'

I left the bar and glanced in the direction the Irishman had pointed, but all I saw was the small grey monument to Grey-friars Bobby. It reminded me of something Iain had once told me, that there were more statues of dogs in Edinburgh than there were of women. I glanced back at the bar and shivered.

'How did it go?' asked Iain when I returned to the flat.

I told him everything.

'There's not a match between those docs and the real world,' I concluded.

Iain returned to his computer while I took to my bed for a rest.

As I lay there thinking, I remembered Dad and unable to control that curiosity I typed the question into my phone: WHY WAS RANALD STEWART SACKED FROM THE SCOTSMAN.

If this email is genuine it cements the evidence of a friendly relationship between Sandy Steward associate Walfrid O'Shea and colleagues at The Scotsman and efforts by Steward to turn a person thought to be a friend of mine against me by referring that person to the police.

It was Dad himself writing about the blogger I had met, Walfrid.

Then there was this on a message board:

I am writing with concern regarding recent reports that several members of the community of online political commentators have been targeted with harassing and frightening actions. Any potentially criminal action that incites fear like those made by Ranald Stewart or seeks to silence a dissenting opinion and collaterally wastes the resources of the police should be given close scrutiny at all levels.

A news item talked of the campaign of dirty tricks waged by blogger Ranald Stewart:

Whisper campaigns have involved Ranald Stewart and Sandy Steward both contacting the police saying that they have identified online enemies of the political process to complain of alleged harassment. Stewart has taken to contacting other bloggers to defame reporters at The Scostman and make frivolous claims of criminal wrongdoing.

Other posts accused Dad of more recent crimes:

Ranald Sewart former journalist turned blogger is a creepy far-left activist. There is evidence that using fake accounts Ranald Steward has engaged in violent rhetoric.

My eyelids were heavy and I didn't feel I'd learned anything, but just before I dozed I did at least see something that I could believe.

Ran Stewart you're a punk for independence who was sacked from The Scotsman for assault on a colleague. Get some help loser.

7. A town called Bastard

Iain Inglis did not cycle as his true calling was to walk. Iain's being was connected to the city by his shoes and it was by travelling on foot that he came to hold such a deep relationship with Edinburgh, and he knew it better than anyone else you could meet. The only other method of transport I had ever Iain praise was the train, which he said also ripened his realisations of space. Iain read the city as a series of signs, stories and historical indications. Graffiti was important to him as an informal set of public signposts but most of all Iain sought out Edinburgh's invisible spaces. He knew every derelict gap and neglected site and he had documented the ruined tracts of land that emerged invisibly between various developments both historical and modern. He loved the Old Town and was constantly angered at how it sold itself to the world. 'There's a real history that isn't celebrated,' he said. It drove Iain crazy that if you searched the term *history of Edinburgh* on the internet you were without exception pointed to pages purveying ghost stories and links to unmissable tours of equally untrue phenomenon.

The next day was the day of the big vote for independence and I told Iain that we would have to see this small town of Blackness for ourselves and he thrilled at the idea and immediately braced himself. As this was a 35 mile round trip I argued strongly for taking the bikes but Iain was doubtful.

'You can only truly cross land on foot,' he said. 'Whether it's urban or rural it doesn't matter. Your feet can follow lines that are unseen. These lines are the truth.'

What Inglis meant was that by any other mode than walking one was trapped by human construction.

'Would you propose a route?' I asked.

'Absolutely,' he replied. 'There is only one way to get anywhere. Take a map and draw a straight line between location and destination and then do your best to follow that line.'

This was the essence of Iain's so-called psychogeography which was a method of dissociation from the human-made and a means of exploration that afforded him a freedom far beyond the normal experience of city living. I'd been with Iain on several such expeditions and walking in this fashion he rose into a unique state of awareness, elevated from that imposed by the city.

'If we walk to Blackness we'll be out all day' I said. 'Longer in fact. We'll not even have the chance to vote in the referendum. We'll have to spend the night somewhere.'

Iain considered it and shook his head. 'I don't care if I miss the vote,' he said. 'I'd much rather be walking.'

But I wasn't having any of it, and I brought him to the foot of our stairwell where I kept two bikes. Iain looked at the second bicycle, suspiciously turning the pedals as if he had never seen such a thing before.

'We'll be there in no time,' I told him. 'It's either that or we take the bus.'

Iain puzzled. The choice was a hard one. Four hours of cycling or one hour of public transport was a tough call for him. In the case of travelling by bus it was the proximity of fellow sufferers that got to Iain. 'Nothing ever interesting happened on a bus,' he once said to me.

'We can leave first thing in the morning,' I said handing Iain a pair of cycling gloves. 'We'll be in Blackness by lunchtime. We can have a look around and get home in time to vote in this epic referendum.'

Iain spent a good minute examining the pedals of my bicycle before he took my gloves and said: 'OK. It could be fun. But don't hold me responsible if we're squashed by a black BMW.'

It was unfair to ask Iain Inglis to cycle so far, that was true. Iain disliked automobile culture which attested to experience of life only in the approximate. In Edinburgh every prejudice that he had formed concerning these road-raging beasts was confirmed. Iain felt cowed by cars which to him were violent and armoured extensions of the human body which had come to take over the city, whereas for myself, despite being no lover of the motor car there had always been a gladiatorial aspect to cycling because we cyclists were all brave Davids battling the Goliaths of the street with nothing but iron nerves.

We set off at 8AM the next day, pausing on Forrest Road

to watch the morning stream as it wound its habitual course through our local bottleneck. It was what was known as Independence Day for Scotland, September 18th 2014 and Iain in particular was keen to see if anything at all was different.

'Look at them,' he said, referring to the passers-by. 'The only reason they actually make it to their destinations is due to a human version of automatic pilot.'

I led the way and was glad to, because it meant that Iain was cycling behind me and I could only have imagined his tortured face. The day was warm and with our senses sharpened by our mission we made good time as we darted our way north-west to the edges of the town. I knew every bicycle route in Edinburgh and in thirty minutes we had covered half the distance. We pedalled against the flow of traffic coming into the city from the north and arrived at Ravelston, from where we veered towards the Firth of Forth along Queensferry Road. As far as Iain was concerned this was an appalling thing to do because this road was the busiest in all of the city, a cement artery that led from the motorways directly to the financial, commercial and tourist centre of the country. When we stopped for a rest at a traffic node at Barnton Iain let me know how he felt about this.

'That's the problem with you cyclists,' he said. 'You'll never win because you think like car drivers.'

It helped Iain's point that he had to shout above the noise to say this. He was furious, aghast at becoming a part of the traffic.

From Barnton Iain and I were virtually in the countryside which to Iain's credit would have been a pleasure on foot but was impossible by bicycle. Our problem with the smaller and safer roads was that much to the understated whispers of 'I told you so' from Iain we were obliged to follow the lines of fields which meant that we'd often end up diverting far from the direction that we wished to take. Following the same course as the motorway for the next hour we arrived at a high point near Dalmeny from where we could take a good view of Edinburgh. Edinburgh has a most peculiar skyline made up of some familiar monuments, framed by Edinburgh Castle on one side and the volcanic crags of Arthur's Seat on the other. Other features were squeezed into this picturesque scene such as the acropolis on Calton Hill which slopes above the cathedrals and towers that make up the twin religions of Christianity and Insurance.

We consulted our map and began to cycle parallel to the coastal stretch of the Forth. There were no settlements on this minor road although the area still offered locations with evocative names such as Bog Wood, Midhopeburn and Hopetoun. This part of the journey was slow and periodically we believed ourselves to be at least within the orbit of the town of Blackness although nothing could be seen. We had left the main road and taken to the more ancient farm roads and expected to come across the outward boundaries of the town at any point. We passed close to a grand residence called Hopetoun House which like many baronial stacks had once been a great estate but was now open to the public. The site of this sandstone heap caused Iain to stop, it being our last landmark en route to our target town.

'We should be close now,' he said, stretching his poor legs. 'We'll go through this forest and on the other side we should be able to see Blackness. How about we walk for a while?'

We wheeled through the trees enjoying the early autumn ambience. Bees buzzed and the soft clicking of our bicycles lulled me into a fine mood. Everything was quiet but for the noise of nature which like a song reached a profoundly hidden part of us.

'I've been thinking of quitting the business,' I said to Iain once we were in the forest and just as deep within our own thoughts.

The requisite few seconds passed before Iain answered and he said: 'You may be right.'

'It's to do with this independence vote,' I said, 'but it's just not for me. All that side of the internet is about popularity. It's not revolutionised media, it's just amplified the way things were before.'

'That much is true,' said Iain. 'The internet is every bit as much a part of the spectacle now as television. Worse it's dragged us deeper into trouble because television was at least passive and couldn't be monitored.'

By spectacle Iain meant the entire gamut of commercial broadcast, everything that he believed suckered the public into the docile purchase of consumption. 'Spectacle' was a favourite word of his and it referred to virtually everything from billboards to car registration plates to supermarket packaging. All of it fell under the auspices of the spectacle and not just the television shows, and it stood in Iain's vocabulary in the starkest contrast to the concept of community, and socialised living.

'Somehow social media just doesn't do it for me anymore,' I said. 'That's why I'm going to start winding it down.'

The forest seemed to contain a mighty rustle like a laugh,

something that suddenly made me want to lie down and stay there.

'We should see Blackness from here,' said Iain as we left the trees, but we saw nothing of the sort and he stopped and pulled his map free. 'Funny,' he said. 'But we must be somewhere further up.'

I joined Iain in poring over the map and we surveyed the plain below while Iain looked up something on his phone. Between ourselves and the Forth was a range of fields, copses and farms with a tidal spread of sand sticking to the coast to the north. Visible in the distance were the dark towers of Grangemouth refinery and on the other side of the firth were the tiny cranes of the naval dockyard. Beyond the cranes rose a roll of hills which indicated to me the ceasing of urban Scotland. Visible in the distance and on the waters of the Forth, more cranes worked on the foundations of a new bridge. However within our view there was no Blackness.

'Let's go,' said Iain and he began free-wheeling down to where the town should have been. I followed him, trying to check my phone, but Iain had gone on ahead and was pedalling like a dervish along the side of a rolling field of wheat, a dash of black hair and a denim jacket beside acres of golden promise. I pedalled fast to keep up, but Iain had predicted my move and he sped away from me, cutting a corner at the bottom of the field and whizzing on to the next small road, this one leading by a park of grass and down towards the firth. I called out because wherever Iain was going it was certainly away from the town of Blackness, although on that count I was feeling lost. Iain was pedalling furiously and I raced after him. I had underestimated Iain as a cyclist — he was going like the clappers. By the top of the next field I was on Iain's tail, and this next stretch of road was uphill and Iain was standing on his pedals and pounding his way up. I followed until we reached the summit in a dead heat, arriving at a crossroads in the middle of nowhere. We rolled to a halt and let the bikes fall into the verge and stood there hands on our knees, breathing deep and fast.

'Where are we?' I managed, looking around. The fields were bordered by dry stane dykes behind which were a row of ancient trees, a cattle trough and a patch of mud. A dense crown of murky smoke suggested Edinburgh many miles away.

Iain panted hard still smiling. 'Welcome to Blackness Swimming Pool,' he said.

I felt a thud as if a pebble had dropped in my stomach. It made sense that we hadn't located our destination, but that was all that made sense. I grabbed my phone from my pocket and scrolled through the maps page to see that Blackness had gone.

'An error?' I said, but Iain, shook his head.

'Too big for an error,' he said. 'Between the forest and the end of the first field, Blackness disappears. Where we are right now is the swimming pool. The door should be there,' he said pointing to a scruffy bramble. 'The town should be all around us. There are shops about half a mile down there where those trees are.'

'They're on the map,' I said.

'Agreed, that makes them real up to a point,' said Iain, '— but they don't quite pass the final test.'

I scrolled the screen on my phone in quiet disbelief before collecting my thoughts and trying a few rational explorations and another map search.

But as I stood at that clarty junction on the hill above the Firth of Forth all I was greeted with were map and satellite representations of what I could see before me. There was no town of 9,000 people, no shops, no swimming pool and certainly no Sanquhar Court.

Hearing the roar of a motor-bike engine we grabbed our bicycles in time to see a large black bike sweep round the corner. The bike slowed and the rider took a look at us before he sped off up the hill.

Climbing on our bicycles Iain and I also began up the hill, although I found myself turning in the hope of seeing the town which we'd perhaps missed by a mile or overshot in some other fashion. Iain knew the exact point at which the town of Blackness had cut out of the map and he stopped and pulled out his phone. I dropped my bike and did likewise.

'You can't see Blackness on the map when you're here,' said Iain, 'but walk up the hill and see what happens.'

Like diviners, Iain Inglis and I walked up the side of this wheat field with our eyes on the map pages of our phones tapping to refresh the images every few steps. On my screen I saw the satellite image of what lay around me, including the road, the trees, the Firth of Forth and even the wheat field. I walked until the town of Blackness snapped into view on screen.

'I have it,' said Iain.

'Me too,' I said.

It was clear enough. On the last refresh the town of Blackness had appeared on our screens right down to the swimming pool. Our maps showed that the town began a mile below us, where there was nothing other than fields and the odd dark patch of trees.

'Let's try it the other way,' said Iain and he began down the road, refreshing his screen and watching closely until we came to a certain point at which the town on screen disappeared.

'This is a curious bug,' I said. 'Should we tell Google?'

Iain stared at me his eyebrows arched in surprise. He glanced into the sky.

'Let's go home and copy as much of this as we can before we tell anyone. I want screenshots and copies of addresses and all the information we can get. I want it documented before we tell anybody.'

A chill crossed the field as we climbed on our bicycles. A cloud from the sea had edged across the land and blocked the light above the fields, and as we began a slow pedal towards the woods the motorbike drove past us once again. We stared at the motorcyclist but his helmet was so inscrutably dark that we could tell nothing of his purpose or intention.

The cycle home was slow and miserable. As we reached the first cement corners of Edinburgh where buses barked and cars waited in long queues, I asked Iain if we could have made any mistake.

'There isn't only a town that's been created there,' he said, 'but all of the people too. I wouldn't worry about your moral issues with persona management. There are people doing worse things than that.'

Just as we had left Edinburgh in the throes of its rush hour that morning so we arrived back in the early evening to the same mess. On the main roads we were buffeted by all sorts of vehicles and on the smaller roads we always seemed to be travelling in the wrong direction.

It was early evening when we returned to our neighbour-hood, where Iain directed me to the Augustine Church just down from our house, in order to vote. Outside the church were campaigners for both sides YES and NO but they barely bothered with us they seemed so awfully tired. It had been several years of grind for them and now it was over.

Inside the church, Iain and I collected our slips and entered two adjacent booths and it was in there that my mind settled.

It had been a long day and I was still surprised by what we had discovered. Our nation had been waiting years to stand where I was now, facing a piece of paper that said SHOULD SCOTLAND BE AN INDEPENDENT COUNTRY? on it, but I had lost my direction and couldn't get Blackness out of my mind. In a way the referendum question was a dud, more like a canvassing of opinion than a referendum that would change anything. I gazed at the question unsure as to whether the paper, the moment, or even the idea had any historical currency. It seemed so mundane an exercise and yet so many people hoped it would change so much for them. I ticked the YES box and left the booth, meeting Iain outside. He smirked. 'Took you a long time to decide?' he asked.

'It was surreal,' I said, and we climbed on our bikes to make the last short trip home.

Once back in Oddfellows Hall I looked up Dad again. I was itching to share our findings with him because I had a feeling that it was what he'd been looking for all along, but Iain was cautious.

'Let's wait and see what we've got,' he said.

Iain went to work while I looked at photos I'd taken of the fields, farms, burns and ditches that disguised the nonidentity of the town of Blackness. Iain had been examining records with care even before we had left, and he showed me what he'd found, a parish register from 1913 which included plans of Blackness which held up well in comparison with the current local layout.

'That's when the first parts of the town were built,' he said. 'There are still streets and roads that're recognisable from today's maps but which in fact are not there at all. Then there are streets and houses from the 1970s and 1980s which show the modern planning of Blackness including Sanquhar Court and the other addresses.'

We looked at the printouts, but the more we examined them, the less sense there was to be had.

'Brigadoon?' I asked, but Iain shook his head, as if in contemplation of a dangerous and incomprehensible enemy.

'More like a town called Bastard,' he muttered.

We worked on and the evening was bright for an hour, before Edinburgh was plunged with no warning into darkness, as the autumn sky has a habit to do in Scotland. Assuming that the best way to create a fake town online would be to copy an existing one, Iain had begun to scour digital maps of the country, looking in particular at towns with a 9,000 or so population.

Headlights on cars glowed on our street for the first time since the summer, and the marching mass of residents that had been on their way home from work changed into a more relaxed crowd. By ten o'clock there was the usual group of worthies propped in the doorway of Sandy Bell's World Renowned Folk Bar singing songs hopeful of independence for our country. Their songs were passionate with the ragged energies provided by beer, and it felt good — so I got up to watch them. I was enjoying it too, until a few minutes later when Iain let out a yell.

'The town's gone!' he shouted.

I remember looking at the clock and can tell you from that yell, that it was exactly four minutes past ten pm on that evening the 18th September 2014 when the phantom town of Blackness vanished, with all its records, and the records of its inhabitants, its roads, its data and of course, its swimming pool. I had never seen Iain so frantic.

I opened Facebook and looked for the accounts of the people that we had tracked down to Blackness, and likewise Iain was trying to locate other records, even those regarding services at Blackness provided by West Lothian Council, and all the while he was saying 'Gone!'

It was uncanny but with each examination I became more nervous of the outcome. I worked with Iain for an hour but we only ever reached the same dead end. What was most upsetting for Iain was that even though the maps and records relevant to Blackness and its people had vanished from the live internet, none of it had been preserved in any cache or any of the various mirrors which exist to keep eternal records of the web. The town was gone and was replaced with an acreage of crops, farms and copses, and so settling in a slump before our largest machine Iain and I began to look for cached versions of the maps and other pages on our own computers rescuing what we could and printing it. I worked as effectively as I could but at midnight the yawns got the better of me and I returned to the window where I watched the later revellers in a half-doze.

The night was long but I couldn't sleep. Many Scots were staying up late to hear the results of the referendum and I was joining them. A mist crossed Edinburgh and in the silence of the night in which I could only make out Iain's typing I entered the national stasis, a waiting state of mind which concluded in my case with a bleak announcement on the radio at about 4AM.

I was on my bed and asleep within seconds and found myself in a gloominess like no other, awake in my dreams and yet with nowhere to turn that did not face the same mist or the same colour black. There was something about that colour black that spoke to me of foul play, and fierce and unmanageable forces at work.

The NO result was awful, and the black coloured ornaments of my dream were the thoughts that even by voting a barely committed YES, I had somehow let it happen.

8. Seventy years of hard work for this!

The depression of the following morning is well remembered by many in Scotland who awoke that fateful day to hear on their radios and see on their computer screens that the result of the national referendum on independence had been NO.

Scotland had been rebooted to the seventeenth century and after a legitimate attempt at achieving political freedom was shackled again to the larger authority of an imaginary state called Great Britain. It had been all or nothing and our country it was thought, had lost it all and gained nothing.

I met Iain in our cold front room where he was still dragging up as much evidence of our discovery as he could, having worked onwards through the night. It was eleven in the morning and he had scrawled a variety of theories on some sheets of paper.

'I had every opportunity to copy this stuff and now I can't

find any of it,' he said rubbing his hands in his hair. 'Lesson is in future I'll copy everything no matter what it is.'

'What have you got?' I asked and I sidled over to where he sat. Iain had documents on at least 100 Blackness residents all of whom had vanished from the internet. To combine with these details he had maps, social media accounts and print-outs of the 1913 and 1976 plans.

'My best guess is that Blackness came into being about a month ago, just when you met your dad,' he said. 'Then it looks like it vanished last night after the vote.' Iain pulled a few sheets of paper from beneath his hoard. 'These are the teenagers I showed you. My guess is that they cast postal votes in the referendum and then disappeared. What was the margin of the vote?'

'It wasn't close,' I said.

Iain thought for a moment. 'These papers are valuable,' he said. 'We should get them somewhere safe. Maybe Blackness wasn't the only town. Maybe there were more towns that voted NO. We can't be the only ones who've got questions.'

'Do you think they could have done that?' I asked.

'It costs a lot to campaign,' said Iain, 'but this would probably be cheaper, especially if there were more towns.'

'Where did they get this 1913 stuff then?' I asked but Iain did not answer, he just kept clicking on through, increasingly more anxious with each new webpage he visited.

'I think you should keep looking for your dad,' he said.

I was giving this some thought when our door buzzer began a repeated ring. Iain and I glanced at each other and I made my way to the door and offered a cautious 'Yes?' into our intercom.

'You boys can you let us in it's an emergency!' said a hurried female voice. It was Mhairi and I admitted her and returned to tell Iain who hustled his papers into a pile and shot me a firm glance.

'Not a word of this,' he said.

I met Mhairi at the door and ushered her in to our hall. She stood with her shoulders slumped. She was half drunk and had clearly been up all night. As soon as she'd regained her breath from the climb she followed me to the living room where she ensconced herself in the same seat she'd taken during our drinking session.

'He's inconsolable,' she said. 'You boys have to help us.'

'Would you like some tea?' I asked and Mhairi nodded. A second later she'd returned to staring at her cigarette and playing with the hem of her sweater and so I departed for the kitchen to prepare us a brew.

When I returned she was nearly asleep, although she pulled herself awake and thanked me.

'He's in the pub,' said Mhairi sadly. 'He's doing his nut. It started as soon as the vote came in and it's got worse. All night and all morning messages and tweets and all laughing at him. All his colleagues are getting it and so are all they guys in the radical movement. It's all a big slanging match but they're going for Barry most of all. Yous have to do something.'

Iain looked up from his keyboard where he was still diligently scraping together what vestiges of the remaining sock puppets as he could.

'Tell him to get off Twitter,' said Iain. 'Switch off his phone and it'll go away. Go offline and the trolls can't get you.'

'He can't do that,' said Mhairi gravely. 'There has to be

something you can do? What is this stuff you've got here? You must be able to do something?"

Iain looked up. He was irritated by Mhairi's interruption and her idea that we could just press a button and our private army would make everything all right.

'I just want to get these bastards,' said Mhairi and she dug her nails into the arm of our chair. 'They can't get away with this.'

Iain and I glanced at each other. It looked like the virtual battles that had blighted the referendum were going to continue.

'Look at this list,' said Iain eventually. 'These are about 100 accounts I'm working on tracking down, trying to find patterns so I can see who is behind them. It's virtually impossible to find a real person behind an account but I always seem to have enough pieces of the puzzle to carry on the next day.'

Mhairi looked at the list. Iain had itemised an impressive array of fake accounts, sock puppets, trolls and other parties that had been doing their best to destabilise the national debate towards Scottish independence. A lot of them had lived their brief lives in Blackness.

'Sounds like the work of that prick Ranald Stewart,' said Mhairi. 'I wouldn't be surprised if he was behind it all.'

'Come on,' said Iain, glancing at me, but she wasn't deterred.

'He's a lying piece of crap,' said Mhairi. 'If Ranald Stewart was a real journalist he would turn up with some evidence and face us properly instead of hiding. But he's a nut or an MI5 plant.'

'He's my father,' I said before Mhairi could blurt out any more inadvertent insults.

'You what?' she managed, but as it sank in a slow smile drew across her face.

Her hand turned her phone so that her fingers fiddled with the ON/OFF key. 'Jesus,' she breathed, 'wait til they hear this.'

'Thanks a bunch,' I said. 'You can't wait to get down there and tweet that you've met Ranald Stewart's son.'

Mhairi's hand turned her phone one last time before she pocketed it. She traced her feet back and forth across the patterns on Iain's rug.

'Still,' she said, looking at me now for a likeness, or a hint of the man they knew as the great idiot. 'I really thought he was a made up dude. That's amazing that you're his actual son. Does that mean you've met him and you know where he lives and everything?'

'Of course I've met him,' I said. 'But nobody knows where he lives.'

'Where is he now?' she asked and I shrugged to indicate that I didn't know. 'You should probably find out,' she said. 'All these Twitter accounts that have been trolling us for years have vanished. Other accounts changed into new accounts, but Ran Stewart's account and his blog and everything about him has vanished too.'

I gulped in an effort to stop my heart from climbing my throat and I opened a browser window and looked for Dad only to find as Mhairi had suggested that his web accounts had been deleted.

'Damn it.'

Dad was gone, and as my head puzzled with the idea, I could not entirely repress the doubts I had regarding his involvement in the vote rigging. Dad's blog was gone too, as if it had been deleted. It made me want to get out and look for him once more, but when I thought of those cold stone closes with the debris of their ghost tours and the sweepings of their tartan trash, I kicked myself for my attachment. When I'd met Dad the month before we'd recognised each other in an instant. Years of change could not erase our recognition. Dad had really been a journalist at *The Scotsman* once. People would verify it. Those that kept insisting that he was not real were denying incontrovertible evidence to the contrary.

Iain and I left the flat with Mhairi and we filed down the stairs and on to Forrest Road. An intolerably bright light seared the sky and we kept our heads down as we dodged the traffic and crossed to the pub. I took a look at the whey-faced passers-by and thought that maybe the place had become a ghost town after all. The city, like the country, was stunned.

For once the music had ceased to sound out in Bell's. Barry and Walfrid sat in the exhausted gloom which was brought on by the failure of their combined efforts to achieve their desired national destiny. Seeing them like that it was clear how much this had meant to them but I was still thinking about what Iain and I had discovered.

'Mhairi says you're being hassled online,' said Iain.

'Aye,' was all that Barry said unable to look up from his pint.

'We've something else though,' I said, 'something we could all look at together. We're not sure if the vote was fair.'

'Of course it wasn't fair!' blurted out Barry and he snorted and grabbed his pint. 'Media manipulation and lies. Fear scaring the wits out of Scottish voters with rubbish about how this country could never survive on its own. How they engineered that I'll never know.'

Iain had our file of evidence on Blackness which he

presented to Barry just as Mhairi plonked herself down with her own drink.

'Look then,' said Iain. 'This is Blackness and it's an entire town and all fake. Fake Google Earth, fake houses and internet profiles. Fake bank accounts and even fake people to pick up the phone if you call them. A fake leisure centre and fake roads. Fake maps with fake shops with fake websites. What I'm thinking is fake voters, 9,000 of them. These people weren't here two months ago and they aren't here now, but they were definitely there in between. And this is just one town. There may have been other towns too.'

Barry looked distraught while the calmer and more methodical Walfrid picked through the papers. Barry grabbed at a few sheets scanned them and dropped them, completing these motions by placing his head into his hands.

'Where did you get this?' asked Walfrid.

'Ranald Stewart,' said Iain. 'I already had some of it but when I saw Ran's list, I could see it had names on it from this same town — Blackness.'

'Ran Stewart?' said Barry, despair ingrained into his voice. 'That idiot? No surprises but he vanished last night just when these trolls started in on me. Either way, you can't trust him any more than the other trolls.'

Mhairi placed her hand on Barry's arm. 'Rans is Alan's dad,' she said.

The look that Barry gave me was not a kind one, an acid stare that was more to do with his confusion than it was to do with myself and my dubious relation to my father.

'Great,' was all he said and he stood up and wandered to the bar where he quietly ordered more drinks.

Walfrid was fascinated with the documents and looked at everything in turn before saying to Iain: 'Have you told the press?'

Iain shook his head. 'Wouldn't know how to. Anyway, I thought this was the age of the citizen journalist.'

'It would be good if that were true,' smiled Walfrid, 'but if this is for real then someone must have seen something. How hard would this be to do?'

'It would be difficult,' said Iain, 'although I've found a few shortcuts they've taken. Like this — they copied the whole of Blackness from another town. I think the one they used is called Ellon, and it's in Aberdeenshire.'

'But the voting?' asked Walfrid.

Iain had his own postal voting slip to hand. 'They took advantage of a loophole which meant that nobody had any idea how many registrations to expect from under 18s, which is why there were so many 17-year-olds living there. The impossible part is accessing these public sites and persuading Google to do it, because you would think that Google would have noticed. It wouldn't be easy to hack into Google maps and edit in a town, but that's what they did. We went to Blackness yesterday and there was no town there. The real town was Ellon in Aberdeenshire. Blackness was just a copy.'

'I see,' mused Walfrid, reaching the end of our notes. 'I can't see any of the newspapers running this story but there's nothing to stop us putting it around and seeing if we can collect any more evidence.'

'Ran Stewart knows,' said Mhairi just as Barry returned with the next batch of drinks.

'Stop talking about that guy,' he said.

Walfrid folded the sheets and returned them to Iain. 'Leave it with me,' he said. 'It doesn't sound like we can prove anything but this is just how an urban myth starts. Freak occurrences that only a few people can vaguely verify. Let me publish a few bits and pieces see what happens. The story can't go away so if we just keep forwarding it eventually the truth might pop out.'

'Eventually!' screamed Barry, causing us all to jump. 'There's no eventually and there's no tomorrow and there's no country and there's no future! Can't you see it? We've lost. There is no Scotland anymore. It's just another part of England, which is just another part of America. We're an amoeba on a flea on an elephant and now they're going to round us up and finish it off. Seventy years of hard work for this! It's over.'

'Now now,' came a voice from behind the bar. Barry's outburst had heightened the hush that came over the room but judging from the tactful nods from each corner it seemed that he may have spoken for more than just himself.

I drank up and left them to it. There wasn't much else that could be done. The hurt was tangible and was mirrored in the face of every man and woman in the bar.

I returned to the flat and began to think things through but ended up staring out of the window, unwilling to face any work.

I thought of Dad and I wasn't alone. Other people on the internet were speculating on why he might have vanished, and the general opinion was that Dad had been a fake that had been invented to disrupt the referendum and start fights with people wherever it would cause the most damage.

The rest of the stuff online that day, I would class as the same banter as before:

YES yous you lost you can all get it up yous fat indy cunts

I awoke and it was evening. The lights were on and Iain was at work and having given up his researches for the night he was arranging a multitude of social LIKES for clients that we had taken on board a long time back. He gave me a slow and depressed wave and returned to his programming. It was eight o'clock and I knew that I was going out again and that I would never be able to tolerate not knowing where Dad was. I knew that I would spend the next two hours haunting the Old Town of Edinburgh looking for somebody that may never be there again.

9. You were Scottish last time I saw you and you're still Scottish now

People are creatures of habit and a person used to doing a thing one way will inevitably find themselves carrying out that action to the same pattern, refining their method with the ultimate goal being that they will eventually be able to carry out what they are doing without any thought whatsoever. So it was with my search for Dad, and each night I worked my way from the volcanic plug of Edinburgh Castle down the High Street to the parliament building at Holyrood.

The upper reaches of the Royal Mile were quiet, where the unconvincing Wee House of Edinburgh sat next to The Bay of Bengal, The Royal McGregor, Highland House, The Whisky Trail, and The Luckenbooth Tax Free Shop. Empty now were the doorways of Wildest Drams, The Glenhas Café and an adjacent shop which was simply titled Italian Style Ribs. Two of these shops were still trading, the House of Cashmere and Taste of Scotland, but tourism had left the Mile as it did each year as the days grew shorter, and although much of the area seemed half open, the lower reaches of the Canongate were simply shut down, like the concrete defences around the parliament.

I passed along the empty affront of the Tourist Mile and walked a winding course through Milne's Court, James Court and Wardrop's Court looking into Riddle's Court and Brodie's Close before moving towards the next stretch.

I saw Ghost Tour Doug leading a group of just three tourists down the narrows of one of these ancient walkways and I continued to think of the words of Robert Burns.

I watched Doug go, and on an impulse, I stepped into a doorway and searched for Dad on my phone. I found nothing of him of course. The internet is a darker and more complex city than Edinburgh, even though I knew that Dad was out there somewhere and in both.

The gloating was in full flow online and although the run up to our referendum vote had been dominated by the positive arguments presented by the YES campaign, this strain had immediately gone quiet. On the blogs the left yapped and the right crowed. The victorious NO determined that Scotland was now a place where every argument was silenced with a reminder that the country had voted to stay as a part of the United Kingdom, as if this was enough to settle anything.

Iain and I persevered in our business but largely I was distracted and each time that I sat down to work I found myself either looking for Blackness online or just plain hunting for my father. In looking for Blackness I came across cached geographical databases and selections of historical records. I found traces of documents referring to Blackness and always I returned to the digital map of Ellon in Aberdeenshire which had been used to mock up Blackness. Each day I showed my stuff to Iain but it made little difference to him.

'I've already seen that,' he would say.

Dad had left a trail of sorts to follow, because often when he'd been in fights with people online, these people would store the conversations and publish them at a later date. People liked winding Dad up because his reaction was always so strong.

Scotland was the same old country except in the face of the NO vote it was more massively depressed than ever before. Mhairi would join us if she was in Sandy Bell's. Once Barry and Walfrid were ensconced in the driving misery of their drinking and the inevitable long haul back towards independence, she would slip away and see if Iain or I had any information for her.

How many more decades would it take to arrange another vote?

Barry and Walfrid hadn't given up the dream and were just as determined that Scotland should be an independent country.

'I've reached a brick wall,' said Iain. 'I've tracked down hundreds of proxy addresses but I don't think they can help us.'

Iain had a long list of names, addresses and map co-ordinates.

'What is it then?' asked Mhairi.

'Whoever was controlling those fake accounts that were supposed to be coming from Blackness, they all used proxies,' said Iain. 'What that means is that they routed their internet connection via another computer. We can identify the proxies but there is no way of knowing where that traffic came from in the first place.'

I looked at the sheet with addresses in China and North America. Most of the addresses were useless to us. Mhairi and I leafed through Iain's pages and put them down sadly. Mhairi looked at all our computer equipment and her eyes lightened somewhat, as if she was asking me: 'can't you do anything at all, with all this stuff?'

I shook my head.

'Iain's right,' I said. 'In the case of these proxies there would only be one hope, and that would be visiting the actual computer in question. If you could get to one of these computers you may be able to scan it for the software that the hacker is using and then track them down that way.'

Iain looked doubtful. 'There's no chance,' he said. 'It isn't even worth considering it's so mad.'

Mhairi gazed at the list and said: 'Could I have this anyway?'

Iain nodded and dug about under his chair pulling sheet after sheet until he had collected a whole armful of pages.

'There are another couple of thousand,' he said. 'Good luck.'

Time passed, and it looked like we had less evidence than we thought. The town of Blackness and its inhabitants were represented by sheets of paper from Iain's printer, and there was nothing left to back them up. With so much random paper in the house and no evidence online, I wondered if I had become a conspiracist like my father, and it was that thought that drove me out each evening.

This was when I had another chance encounter with somebody that I remembered meeting before.

It happened when I tired of walking that I often found myself standing in the mouth of one of the closes, half in the shade and in the night, watching the world and waiting for the chance to be surprised by my father once again. October had passed and I was waiting in the mouth of Burnet's Close and watching the world come and go, with the vague thought of those now-past independence debates still flickering like a low flame somewhere within my soul. I had edged myself into the gap of Burnet's Close so that I was unseen from the Royal Mile, and as this close was little used I felt I'd found the ultimate safe place from which I could watch the Old Town and its people. Somebody had tacked a piece of paper up which said WELCOME TO THE FESTIVAL OF DARKNESS, a note which at once made sense but seemed to suggest something sinister, perhaps a twisted glee in the privations and miseries of the coming months.

As with most nights I had little expectation of seeing my father and at about half past ten I turned and headed down Burnet's Close which along with Covenant Close and Old Assembly Close formed a steep-sided stone warren which ran down towards the ancient deeps of the Cowgate.

The light was poor and the lamps above the dirty steps and back doors failed to shine enough to let me see my way. In the darkest part of this warren which is a small enclosed square I was stopped by a familiar smell and a dark red glow which caused my heart to skip a beat. I instantly recognised the dark red glow as belonging to a cigar.

'You'll never find him,' said the cruel old voice behind the cigar. I recognised it as belonging to the old Queen's Counsel I'd spoken to in James Court. I peered into the doorway where he stood, but I could see nothing but the red glow of the cigar and hear the rough breathing of its owner.

'What are you doing here?' I asked crossly. Although I couldn't see him I didn't want to be any closer to this foul old man of law.

'We are still celebrating boy,' he replied with a chuckle, and I caught a glimpse of him as he inhaled and the cigar glowed hotly for a second and emitted a low crackle.

'Why would you celebrate?' I asked.

My old friend choked up another short-lived laugh. 'You'll all learn your lessons,' he said. 'How to play the game and who your opponents are, and what's at stake and what needs to be done. You YES guys might feel you won the public debate, but you didn't do any proper work. You didn't ensure your victory. The NO people did and that's why they won it boy. A lot was done, so of course we can celebrate. Anyway lad, you were Scottish last time I saw you and you're still Scottish now so I wouldn't get too upset. We're not going to throw you out or anything.'

'Have you ever heard of No Scotland?' I asked, peering into the space where the old boy waited, but he didn't snap at the bait.

'What are you looking for son?' he asked. His voice was gentle now as if he were trying to inject a note of kindness after having put me down.

'I have to find Ran Stewart,' I said but from behind the red glow of the cigar there came a huge sigh.

'I can assure you,' said the stranger, 'that there is no such person. You're looking for a ghost. You're looking for a meta-phor. You believe that if you find this person then somehow questions will be answered — but he's not real. You're looking for the answer as to why the YES party lost the vote but you won't find it. I've already told you that NO was prepared.'

'He's my father,' I said. 'I know he's real.'

The stranger paused at this idea, but he still wasn't taken in.

'You're an interesting case,' he said. 'But Ranald Stewart was invented by some journalists. The character of Ranald Stewart began as a way of spreading in-fighting among the nationalists and co-ordinating smears across parties. Then Ranald became popular as a whipping boy on the internet. Everyone would start fights with Ranald and that's how he got his reputation. He was quite a character but his real achievement was posing as a concerned citizen because he discredited so many people. Ranald's handlers had a few accounts which were purporting to be teenage girls that would flirt with public figures and that was how it started. Young girl gets in touch and says she wants to be a politician when she grows up. Then she becomes Facebook friends with him or something similar. Then over months it would get a bit more intimate, a few suggestive photos and all he has to do is LIKE one of them and they move a little closer. Soon they're exchanging meaty texts about masturbation then that's it. Job done. Journalists would be conveniently informed and the man in question would lose his job.'

'That's what Sandy Steward is accused of doing,' I said. 'My dad definitely used to work at *The Scotsman*. I've seen him there when I was a young. He wouldn't do that sort of thing. That's Sandy Steward you're talking about.'

'Listen to yourself,' said the old QC. 'Ranald Stewart? Sandy Steward? Fake accounts? The most likely scenario young man, is that they are both false and that there is nobody there, and that if there is anyone there, then it is one and the same. All a part of the illusion you call No Scotland.'

'But Sandy and my dad hate each other,' I said. 'They're enemies. They could hardly be the same.'

'Have a look at it objectively,' he said. 'All of these things are tools. I'm sorry that your dad has the same name as this sock puppet they created. They killed him off at the right moment.'

I pressed against the wall of Burnet's Close. Across the yard the cigar tip glowed and I heard a flask being unscrewed and there was a flash of light as a shot of whisky was tipped back into this fellow's mouth. I backed away following the dull-grey stone down towards the Cowgate all the while watching the red tip of the cigar until I turned and ran.

The faded hues of the close gave way to the brighter lights of the Cowgate and I stopped to consider what had happened. In the Cowgate it was Saturday night and stag and hen groups wandered the roadway, laughing and singing. Behind me in the close I could see nothing of the man who had been with me a moment before.

Back at the flat I was met by the full complement, Barry, Walfrid and Mhairi, and a rather upbeat Iain. It looked like they had been searching the lists of proxies and had news for me, but I was nearing that end-state in which I would no longer care for these deceits, false trails and repeating circles. Privately I had been down-scaling our social media work but despite this it had grown so large that I was sure I'd never quite escape.

'Breakthrough,' said Barry firmly. He had reasserted the revolutionary fervour that had been so appealing in him before the catastrophic independence vote had broken his spirit. 'We've been looking through these addresses and guess what we found.'

'Look,' said Walfrid. My four friends had covered the living room with paper, there were pages with these proxy addresses on them everywhere although they had no problem finding the one they were looking for.

'Working on the idea that we had to physically access one of these computers, we listed all the ones in Scotland, England, Ireland and Wales,' said Barry.

Barry was flashing a handful of pages before me but I still didn't see the point.

He continued. 'Fifteen of these computers used for disrupting the vote are in Scotland and we have street addresses for ten of them. According to your man here all the computers on these sheets were used for either voting, or registering to vote. All the fakes that we've researched can be traced to one or more of these machines, and that's why we've got to actually track one of them down.'

'It's crazy,' I said. 'I won't be a part of it.'

Barry flicked through some more pages and showed me what he meant.

'The computers that we suspected of registering fake voters included some at addresses from Glasgow all the way to the Highlands,' said Iain. He raised one of the sheets on which an address was circled more strenuously than the rest. 'This one is interesting,' he said. 'Most of the computers on these lists are in private addresses or in offices and other businesses, but this one is in a guest house in Inverness, which happens to be owned by someone called Sandy Steward. So we're thinking that one of us could travel there, and stay in the guest house and get access to the computer.'

'No way,' I said, but I did give the sheet a good look.

It seemed like they had narrowed the address down by matching the IP with other traffic, and according to what they had assembled that was publically available, the computer they'd highlighted seemed to belong to the small guest house from where Steward ran his hillwalking blog.

'All we need to do is go to the guest house, and if we can get access to the computer there's a chance we could find some evidence,' said Iain. 'We'll probably get data about Blackness if it or any of the fake people were being served from there. It could be amazing.'

'Thing is,' said Walfrid with a pleading smile, 'none of us would know what to do. You have to be the one that goes there to find the computer.'

'No way,' I said.

I glanced at Iain but he wasn't backing me up.

'This is a great idea,' he said. 'We even phoned up the guest house and booked you in. Once you get on that rig you'll be able to crack it.'

'Give me a drink,' I said dropping into a chair, and everyone moved at once keen to soften the impact of the mission they had just thrust upon me.

'I'm not going,' I muttered receiving a round of entreaties to act otherwise.

'It's a brilliant chance,' said Mhairi. 'We can nail these guys!'

'Completely,' said Iain with a confidence that caused me to shrug further within my chair.

He poured me a drink from their open bottle of corner shop plonk and placed it beside me.

'No,' I said. 'I'm not doing it. And that is final.'

10. The shortest ever bed night in the historic Highland capital

The next morning, armed with the pirate software with which we would capture the rogue computer, I left for Inverness. I admit that I was scared that I might be on my way to meet Sandy Steward, about whom my father had written so much.

'Just get up there,' said Iain, 'plug this into their computer and your job is done.'

Leaving Edinburgh I could see why Iain relished train travel. Only by rail could a person see the dead areas of civilisation, the plantations of weeds where kids had climbed to spray graffiti and all the precious decay of the past and the warehouses and brick outhouses, the remnants of machines and factories and entire industries that hadn't been seen for decades. Documenting these dead spaces was key to psychogeography.

From the coast of Fife I could see Edinburgh for what it was — a mountain with a suicidal crag beneath which were dotted four smoky miles of buildings over which propped a tiny castle. Between the towers and hills a multitude of spires hinted at a much older civilisation, betokening a town of maybe 300 years hence, not a modern electropolis. That smoky haze across the water was like a vision of an older Edinburgh, something dirtier and colder and with evil intentions riddling it like tooth decay.

The train ran the coastal stretch of Fife and by the time the sun had turned gold and was drying off the mist and mildew that clung to every rooftop, fencepost, lawn and chimney, we were passing the Firth of Tay which in autumn colour was a patchwork of gold and brown.

Scotland is without doubt a land of ruins, from walls, castles, fortifications, farms to random outhouses the entire country is crossed with them. Each ruin is home to fronds of moss, silent stuff that grows without notice, far removed from the pylons and roadways where people are most often found. In essence Scotland is a place of wild beauty where humans were always intended to spend their time in communion with rivers, rocks and its many beautiful forests and beaches. Everything in that land is untouched. That real Scotland is a place of silver stones and constantly changing hills and fields. There is a natural tapestry in the wilds of Scotland that those with their heads wrapped in the wool of Edinburgh, and the close-knit pretensions of its businesses and bars, will never see or know.

The train passed between waterfalls and lichen-gorged rock walls, trees as ancient as the frost itself and heather textured slopes. When we rose to the hills and crossed the

Highland line then Scotland became something else, a place of foreboding. The Highlands are devoid of buildings and as our train passed between the mountain crags it began to snow. To see that snowy country you would have thought that nothing could have lived there, and yet the snow textured the land with such delicacy that the hills seemed from the train window to have all the vibrancy of an animal hide.

Then there was Inverness which we drew into slowly. I emerged from the station to a rather tired and wet town of dark windows and old buildings, a place which seemed exhausted and cold.

It didn't take me long to find my destination, a squat guest house on a part of the town they call The Crown. The Crown was an outcropping of rock at the top of a steep slope called Stephen's Brae and up there with a vague view of the Moray Firth was a semi-circle of various shaped buildings. I watched our target from afar. It was a fat whitewashed house with a corny sign which read 'Bide Awa' in the curliest letters possible underneath which rested a retractable section of painted wood which read VACANCIES. Blinds concealed the contents of this small guest house which was wedged between two larger buildings. Next to the Bide Awa was a derelict family house with a creased face of sandstone and on the other side was a small mansion house on which window frames peeled and flaked paint into the wind.

With nothing else for it I walked to the door of the Bide Awa. My fingers brushed the screen of my phone until I found Iain's number. I pressed to ring him.

'It's Alan,' I said. 'I'm in Inverness and I've found the place.'

'Great,' said Iain. 'A nice journey?'

'I'll let you know as soon as anything happens,' I promised and I pressed the bell on the guest house door.

A fearful noise as that of a dinner gong sounded within, along with the barking of a dog and a male voice urging that yapping beast be quiet.

Then the door opened and I was met by a tall man with a most serious expression across his fearful face. The man had no hair but instead a powerful grey bald head with a silver goatee beard, trimmed to a scientific neatness. He wore a tan leather jacket and did not look pleased to see me.

'Welcome,' he said and I placed my bag on the floor. He extended an arm towards his living room where I was bid enter. I followed his lead into the living room where there were two tourists kagouled in modern Highland fig, which is a set of waterproofs and gaiters.

'Good day,' they smiled and I immediately heard that they were German.

'Hi,' I said, unsure whether to sit down or not.

The Bide Awa was normality incarnate. There were china ornaments and a fireplace with brass tongs and a poker, and on each cushion was a cover knitted to a Highland theme such as the thistle or a Highland cow. Magazines and brochures lay on a coffee table, also themed with the sights of the North, such as the Caledonian Canal, the wild heather hills and the Loch Ness Monster. The sole oddity in the living room was a set of three mirrors, each on a different wall, which enabled all of us present to see ourselves duplicated several times over. A small woman with a friendly smile stepped in.

'Hello,' she said in an English voice. She was one of

several thousand Essex ex-pats that had escaped the English conurbations to work a guest-house in the Highlands. 'I'm Annie,' she said, 'pleased to see you.'

I shook her hand and she opened a guest book which she bid me sign. I hadn't discussed any of this with Iain specifically but I assumed that a false name would be in order and so I wrote Colin Cairney in the book and followed this with a false Edinburgh address which I scribbled badly. I returned the book to Annie as the man of the house returned, and it was then that he offered me an accepting grimace and said, 'I've popped your bag in your room.'

The husband squeezed past his wife so that we were all in the living room together with everyone looking at me.

'You have a dog?' I inquired and the husband nodded.

'It says so on the website. I hope there isn't a problem?'

'No,' I assured him, and I took a step back to see a little more of the room. It occurred to me that I should not under any circumstances sit down as this would trap me in further conversation, possibly even with the Germans, and so I pretended to look out of the window.

Finally the husband, the man I assumed to be Steward said: 'What brings you to Inverness?'

'A job interview,' I said confidently. I had at least prepared an answer for that, and so far so good.

One of the Germans perked up. 'What is your job going to be?' he asked.

'It's computers,' I said and I left it at that because experience had shown me that this was often enough to stop any line of questioning.

'What time is the interview?' asked the husband, and as

this was not a question I had prepared for I wasn't sure what the answer was going to be until I'd delivered it.

'I've already had the interview,' I said.

The others were interested but it was Annie who got in first.

'How did it go?' she asked and I calmly nodded with a cheesy smile, saying that I thought it went very well and that my chances were good.

'Why are you staying the night in Inverness then?' asked the man who had returned to a gruffer demeanour. I couldn't criticise him. It was a good question and one that I'd brought on myself.

'I thought I'd have a look around the town,' I said, but the husband looked most sceptical of this notion and gazed at me with dark and angry eyes. I glanced out of the window. It was a wet day and the buildings were a carbon black beneath the stone grey sky. 'I may even get going just now,' I said and I clapped my hands together, hoping to smile my way out of the room.

'Of course,' said Annie and she folded the guestbook. 'Would you like to pay first?'

I followed Annie and her husband out of the room. Sandy Steward — if it was him — seemed too large for the place. His head reached the doorway and the furniture seemed fragile in contrast to his bulk. I gave the guesthouse owner her money and I looked down the hall to see a workstation set up beneath a dormer window, in which was a computer monitor and a stack of maps and guides. Now that the guesthouse had my money I piped up casually: 'Are guests permitted to use that computer? Only I forgot to send these people my CV and I said I'd do it today. I'd really appreciate it.'

Although Annie seemed to be happy with this I could see immediately that the computer wasn't hers. She was about to wave me on when she caught her husband's eye and it was not a bonny welcoming eye. The husband frowned. The computer and its accessories were set up with the mechanical precision of a circuit board, even the mat for the coffee cup was perfect.

'The computer's not for the guests,' he said, but his wife was about to crack the chain of command, I could tell it. She nudged her husband and although he looked at her with a stone gaze intended to reaffirm his answer, she led me down the corridor and settled me in the swivel seat. I glanced back and I showed the husband my thumb drive saying 'The CV is on this.'

Of course there was no CV on there. What Iain had prepared on the thumb drive was a lethal package for me to load and execute. Once loaded, these files would install remote control on this computer and Iain would find the rogue software that we were hunting for, or at least search for evidence of Sandy Steward's persona management efforts.

'Thanks,' I said and I sat down and opened my email as normal while the owners watched. Annie was directly behind me, so I carefully swung the chair round and said 'This is very kind of you,' before returning to the vagaries of my pretence.

The couple drifted away towards the kitchen where they were met by the dog, and I slipped Iain's thumb drive into the computer and okayed the autoplay and executed his files, and I was done in less than twenty seconds. When Iain's remote was installed I removed the drive and returned to my email, glancing over my shoulder just in time to see the husband exit the kitchen to watch me.

'Nearly done,' I said cheerily. Iain would now be going through the computer and looking for that vulnerability that had caused this machine to take part in the national scandal of our cheated referendum. I stood up and swiped the thumb drive into my pocket and said to the owner: 'Thank you very much. I guess I'll be back later.'

'Yes,' he said and he showed me to the front door, from where he watched me as I headed along The Crown in the direction of Inverness Castle.

It wasn't the best day to visit the bygone Jacobite stronghold of Inverness, but I made the most of it and had seen all of the town centre in twenty minutes. I texted Iain but he had found nothing and so I stared into the waters of the River Ness which coursed through the town. The Ness seemed to be faster and stronger than any river I had ever seen.

After this staring contest with the river I thought I might as well wander over to have a look at the dumpy castle which stood at the highest point of the town, and I climbed The Crown again to take a look at it. As I arrived my phone rang and it was Iain.

'What's the score?' I asked him, but his voice was grave.

'There's nothing on that machine,' he said quietly.

'I loaded the software,' I said, 'so keep checking it. There has to be something there.'

'The registry is intact and the whole thing is clean,' said Iain. 'I had a good look at it but it's definitely not infected. The only person gaining any sort of unwarranted access to that computer is me.'

I paused, sick. People passed along The Crown. They all seemed to be fairly well-aged and pensionable around here.

It wasn't raining but water trickled down the gutter in a slow swirl.

'Do you mean we've just jacked a perfectly legal computer?' I asked.

'It looks that way,' said Iain. 'But I don't get it. It's definitely Sandy Steward because the hillwalking blog stuff is there. There must other computers in the house or I don't know what yet. Certainly that rig is clean.'

Further along The Crown stood the Bide Awa guest house, tucked like a fat white loaf between the two taller buildings. I had no doubt that it was time to return to Edinburgh and flee from this uniquely constituted crime scene.

Why had I listened to Dad? This happened on the internet. Sometimes situations took on a reality that was entirely assumed. There could be several answers to the mystery of those proxy addresses but even so there was now no doubt that Iain and I had illegally hijacked a private computer and that it was time to leave.

Inside the Bide Awa everybody was still in the living room. The Germans were talking about motorcycling and the owners were drinking coffee with them. Sandy Steward in particular was surprised to see me back so soon, and he shot a half smile in my direction.

'He's done Inverness already,' he said.

'Impossible!' said one of the Germans much to the delight of Annie.

'Have you seen the museum?' she asked.

'I'm afraid I have to leave,' I said. 'I'm going to get a train this afternoon. There's been a change of plans and I need to get back to Edinburgh.'

The Germans were crestfallen. 'You have not seen Loch Ness,' said one. 'And all of Inverness. It is a great city with a clean environment.'

'Good restaurants,' said the next.

'Historical sites around the city and pubs,' said the first.

'Relaxed living,' said the other.

'I'm sorry,' I said, and smiled nervously.

With a sigh the husband stood up.

'I'll get your bag,' he said. 'You never even saw your room.'

As Annie blushed, I could tell that the question of my already having paid was going to be an issue, but I wanted to assure her that I would be happy for them to keep the money. I was about to say so when the husband appeared with my bag. He blocked my path to the door and stood so close that I began to fear for myself.

'Do you always give false names?' he asked.

I waited, for there was no answer. There had been too many lies for me to back down, but I didn't have time to develop a new story. It is in the horns of this exact kind of dilemma that the truth usually works the best, and yet I barely knew how to explain what I had done.

'What is your real name?' he said still blocking the way. I glanced him up and down, from his strong shoes to his belt buckle, to his powerful domed head.

'I should ask what your name is,' I said. As a rejoinder it was a challenge, but a part of me had regressed to the point where verbal inquisitions would be impossible and so I could think of no other tactic other than to return the questions that were batted to me.

'My name is Sandy Steward,' said the husband. 'And what is yours? It certainly isn't Colin Cairney.'

I stared into Steward's black eyes and felt my heart tighten, my stomach churn and my feet freeze. A second later my body rushed with adrenalin and I flushed, gripping my bag even more tightly.

'It looks like you know my name?' he asked, and although my voice croaked, I could form no words. What could I say? 'Are you the same Sandy Steward that runs an army of Twitter accounts, and was trying to cheat the referendum vote on independence?' I only had Dad's word to go on for that. Are you the same Sandy Steward that co-ordinates the secret group No Scotland and helped create false towns, false people and false votes? I pulled out my phone and switched it to camera mode and with all the bravery I could muster I pushed past Sandy Steward and reached the front door of the Bide Awa.

'Do you know my blog?' he asked. 'Is that what you are interested in? Why did you tamper with my computer? What are you doing? Are you trying to steal something?'

I tried the front door, but I could not work it. I turned to my host, my captor.

'What I can't see is why my blog might interest you,' said Steward slowly. 'But I have a feeling you're a real life troll come to try and break into my computer. That is serious. Do you know what I've had to put up with for years? Smears, accusations, phone calls, threats and that madman Ranald Stewart spreading stuff, or saying how I was pretending to be a little girl to entrap people, or how I'm connected to Donald Phiggs, and saying that I was creating false voters. I've had this for years. You trolls are criminals. You're sick little bastards!'

I fumbled at the door. There was a trick to the latch and Steward wasn't telling me what it was. He was closing in.

'A real life troll,' he said. 'You people are scum. Have you got nothing better to do than attack people? Now you are coming to my house? I'll see you arrested for this.'

'No Scotland,' I said. 'Are you in No Scotland?'

'What's that?' he asked me. He was furious and it seemed to me in my distress of mind that he was even larger than before. 'That's another Ranald Stewart fantasy!'

My fumbling succeeded in releasing the door and I squeezed through the gap. I faced the enemy and backed away, while behind him his hound yapped and yelled.

I pointed my phone at Sandy Steward and snapped. I took two photos of Steward but my camera incensed him and he pulled his own phone free. From the off I had felt reserves of anger within this man but I had not witnessed their turmoil until that moment when I photographed him and he began to follow me shouting: 'It's me that should be photographing you, you little prick!' — and he came for me and I ran backwards, first with my bag over my face, and then with my bag on my shoulder and covering my head. 'I am not involved in your battles!' he shouted down the street after me. 'I'd like to staple the truth to your chest, you little numpty!' he yelled.

Steward's phone snapped images of me with my coat over my face, and my bag on top of my head, and my hands held in front of my eyes, as I worked my way along the street towards a shaft of steps which would lead towards the High Street. I waited at the top of these stairs, frightened of what I'd done.

At the door of the Bide Awa, Steward was staring at me.

The two German visitors were at the gate and watching the show in curiosity, interested by our host's fury and my strange retreat. Perhaps they were musing on the shortest ever bed night in the historic Highland capital. The Germans gaped in wonder, photographing me, awed with the variety and excellence of entertainments supplied by their Scottish hosts.

I rushed down the winding stone stairs of Market Brae Steps and reached the High Street, taking the nearest alley and running past a filthy stack of wet bins bags and back doors where cigarette ends had washed up in a mush. From there I dashed into Inverness Victorian Market and once I had taken a few corners I stopped. From within this arcade I made steps towards the station and thought through the events of the last hour.

In the doorway to the station I waited with my back to the crowd as darkness edged over Inverness and the town lit itself against the night. Wherever I looked someone stared back at me and inside the station it was worse, and I was not sure who was looking at me and who was not.

There was a crowd for the Edinburgh train and I didn't trust any of them, and this included a couple of guys in suits who stood with briefcases. When the train doors opened I made sure that these guys boarded before me, and I parked myself at the opposite end of the vehicle from them.

I pressed back into the seat as the train left the station. The track split and another line tailed away towards Aberdeen and my little train began to climb into the Highlands past the black spikes of many trees. Ten minutes later and the only thing I could see in my train window was own reflection returned. Alan Stewart looked troubled and tired that much was fair to say. Alive yes, and breathing, but I felt like the world could run out of air at any time, everything felt that fragile.

Who were these people on the train? Nothing to me, and yet everywhere I looked I seemed to catch somebody's eye. Later, all I could see were the headlights of lorries on the A9, the great northern highway, and I felt a deathly chill of gloom descend. Nothing had changed in Scotland and its heart still beat. Thousands of people had tried to change things, but they had tried online perhaps thinking that support for the future YES version of Scotland merely involved clicking some LIKE buttons. Barry had proved that to me weeks before. My phone rang and I saw that it was Iain.

'How did you get on?' he whispered.

I looked around the carriage but nobody was near enough to hear me. Outside was immense nothingness. We were crossing the hills.

'We just broke into someone's machine and he will definitely report us for it,' I said. 'We didn't find anything and if you think about it all we have done is taken my dad's word for something and then committed a crime. Dad has been trolling this guy for years. Our sympathies should be with Sandy Steward.'

'OK,' said Iain. 'I'll see you when you get in.'

And with that Iain hung up and I returned my gaze to the outside world which was a sheet of blackness on which was reflected several of the train's interior lights with my own guilty face at the bottom, staring back.

11. Everyone LIKED that we had been robbed

The cold light of day is no mere idiom in Scotland. After the month of October a body wakes up in Edinburgh warm from the neck to the feet with anything that extends out of bed suffering from a high probability of being thoroughly chilled. It is a process which becomes more critical as the dawns grow darker, and a bitter exhaustion takes over.

'I'm sure they'll find us,' said Iain when I encountered him the next day. Iain was deep within a nest of blankets, a warm pile from which his hands emerged to type on his keyboard. 'If Steward reports this, they'll track us down and what are we going to say?'

I checked my email and my Facebook and my Twitter and my Gmail, then my Google Plus and my LinkedIn and my AIM. Then I looked at some printouts I'd made of Dad's blog before it disappeared and I browsed the logs he'd posted of one of his Twitter battles in the month before he'd disappeared.

Most of Dad's last day online had been spent tweeting at Sandy Steward.

> **WTF Sandy, are you denying you posted that? Be a man. You're going to go to jail eventually Sandy.**

> **You can't get away with this harassment forever.**

> **You know well the only thing stopping me from reporting you is that I'm a journalist but your harassment is going too far.**

> **Sandy you deleted those tweets like the gutless work you are**

> **#YES voters Sandy Steward's illegal activities online began in 2011 when he intimidated folks engaged in protesting nuclear weapons in Scotland. At the time, he was running a political campaign business, where candidates running for office as high as the Westminster parliament had hired him. He disguised himself as Super Soutar (an avatar on Twitter depicting a person in a super-hero mask). He scoured the social media world using this pseudonym, threatening, intimidating and provoking people interested in independence.**

Later Iain and I locked up and went our separate ways. Iain went shopping but I didn't want to be at home because I was now scared of the police coming to speak to me about what I'd been doing at Steward's house. What we had done was illegal and it had a name — network intrusion — and God knows what else we would be charged with. I could believe what Dad had written as much or as little as anybody else, but, in the absence of any evidence, accusations weren't enough to build any kind of argument.

Edinburgh mid-morning was quiet and I visited a bicycle shop and spent a while worrying over the cost of new chrome gears and disc brakes for my trusted cycle. Every five minutes I looked over my shoulder. Since I wasn't online it was almost like no time was passing or if it was, then time was passing frozen in blocks. Between us Iain and I had a dozen computers working on this internet business but it was lousy the way the enterprise had distorted my own view of the world. The idea returned to me again as I left the bike shop and wandered inevitably into the Old Town.

A plan formed. First, I thought, don't take on any new business, and secondly finish the jobs that I have taken on. Then, I thought, archive the sock puppet accounts starting with the most recent. In most cases, I thought, I won't be able to delete the actual accounts because deleting them would mean erasing their LIKES and the support they've offered products organisations and events. But I will still be able to quit, I thought.

I repeated these steps to myself as I climbed the stairs to our door exactly as I would present them to Iain. No more new jobs and finish the old jobs, then commence the archiving. I walked into the flat with this on my mind, but these thoughts drained away when I saw what had happened. Everything was gone and Iain stood there with three men, one of them a uniformed policeman the other two, without doubt plain clothes. My jaw hung for a moment while the three surveyed me in return. Iain shook his head. Our front room was empty and everything bar the wires and a couple of terminals had vanished. Wells of dust had been revealed across our desks where the computers had sat and without our machines the room was derelict, a sad sight and a ruin.

'Everything,' said Iain, and instinctively I gripped my phone which was deep in my trouser pocket. The phone was all that was left. I ran to my bedroom and ducked to look beneath my bed but the laptop that I kept concealed there was also gone. Back at the front of the house the police people stood in solid contemplation of our loss.

'I'm sorry Mr Stewart,' said the plain clothes in the blue coat. 'Your colleague reported this an hour ago. We've asked downstairs but nobody saw anything. None of the traders have been able to offer us any immediate help. It looks like the people that did this knew exactly what to go for. The lock was broken and they seemed to have loaded up quickly.'

The policeman's face showed no sympathy. Instead he stared at me like I was the criminal. Maybe he was waiting for me to say something, but his look bothered me, or maybe I was too guilty to speak to him. The policeman had one of our printouts in his hand.

'Did you have a lot of paper here?' he asked.

I nodded.

'I thought that,' he said. 'It's odd that they took that too.'

I glanced at the scrap that was left.

I glanced at the scrap that was left. These were printouts from Dad's work.

'Can you think of anyone who would have known about your movements and may have taken advantage of that information?'

I glanced at Iain.

'I couldn't think of anyone,' he said.

'Were you insured?' asked someone.

I could tell that Iain was irritated by this question as if somehow the police were using it as an excuse to leave. Mine was a different feeling and it was one of panic, as if the oxygen supply were running low. Questions were forming. How would I recover passwords not to mention the data that I'd collected but not backed up? I found myself blinking. The questions had gone for lack of answers and in the space that was left my mind was as empty as the room.

The police filed out. They gave us cards, paperwork, leaflets and a letter from the local community policing officer. They gave us a brochure which had listed on it the police stations of Edinburgh and they gave us questionnaires concerning the crime, our reaction to it and our opportunity to assess the police response on a scale of Poor to Excellent. Then they gave us return envelopes for our forms and personal cards and a website address to use if anything occurred to us that could help investigate this crime, and with that they walked silently to our street door which they closed gently behind them.

'How could nobody see anything?' asked Iain. We stared at the empty room remembering how it had been. 'That's a busy road out there so whoever did this would have needed a car or a van. It's the sort of thing you'd notice. The odds of getting away with this are low.'

Suddenly he flopped down on a chair and closed his eyes. His hands covered his face as he buried himself in a tight ball of remorse.

'We're never going to see them again,' he said and his fingers parted and he looked up at me, his eyes watering red. 'We haven't got any computers,' he whispered.

I plugged some numbers into my phone. I tweeted that we had been robbed and then I informed Facebook, and having done so I felt slightly more human and over the next few minutes I responded to people's messages and thanked them for their support. Of course everyone LIKED that we had been robbed. Iain however remained buried behind his hands rocking back and forth.

'People will lend us some computers,' I said. 'Or we'll go shopping for spares. Charity shops and old motherboards, anything we can get our hands on.'

Iain removed his hands from his face. He was tired and scared. 'Whoever they are, No Scotland has friends in high places with great big erasers. They can bankrupt and break you before lunch,' he said.

'Let's go downstairs and ask if anyone saw anything,' I said, but Iain shook his head.

'Nobody on the stair saw anything, and none of the shops did either, apart from one guy across the way who saw the stuff being put in a van. But there is so much loading goes on here it didn't occur to him it was odd.'

'What about the street cameras?' I asked. 'There are cameras all over the place. One of them must have picked up something.'

'The cops said they'd look into it,' said Iain. 'What is it with those guys? They sent two uniformed police and then those two detectives came. All that was within an hour.'

'Dedication,' I said and I stood up. 'I can't take this

anymore though. I want to track down Barry and the others. We need to find out what we can do with what we've got left.'

Iain however wouldn't move, unable to leave as if there were a vital clue he'd overlooked.

'What have we got left?' he said.

'We've got what we know,' I told him. 'Evidence will have to come later.'

12. You are made up computer people with no heart, and you don't care about anything

Evening again. All I had by way of devices were my phone and the thumb drive that I'd taken to Inverness. The thumb drive was empty save for the remote access software that Iain had used and there was nothing important on my phone, just photographs and text messages. I didn't have to worry about our business. Without our computers, Friendly Social Media would cave in in less than a week.

I was at my lowest ebb, wondering how long it would be before I began to feel better about anything. I had wanted to quit the business and fate had ensured that my wish had come true.

I walked down Candlemaker Row resolved that I should leave Edinburgh and forget my father and return to seeking the security of employment. I trudged towards Edinburgh Castle compiling these thoughts and now not even sure if we had anything to go on at all. There had been Dad's accusations, and the work on Blackness Iain and I had done. Some of that was backed up, but most of it was not.

As I climbed the wynd between the Grassmarket and the castle, a nonsense verse from my childhood sprang into my thoughts, something I hadn't heard for twenty years.

Sandy Still belongs to the mill
And the mill belongs to Sandy still;
Sandy Still belongs to the mill
And the mill belongs to Sandy.

The song was something from the Borders, a point of contact with my childhood. I was amazed at my mind for storing this so long, and I was even pleased that it had chosen now to return the data to me. I really had not heard Sandy Still in all those years. I had never known what Sandy Still had meant, but maybe that was what had kept it so fresh in my memory. The song was a mystery, and Dad, the very quintessence of fatherly fun, had sung it to me, just as it had been sung to him.

I was thinking these very thoughts, and had just reached the gates of the castle, when my sleeve was tugged and I was pushed brusquely away from the road. I had no time to act and although I was sure I was about to be robbed or mugged I suddenly saw that it was Dad who had collared me, and I gasped as he began to pull me away, down from Castlehill.

I tumbled on wordless until Dad shoved me into a doorway, and looking behind me into the street from whence he'd ripped me, he checked to see if he had been spotted. Dad's eyes darted to meet mine, and as befitting a man as paranoid as I knew him to be, he held me tight by the lapels of my jacket and stared into my eyes.

'Where have you been?' I asked. 'I've been looking for you for months.'

'I've been in the house,' said Dad. He wasn't letting go of me. 'I never go out and I haven't spoken to another soul in ages. I deleted my accounts. I'm out of the game. I'm leaving town.'

'Just when I was getting to know you,' I said.

Dad didn't respond to my sarcasm. 'There will be no internet where I'm going,' he said. 'My work's done, though I can hardly call it a success. Sandy Steward and No Scotland won.'

I tried to free myself from Dad's grip but he was strong and wouldn't part with me, and instead he turned me towards James Court and began hustling me down the narrow path between the buildings.

'People were saying you weren't real,' I said as I tried to stay upright. 'People said you were a troll account or a sock puppet. There was no dox on you and no photos so people accepted that you weren't real.'

'Not real?' said Dad. 'How could I be not real? You've met me. You've seen me. I'm your father.'

He pushed me on and we came to a stop in a tiny doorway.

'Of course you're real,' I said. 'But people believed those lies.'

Dad let go of me and looked back. While he looked nervously behind us, I took in every aspect of this stranger, the small marks on his face, the hairs above his eyes, a rough pockmarking that covered his cheeks and the redness of his ears.

'Since I left the newspaper that's all I've had,' he said. 'There are stories they won't cover no matter how obvious they are. Instead of people reading my work I've had years of references to my sanity, smears, complaints, publication of personal information and publication of false information, allegations of criminal activity, whisper campaigns, stupid legal actions and then finally the word is that I don't even exist. There's no record of me at *The Scotsman* and every day until I closed it my Twitter account was bombed with abuse from Sandy Steward sock puppets.'

'How do you know it was him?' I asked.

Dad frowned. 'Ever since I uncovered Sandy and his army of socks he's been harassing me. He's the guy behind No Scotland. I know who they all are. Remember that list I showed you? There were people on that list who voted in the referendum and they weren't even real.'

'We know about the fake votes,' I said. 'We went to Blackness.'

'What did you see?' asked Dad.

'Nothing,' I said. 'There was no town. It was made up. So were the people.'

'I knew it,' breathed Dad and he looked skyward and after a second seemed to realise what he'd done to me. 'Are you all right?' he asked.

I nodded.

'I should have gone myself,' he said speaking with a contemplative slowness, as another piece of the puzzle slotted in to place. 'But I didn't know which of the towns were real.

There were a few towns like that. Towns full of NO voters and trolls as far as I could see. Blackness wasn't the only one. I've been working on this story for years. Nothing but this. I didn't even know what I was researching but as soon as the hate posts started and the smears began, I was hooked. I wanted to know what was going on but I had no idea it would lead to this.'

'What did it lead to?' I asked. 'Vote rigging?'

Dad nodded. 'They spent years manufacturing these towns. Then they won the vote and the voters disappeared. Evidence is thin on the ground now, and I guess it'll be less so since they stole your computers.'

'Who stole them?' I asked.

'Steward,' he said. 'Or someone like him. They have the money and the protection. I've been outside your flat, there are a couple of good hidey-holes across the way. That's when I saw the van arrive and I guessed that all was your stuff they carried away. It took them two minutes. You can be sure that since they took your stuff they're going to be watching you as well.'

'The police aren't involved in this,' I said, but Dad shook his head.

'I don't mean the police,' he said. 'Any access to online documents you have on those computers will be compromised, but we're not going to give up that easily. No way.'

I looked over my shoulder noticing that Dad's eyes had widened and we both found ourselves staring at a young man in a suit who was watching us from nearby. The man smiled, embarrassed, and he moved on, leaving Dad staring into space, looking left and right, glancing up and then behind him. He hustled me along a little further.

'Will you try and get another job in journalism?' I asked but Dad looked incredulous.

'Are you joking?' he asked.

'It says on your blog you were unfairly dismissed from *The Scotsman*. That's what you say — unfairly.'

We were at a corner in the close where the back door of a restaurant afforded us another concealed space. Dad let go of me. 'When I worked at the paper they asked me to edit the digital back catalogue. I was supposed to look for critical pieces about Donald Phiggs and delete them or soften them. It was political imperative because Phiggs was investing hundreds of millions into Scotland, so someone wanted to make him into the good guy. That was the digital archive of the paper, and what I didn't know is that it gets edited the whole time. I refused to do it and there was a fight and I'd been drinking and I punched another journalist. But that is not official. None of that happened. The punch didn't happen. The editing of the digital archive didn't happen, but guess what Alan? It's still going on. I have a copy of the newspaper's entire website from when I left and it's different now believe me. They've changed the news. They'd like to get my copy back because it doesn't include all the backdated revisions they've made. Looking through it all, I'd guess that Phiggs' investments into Scotland came with strings attached, and I think some of that money is funding No Scotland. It says that on my blog, and that's my argument. I signed off to a silence and the moment I start talking about it they say they'll sue me and press charges for the assault. In the meantime they don't know where I live. I have so much info on No Scotland but I can't leak it because I hacked it or stole it. Anyway if I do leak or publish anything, they'll come for me with that assault charge. They'll bury me. They don't know anything about me other than that Twitter account and my old blog, and they can't trace that and that's the way I want it. That's why they persuade people that I don't exist. I don't have a credit card or a bank account and the flat is in a false name. I might as well not exist, and soon I won't.'

'I'm glad you're off Twitter,' I said. 'You were embarrassing.'

'That was my job,' said Dad. 'I was there to find the truth.'

Dad stared at me in earnest. His face was an accurate reflection of the persona he had been online in which he appeared to take everything seriously and had no sense of humour. Dad lived with the strong belief that everybody was out to get him and I watched him for a moment, feeling for a deeper connection, separating the man from the machine. He was nervous and erratic and spoke quickly and in several directions at once, very much like his online self.

'I want to help you,' he said eventually. 'Take this link,' he said and he gave me a slip of paper with a long web address on it, a user name and a password. I turned the paper in my hands and was about to ask him a question when Dad shushed me.

'Put it away,' he said. 'Be careful with it. Log on to that address and you'll find all the evidence you'll need to take this investigation public. I have chatlogs, screencaps, emails and account details for the so-called citizenry of Blackness and other towns. Made up towns Alan. Together it adds up and there's the link. Don't share that link anywhere. Try and memorise it if you can. Don't get caught with it whatever you do.'

'What have you got against Sandy Steward?' I asked.

'Nothing,' said Dad, and he glanced around. 'Just that I know he is behind it, though he's careful about what evidence he leaves.'

'It looks like you're just harassing him for no reason,' I said.

Dad snorted and tugged my arm. 'This way,' he said, and we were on the move again, now heading down a narrow pend towards James Court. I followed him and I noticed his head was turned slightly to the wall, presumably so that no person nor camera would catch a full view of his face.

'Steward has written how-to guides on phony identities and how to hide your activities online from not just the general public but from the law,' said Dad. 'He runs No Scotland and that's funded by Phiggs through groups like National Convention. He has this dopey blog about hill-walking but that's just a pathetic front. He doesn't have a quarter of a million followers interested in hillwalking, that's a fact. How do these groups get any of their money? Weird donations from on high. Money given to one group and then spread in small amounts to individuals who secretly form another group. Sandy Steward is one of them, an unemployed e-thug whom no legitimate political candidate would ever associate with. Follow the evidence and let it lead you where it may. The links between these people are out there. The towns that the fake voters lived in existed for a month which was long enough for them to register and vote. Then they vanished like in a fairy tale.'

'So how many are involved?' I asked.

Dad shrugged. 'Steward is a master of black operations and dirty tricks. He's the one who starts the whispering campaigns and the smears. It's Sandy Steward that plants the fake stories about me. He never has any difficulty finding others to work for him.'

'I met him,' I told Dad. It was an admission that firmly grasped Dad's attention.

'What?' he asked.

'I met him in Inverness,' I said.

We came to a stop in a patch of darkness under one dim lamplight.

'Even I've never met him,' said Dad, 'and I probably know more about him than anyone. That scumbag. How did you meet him?'

'I went to investigate Blackness and where the votes came from, and ended up staying in his guest house.'

'The guest house is real?' asked Dad.

I nodded. 'I'd never heard of the guy until I read your tweets,' I said. 'The funny thing was that when I met him, we had a disagreement, let's put it like that. And while we were fighting he said he'd like to staple the truth to my chest. Did you ever hear that before? I did. It was something one of your trolls said. That was an exact insult used by one of the fake accounts that was attacking you, I'm sure of it.'

Dad eyed me up and down as if remembering who I was. Now we were both nervous, scared of who might be watching us.

'I have to go,' he said. 'I think there's enough at that link to prove that a sock-puppet army registered tens of thousands of votes. Steward's involved and maybe that line from him proves it, but there are more than just him at work on this.'

Dad peered into James Court. This is where I'd somehow

pictured him, hidden out in one of these high-gabled blocks, so many rooms with so many tiny windows, each one barely the size of human face.

To me the coast looked clear and there was a pause while both Dad and I looked in different directions. James Court is handsome after dark and lit by foggy lamps attached to the old stone buildings. It is a place of glorious nooks and archaic stone overhangs which create hundreds of recesses which you feel you could read like ancient history alive.

A footstep behind us indicated that we were not alone, and I turned to face the red hot point of the cigar which belonged to the old QC who stood at the back of The Jolly Judge tavern with a smile of satisfied curiosity. Dad's face dropped in horror.

'Ranald Stewart,' said the old QC.

Dad pulled me away, his face paling awfully. 'That's one of them,' he said to me.

The stranger with the cigar already had his phone out and had turned to the door of the Jolly Judge, while Dad was running up the nearest close and back towards the Royal Mile. I let Dad go. The experience of meeting him had been deep enough but it was over again, and I was alone with the cigar smoking QC whose face seemed infinitely cruel.

'I'm impressed,' he said. 'You have a wanted criminal there.'

'Wanted for what?' I asked. I looked across the black slabs of the court in the direction Dad had taken. From the opposite direction there appeared another man in his forties, non-descript of face and wearing black. He seemed to indicate something to the QC and passed us, crossing James Court in the direction of the Lawnmarket. This man had been following me, it was clear from where he had emerged.

'Ranald Stewart is wanted for fraud,' said the old QC. 'Not to mention internet threats, network intrusion, stealing emails and I am sure tax evasion and harassment and many other charges too. You did well to capture him.'

I stared into the space vacated by Dad with the same plunging feeling in my stomach I'd had when he'd left me before.

'I didn't catch him,' I managed. Then: 'Who is Sandy Steward?'

'Sandy is an innocent blogger victimised by your father,' he said. 'Did you not access Sandy's machine yourself and did you not fail to find anything of substance?'

I paused because it was better to say nothing. Everything I did had been recorded and everywhere I had been was noted, from the train tickets to the street cameras, to everything I had typed into every computer and phone I had ever owned.

'Did Ranald Stewart give you anything?' asked the QC and although I shook my head he stepped closer, following me as I backed away from him. 'Put your hands up, and open your jacket then,' he said.

Slowly I did so and the QC with the cigar roasting in his face, touched me up and down, pressing my pockets, running his hand around my front and even patting my legs. He found Iain's thumb drive in my pocket and nudged me, asking me to pull it out, and he took it and seemed satisfied.

'My lad,' he said, resuming his vile leer. 'Officers of the law will be here in minutes so let me do you a favour and ask you to leave before you're dragged any further into this.'

'Why would they want my dad?' I asked, and like they were the lenses on two dark cameras I felt the QC's eyes widen as he digested this latest question.

'Ranald Stewart has masterminded a campaign of mis-information, false accounts and internet stalking. He's been harassing referendum campaigners as well as politicians lawyers and journalists. So I think they'll probably want to put an end to it by locking him up. Having lost the referendum, extremists like him are laying the blame wherever they can, making up stories and spreading accusations.'

'Stories like entire towns that have been made up out of nothing?' I asked.

'Precisely,' said my friend, and he squinted out of the darkness with one strip of cigar light glowing. James Court was deathly still and the QC tilted his head so that he looked at me from over his glasses. 'As a Queen's Counsel it is my job to listen with all my concentration to any case presented by the Crown and deliver my response to it to a jury. Always that involves a thing called evidence, and there is a lot of evidence against Ranald Stewart. He has stolen information, and he has issued threats, and all of that will be proved.'

'Even if he had to steal it, he has got it,' I said.

'Stolen evidence, even if it exists, counts for nothing,' said the QC, and having reached the completion of his cigar he dropped it on to the slabs of James Court and glanced in the direction of the Lawnmarket from where I now heard footsteps. 'Nothing goes unrecorded,' he reminded me.

I didn't wait, and without acknowledging this last remark I took the narrow gap out of James Court, passing two police-men as I did so. The policeman gave me a look but judging from their hasty glances I guessed that they knew who they were after.

There was however nowhere for me to go but home and so I crossed the Royal Mile and entered the first available close, but here I almost ran into another policeman who was scanning the walls and windows and speaking on his radio. I wondered if the QC had been correct in his statement that nothing went unrecorded, because I knew that all such authorities as this police now often carried about their person, or had embedded in their headgear some kind of recording device, or a bodycam it was so-called, a camera that would in this instance have caught my own furtive passing.

A minute later after descending this dark stone corridor I reached the Cowgate, which was dotted with clusters of drunken human traffic, causing me some more anxiety, given the concealment that I sought. From there I crossed to the Southside and began to work my way home. I had no doubt that the police would catch my father and I was worried that when the QC searched Iain's thumb drive and found that it didn't contain what they were looking for, they would return for me to establish just exactly what Dad had passed on.

Although I didn't see anybody who seemed to be specifically watching our flat, I still didn't want to go there so I pushed the door into the Forresthill Bar (yes, that's what Sandy Bell's used to be called) and saw Iain and Walfrid nested at the nearest table. Before them were two untouched pints so I purchased a third and joined them, removing the paper Dad had given me and showing it to Iain.

'What's that?' asked Iain though he barely looked up, troubled as he was by the apparition of his fingers on the table.

'It's my dad's link,' I answered. 'He says it's the file location of his evidence. We have to start reporting this now.'

With deliberation, Walfrid produced a tablet computer from his pocket and typed in the address, and while we waited for Dad's page to load I looked around the bar.

As with the rest of the country the gloom was manifest now that the dream of independence for Scotland was over for another generation. It had seemed that people in the country had been behind it but that had been an illusion bolstered by the internet. Now that the dream had ended, the repercussions had begun, and the world of the week before which had all been about the joys of YES was extinct, run down and destroyed by a bulldozing loud-laughing majority which had appeared from nowhere and said NO.

Even bloggers like Walfrid couldn't face the prospect of writing the inevitable What Went Wrong articles and had resorted to gazing into pints of beer in the hope that soon their memories of defeat would also be clouded. People still dredged up stuff that Dad had written in the hope of an answer but nobody believed his tales of imaginary e-towns, and certainly nobody believed in No Scotland.

I tried to remember where I had heard about No Scotland from, but it seemed to have all come from Dad. I'd bought so much in accepting that one concept, but when I checked it online there was nothing but the oddest items of hearsay concerning it, and it all came from Dad's conversations and Twitter battles.

There is no such thing as No Scotland. I can't find anything on it.

You might look into it at some point. Sometimes have to hack for data.

Is there some place on the web where all this shit is?

I write about it but it gets taken down.

Who takes it down?

The law sometimes, sometimes the service providers. There isn't a No Scotland website because they pretend they do not exist. But they do exist. Some of the members are in law or public relations

Sandy Steward says you harass him.

Sandy Steward is a sadistic thug who brags about trying to push his victims to go nuts, commit crimes or harm themselves.

That sounds like something Sandy Steward would say.

You ARE Sandy or one of his socks . . . most of your followers are his allies . . .

'There's a lot of stuff here,' said Iain as he scrolled through Dad's work.

'That's good,' I said. 'Did they steal the printer?'

'No,' said Iain. 'What have you got in mind?'

'Give me an hour upstairs and I'll make hard copies of what Dad's left us,' I said. 'We can work with that while we're offline.'

'Has it got that bad?' asked Walfrid.

'It has,' I said.

Walfrid looked into the screen and Iain and I drank for a few minutes, all of us in separate thoughts until finally Walfrid spoke, gently clenching his fist, a determined sign that in his mind none of this was over.

'Very well,' he whispered, 'let's go for it. We can set up at my place and hammer it out. Let's go there tonight after you've printed the stuff. Let's do it as discreetly as possible and assume the worst. You guys go to your house and get what you need and leave your phones and then we'll walk to mine.'

'Where do you stay?' asked Iain.

'Near Lauder,' answered Walfrid.

I was about to protest because what Walfrid was proposing was a seventeen mile walk through the night. Iain however had perked up as there was little that would please him more than making that kind of trip.

'When do we start?' he said.

Walfrid leaned in. 'If we set off now we could be there by morning. Just let's be careful and keep a step ahead. Maybe we can prove what your Dad was saying and get some decent evidence that these towns were invented by No Scotland.'

'Are you sure we need to walk?' I asked, but Iain and Walfrid nodded.

'It's the only safe way to travel,' said Iain.

We finished up, and were crossing the road, when Barry appeared before us, his anorak flapping behind him and his eyes raging. He was drunk and he pointed a finger at us.

'This was your fault,' he said quietly, but the force with which he spoke was awful. At first I wasn't sure who Barry was speaking to, but deep down I felt that it was myself. 'All of you did this,' he said, 'all of you with computers, blogs, Facebook, lies, LIKES, nothing is real and you just sucked us all in and ruined this, made it into a joke with bits and pieces of truth that don't amount to anything, just stuff people click to get attention. This is your fault because none of it is real. Nothing you do is real, you are made up computer people with no heart, and you don't care about anything!'

'Barry — ' Walfrid interjected, but he was shouted down.

'Fake people!' he yelled. 'Fake money, fake work and fake places. All your computers are is excuses to creep on people's lives. You've shut down everything. You've let the bastards take over and let them do what they want and they've turned you into their wee machines. You've ruined everything!'

Then Barry sobbed. Walfrid stepped up and put his hand on Barry's shoulder, but his attentions were shrugged off. We looked at each other, and as Barry turned we all gaped at him, almost waiting for him to finish.

But Barry didn't finish. He shook his head and took off in the direction of the city, and I speak for myself at least when I say that I was ashamed and glad I had no computers any more, glad that I was unattached and ready to see what would happen when I was disconnected entirely. I watched Barry pass the statuette of Greyfriar's Bobby, which predictably and even at this late hour, was being photographed by a young couple of tourists, whom we saw grabbed Barry's attention.

'Can you see his wee boaby?!' yelled Barry, frightening them out of their skins.

Then he was gone. Walfrid Iain and I exchanged guilty looks, before I switched my phone off for the last time, sure that wherever I went next, I wasn't going to be tracked that way. Iain did the same and then Walfrid did it too, and in less than a minute our phones were in pieces, with the batteries in one hand and the dud remains in the other.

Could a person even exist without a computer or a phone? We looked at each other and we did not know.

How long could a person survive, unable to apply for a job and without email, unable to register for any service?

How long could a person even be without a phone, without a number, without a web location and without the means to verify themselves or even communicate with their family?

I did not know but soon I would see.

We climbed the stairs to pack for our long walk, and logged Walfrid's computer on the internet, before we proceeded to print what turned out to be 1600 pages of material that Dad had collected — our work for the next week.

13. Self-determination is real

At last we know what it was all about. Mainstream media, legacy media, call it what you will, maybe just *the* media, wouldn't buy it at first, but it goes to show you what you can do with a simple blog in this day and age.

Confining ourselves to Walfrid's laptop, we wrote our story and published it ten days before the larger news organs would touch it. I was the one who put the finishing touches on the story and so it was my name that appeared at the top.

BREAKING: NO SCOTLAND VOTE WON BY MASS USE OF FAKE INTERNET ACCOUNTS

By Alan Stewart

There is a small town near Edinburgh called Blackness which has a population of 170 people, although for a period of twenty days this year, the population of Blackness soared to over 9,000. This

was because a network of computers activated fake accounts of fake people that claimed to live there, registered these accounts to vote in the Independence Referendum and then deleted them after the votes were cast.

There is reason to believe that Blackness was not the only false town which operated like this, and as many as fifty thousand extra NO votes may have been cast on 18th September, skewing the result and ensuring an emphatic victory for NO.

This came to light through the work of blogger Ranald Stewart, now under arrest after he stole data from among other places a campaign group known as No Scotland. No Scotland it is alleged were the group which operated these fake accounts and helped build the network of infected computers which served false data, such as the maps and images which showed these towns.

We, along with Ranald Stewart, allege that No Scotland employed a team of cyber-extremists who co-ordinated these attacks from their computers.

In an exclusive on this blog, Ranald Stewart uncovered evidence that through The National Convention, an arts organisation which campaigns to register young people to vote, funding was provided for a secret group known as No Scotland. Those involved in funding No Scotland included billionaire investor Donald Phiggs.

It was impossible to say if Dad would have been proud of my work as he'd been arrested that night in the Old Town, a fact that was announced by the police two days later, by which time I was in the wilds of the Scottish Borders, living in a place with no internet, no telephone, not even a television.

Dad was charged with harassment and hacking, and he also picked up some charges for fraud because some of the data he'd stolen had included credit card numbers, a fact he hadn't even been aware of. Then they threw some other stuff at him including tax evasion, threatening an officer of the law online, and he was denied bail because they didn't want him anywhere near the internet.

I kept well clear, although I did write to Mum and tell her what had happened, but I didn't know if they'd be looking for me now, so I just kept my head down and worked with Walfrid and Iain on the stuff.

I had been without the internet for ten days, something a normal person would find refreshing. For myself, I imagined that most people would be thinking that I had died, so used were they to seeing me on social media. I had no computer and I wasn't using my phone, but instead I had a portfolio of paper, everything we'd printed, huge sheaths of the stuff which I guarded around the clock. When I walked to the local shop in the small town of Lauder, the paper evidence came with me in the form of a large bulge on my back, and when I slept on Walfrid's sofa the same bulk of pages were always at my feet, tucked in a plastic bag. We had tried photocopying the evidence but the tiny copier in the village shop could only handle so much, and so we kept on reading what we had. The documents had become even more important still, as the archived version of Dad's work had been removed the day after he was arrested, so we were mighty glad we'd printed it.

Ten days after leaving Edinburgh the moment had come.

Our final task was releasing our blog article which we hoped would start others talking about the fraud. We had no plan after that other than a dream that people would talk about it so much, that it would eventually cause the Presiding Officer of the Scottish Parliament at Holyrood to ask for invalidation of the September 18th Scottish Independence Referendum 2014. That is what we hoped for, at least.

'I'll upload it,' said Iain.

'What are you going to do?' I asked.

'I'll walk back to Edinburgh,' he said. 'I'll maybe use a public computer but on balance I think it might be safer to crack the wi-fi of a random person and upload it that way. Walfrid will walk me part of the way and you can stay here and take it easy.'

'What if no-one sees the article, or it gets taken down?' I asked.

Iain thought. 'Our social media empire would be handy now,' he said. 'I'll see what I can do.'

I watched Iain and Walfrid leave, and I felt the satisfaction of a job done. I had absolutely no money and I had been living out of Walfrid's cupboard for a week, and although it was pleasing that job satisfaction was still a possibility, it appeared that paid employment was out of the question.

Two months before, I'd not seen my dad for many years, and I had never heard of Blackness. Both Dad and Blackness were gone now, leaving a trail of conspiracy, and I had moved from general indifference regarding politics to feeling that I could make a difference. What's more I felt that I had come to an acceptance of the fact those in power would do anything to keep their filthy hands on it.

With Iain and Walfrid out of sight I sat at the front door of Walfrid's house, and wondered what I would do next. I felt the fine delirium of the country air and stared towards the nearest hill, feeling a strange kind of mixed confusion. Everything was good, and still something was missing, and I wondered what it could be.

Was it because I could not share the moment with anybody? Even then my own mind was working on how I might have access to the internet — or better still, I thought as a new idea slid insensibly out of nowhere and into my mind — I wondered what I would do if I could get an internet of my own making.

I looked down.

The earth, I thought. Iain had been right about when he'd said that soon our skin will be used to transmit broadband around our bodies. But then there was the earth, which was also a reasonably energy-efficient conduit for transmitting electricity. The earth could, I thought, also transmit data. I remembered reading about a ground based communication system, which used a mic, an audio preamplifier and a trans-former. The preamp boosted the audio data from the microphone and the transformer acted to match the amplifier to the grounded element, creating a system that in lieu of using wires to connect telephones or modems, used the earth as a conductor.

Without the internet it was hard to find most of the information I was looking for, but I did manage to search Walfrid's reference books enough to locate the natural frequency of the earth, which was 33Khz. With the right kind of electrodes and correct ground element spacing, I thought, broadband could be sent through the earth, allowing for a wireless system that could transfer data at a speed that would rival anything most people had in their homes.

All it would take, I thought, would be some electrodes, maybe a foot and half long. If these electrodes were stuck in the earth as transmitters and receivers, then low-frequency broadband in the form of electromagnetic waves could travel through the ground without any outside interference, assuming there were no metallic objects in their path. Ground composition, water table and water and sewage pipes would all effect the ground radiation pattern I envisaged. But unlike telephone lines, which were our current favoured method of connection, an earth based data communications system would need no conditioning or complex laying of cables. It would actually be the perfect way to spread free broadband to the wilds of our country.

I still had Dad's link in my pocket and I began to sketch upon the scrap of paper, imagining metal electrodes coated with silicon, something which would allow our own broad-band to be sent and received.

The idea was compelling and all but deafened my thoughts, and I began to wonder about security. Of course, such an internet would be completely unsecure, as the signal would travel in all directions at once and could be picked up by anyone with the right electrode, but I'd always personally put technology before security. Everyone could use encryption, I thought, and so no data would ever be sent to internet providers, or external services of any sort. Now what sort of internet would that be! Depending on the condition of the soil, the actual mileage of such a broadband would vary greatly, but there is no limit to the amount of electrical current you can pump into the earth. You wouldn't want to feed too much electrical current into the ground, but you could still get away with plenty, and unlike the telephone system, your ground wave communications link would never be out of service.

Now that I had had the idea, everything seemed clear, and in a series of visions and intuitions I began to map it out. I almost wanted to run after Iain, chase him down and ask him if he'd ever thought of this. I looked around me, giddy and swelling with satisfaction, and I wanted to start experiments immediately. There was absolutely no reason why it would not work. That cold day, that late winter moment in Lauder, that was the moment that I first dreamed of it.

Fate would keep me unemployed for a little longer, I realised, and an hour later I had all but finished my first sketches of what the electrodes would look like, and what they would need to work.

The telephone first, and then the television, and the microwave, the decimal point, the facs machine and the refrigerator — they all claimed Scottish pedigree and origin, and now there was my own radical free and unsecure internet.

I was to take my place in the enormous history of invention and discovery, everything that had in short come from the ingenious and forward looking people of Scotland.

Iain, Walfrid and myself — we alone had the evidence that a concentrated and combined effort had been made to cheat the people out of their right to self-determination, and we would hold on to that evidence, and share it where we could, until such time as my dad was freed, and with him, the people of our country.

Self-determination is real, I thought, as is the determination of those in power to ensure that the status quo is carefully maintained.

They had sabotaged the voting process, just as they had swamped the internet with spying mechanisms and controls. Nothing was as it should be, but if my theories were correct that morning, we'd be changing that as soon as my friends returned. We'd start up a second internet, one perfect for our island nations, conducted entirely through the earth.

MARGARET OLIPHANT
(1828-1897)
NON-FICTIONAL WRITINGS

A BIBLIOGRAPHY

Compiled by JOHN STOCK CLARKE

----oOo----

Victorian Fiction Research Guide 26

Victorian Fiction Research Unit
Department of English
The University of Queensland

ISBN   0 86776 737 5
ISSN   0158 3921

Published by
Department of English
The University of Queensland
Australia 4072

VICTORIAN FICTION RESEARCH GUIDES

Victorian Fiction Research Guides are issued by the Victorian Fiction Research Unit within the Department of English, The University of Queensland.

The Unit concentrates on minor or lesser-known writers active during the period from about 1860 to about 1910, and on fiction published in journals during the same period. Among the **Victorian Fiction Research Guides** currently in preparation are bibliographies of Ada Cambridge, 'Sydney Grier'|Hilda Gregg|, and L T Meade, and indexes to fiction in **The London Journal**.

We would be interested to hear from anyone working on bibliographies of these or other authors of the period, or on indexes to fiction in journals of the period. Any information about the locations of manuscripts, rare or unrecorded editions, and other material would be most welcome. Information about gaps or errors in our bibliographies and indexes would also be appreciated.

The subscription for the current (seventh) series of **Victorian Fiction Research Guides** is $40 (Australian) for four **Guides**; single volumes $12. Copies of earlier Guides are available at the following prices: Series 1,2,3,4,5: $25 (single volumes $7); Series 6: $35 (single volumes $10).

Orders should be sent to Dr Barbara Garlick and editorial communications to the general editor, Professor Peter Edwards, both c/- Department of English, University of Queensland, Australia 4072, fax 7 3365 2799; email b.garlick@mailbox.uq.edu.au.

Margaret Oliphant, from *The Bookman*, Aug 1897: 114.

CONTENTS

Introduction   1

Bibliography

    Abbreviations, Acknowledgements   16

    A   Non-fiction   18

    B   Articles   35

    C   Poems and Plays   66

    D   Manuscripts   67

Appendix: Foreign Classics for English Readers   76

Addenda and Corrigenda

    Addenda 3 to Margaret Oliphant's Fiction
    Victorian Fiction Research Guide XI   77

THE LIFE OF

EDWARD IRVING,

MINISTER OF THE NATIONAL SCOTCH CHURCH, LONDON

Illustrated by his Journals and Correspondence.

BY MRS OLIPHANT.

"Whether I live, I live unto the Lord; and whether I die, I die unto the Lord: living or dying, I am the Lord's." Amen.

Third Edition, Revised.

LONDON:
HURST AND BLACKETT, PUBLISHERS,
SUCCESSORS TO HENRY COLBURN,
13, GREAT MARLBOROUGH STREET.
1864.
The right of Translation is reserved.

Title page of the third edition of **The Life of Edward Irving** (see items 7, 8).

Introduction

I

Mrs Oliphant, says Mrs Q. D. Leavis, was "important as a case-history of the woman of letters in the nineteenth century".[1] We think of her now as largely a novelist. But in her day she was equally admired as a biographer, and much of her non-fiction was frequently cited as essential for an understanding of her as a writer. She took an interest in urban history, the lives of religious leaders, and literary history, and in her mature years she regularly reviewed books in *Blackwood's Magazine* and other periodicals. She was almost as prolific as a writer of articles and book reviews as she was as a novelist. Accordingly, whoever wishes to form a complete picture of Mrs Oliphant as a writer needs to bear in mind the contribution made by her non-fiction to the completion of this picture, and to a fuller understanding of her literary personality and her cast of mind.

II

Mrs Oliphant's first work of non-fiction, *Sundays*, was published when she was 29. It has been given no attention by any biographer or critic, until Elisabeth Jay made brief mention of it in her recent book *Mrs Oliphant: "A Fiction to Herself"*, so, although it is in most ways an undistinguished book, it is worth a brief mention here, especially as it has a significant role to play in the development of her religious views. Its main purpose is to survey the Christian year and to recommend regular rituals for the celebration of events in the calendar. As a Scotswoman living in England she had come to feel affection for the traditions of Anglicanism, even though she retained throughout her life her loyalty to Presbyterianism; and in *Sundays* she expresses a regret that Scotland, as a result of over-reaction to Roman Catholicism, has disregarded the events of the Christian Year. Thus, so early in her career, she shows the broad-minded attitude to the different Christian sects that was to characterise her later work. Her Christian faith never faltered, except perhaps at the time of her daughter Maggie's death, but she was happily able to respond to Anglicanism, both High Church and Low Church; and after her long stays in Italy, France and other parts of Europe in 1859/60 and 1863/65 she became equally sympathetic to Catholicism.

In *Sundays* Mrs Oliphant showed her sympathy for the movement towards reformation in the Church of Scotland, associated with such names as John Tulloch, Principal of St. Mary's College, St. Andrews, who became her friend three years after the publication of the book. One of Tulloch's special concerns was the softening of Scotland's strict sabbatarianism, and in the introduction to *Sundays* Mrs Oliphant speaks of "our gloomy Sundays" and stresses in some detail that it is possible to worship God with cheerfulness.[2]

In other ways *Sundays* is of interest to students of Mrs Oliphant's work. Themes which were to be of importance in her future work, especially her novels, make an appearance here. She complains of the current trend towards institutionalised charity, which inhibits genuine human compassion.[3] She speaks with ironic disillusion of the tendency of all human ideals to lead only to

disappointment, prefiguring the ironic tone of her finest
novels. She shows understanding of the capacity of many people for
obsessive self-torment; this is echoed by her treatment of some of
the most interesting characters in her mature novels. And she speaks
of the difficulty that most people find in thinking, which is usuall
represented by "a reverie, disconnected, broken, full of sudden
starts and pauses, sudden pictures suddenly disturbed, a kind of
panoramic contemplation of everything hovering within our mental
range, which we dignify with the name of thought".[4] This point of
view is expressed in many of her novels and indeed is to be found
earlier than *Sundays*, in the novella *John Rintoul*, 1853.

III

     Mrs Oliphant's second work of non-fiction was her biography of
Edward Irving, published in May 1862. As a proud Scotswoman and a
deeply religious woman she had long admired Irving, the Scottish
revivalist religious leader who became one of the most eagerly
sought-after preachers in the London of the 1820s, and founded the
Catholic Apostolic Church. The biography was carefully researched,
with many letters to, and interviews with, people who had known
Irving - including Thomas and Jane Welsh Carlyle. It brought Mrs
Oliphant fame and also some notoriety, because of her eager
championship of Irving in his disputes with the Scottish Kirk.
Irving has so crucial a role to play in Mrs Oliphant's
development as a writer that more attention must be given to it than
to any other of her non-fiction.
     Edward Irving was one of the most extraordinary characters whom
Mrs Oliphant ever described, either in novels or biographies: a man
of powerful personal magnetism, driven by an obsession, an *idée fixe*
egotistical and credulous, his credulity fuelling his egotism, his
egotism closing the door to any critical self-observation, except
according to the stereotypes of conventional piety; this egotism
strangely coexisting with self-abasing humility; anti-intellectual,
with little capacity for systematic thinking, or for prosaic
rationality, an unassailable conviction of the rightness of his
views, and an entire inability to heed advice. Mrs Oliphant describe
him as "impracticable", "impatient, eager, visionary", "thought or
calculation of prudence not being in the man", "a primitive Pope or
Bishop, as, indeed, he felt himself to be", holding to his "primitiv
standing ground ... as if he had been born in the days of Moses or
Abraham".[5] He makes a long journey from the austerities of Scottish
Presbyterianism to an idealistic, revivalist, visionary, evangelical
inspirational, prophetic, theocratic, millenarian new religion, with
its sights set on the Second Coming, heralded by the presence in
Irving's congregation of supposed prophets endowed with the gift of
"Tongues". "He had left the calm regions of philosophy far apart and
behind".[6] And he makes another journey from the massive popular
support of the public and of his ecclesiastical superiors to public
ridicule, hostility and suspicion, and to rejection by the
Presbyteries of London and Annan[7] for supposed heresy, leading to hi
unfrocking.
     Reading *Irving* is not a comfortable experience as a result of
Mrs Oliphant's style, too often rhapsodic and rhetorical, with
Carlylean rhythms, and over-elaborated sentences relying upon
the cumulative effect of interlocking subordinate and co-ordinate

clauses. But at other times she adopts a quieter tone, in which humour is allowed, with a gentle detachment from Irving which is too courteous to be irony, although irony does at times break through her defensive approach, for example "His was not a mind judicial, impartial, able to confine itself to mere evidence"; the word "mere" quietly and effectively highlights Irving's irrationality. And Mrs Oliphant recognises Irving's occasional "illiberality and intolerance", regrets that in expressing his views he can be "strongly defensive and belligerent", and notes the "all-believing admiration ... admiration too great" which Irving aroused in his hero-worshippers.[8]

In the last five chapters, where Mrs Oliphant has a classic tragedy to narrate, her instinct for the dramatic comes into full play, and she highlights the hubris and hamartia which Irving's story so richly illustrates. "Whom the gods wish to destroy they first make mad." These chapters contain some fine examples of sustained eloquence, for example the opening of volume II, chapter 4 (chapter 16 in the one-volume editions), and are remarkable for the clear inevitability of their narrative line, although this is much encumbered by tedious theological detail. But the tragedy, rich in tragic ironies, maintains its impact upon the reader.

The writing of *Irving* had a direct influence upon Mrs Oliphant's subsequent novels. Of special interest is her analysis of the mental processes, both of Irving and of his more rational colleague Thomas Chalmers, noting Irving's moments of self-examination, and strikingly examining the mutual incomprehension of these two very different men. "The one man was not able to judge the other with such an astonishing gulf of difference between"[9]. We hear much of this "gulf of difference" in her mature novels; her insight into the states of mind of Irving and Chalmers prefigures a wealth of similar insights in the novels. And she speaks with confident authority from her developing experience of human nature, as when she comments on the "disench-antment which, next to personal betrayal, is perhaps the hardest experience in the world"[10].

IV

Irving had given Mrs Oliphant a taste for biography and it is not unreasonable to say that almost all the non-fiction she subsequently wrote was essentially biographical in character. She published three more biographies as conscientiously researched as that of Irving: of the Count de Montalembert, the liberal French Catholic reformer (1872); of John Tulloch, Mrs Oliphant's friend, an important Scottish religious leader (1888); and of Laurence Oliphant, journalist and traveller, and possibly a distant kinsman of Margaret Oliphant (1891). In addition, there were three minor biographies, compiled from existing authorities, and included in series of volumes published on particular themes: Francis of Assisi (1868 for The Sunday Library for Household Reading), Thomas Chalmers, a leading figure in the history of the Kirk of Scotland (1893 for English Leaders of Religion), and Jeanne d'Arc (1896 for Heroes of the Nations, an Anglo-American series). To this list must be added Savonarola, the fifteenth-century Florentine monk, to whom the five finest chapters of *Makers of Florence* (1876) were devoted.

These biographies all have in common an interest in strong

religious faith. The apparent exception to this, Laurence Oliphant, is not an exception at all. Mrss Oliphant is evidently much more interested in the entangled development of Laurence's religious opinions and of his baffled self-examinations on the subject than in his political and military exploits. The natural and inevitable climax of the biography is the sequence of three chapters describing his religious conversion, and his subsequent strange, obsessive subjection to the American evangelist Thomas Lake Harris, who introduces into the biography a note of tragedy reminiscent of *Irving*, and poses questions, as does *Irving*, about the nature of obsession. The last two chapters, describing events subsequent to Oliphant's bitter crisis of disenchantment with Harris, centralise, at times rather tediously, the further development of his religious opinions.

Many similarities of theme unite these eight biographies, although thirty-four years separate *Irving* from *Jeanne d'Arc*, years in which Mrs Oliphant developed and deepened her skills as a novelist, and came to understand more thoroughly her responsibilities as a biographer. Most of the biographical subjects are driven by powerful religious belief, which they follow to extremes of asceticism or to the creation of new religious movements which promote passionate loyalty among their followers. All of them possessed a remarkable gift for inspirational eloquence, or, to be less charitable, emotional rhetoric, especially seen in the sermons of Irving, Chalmers and Savonarola, and in the political speeches and writings of Montalembert, but also in Jeanne d'Arc and, more lyrically, in Francis of Assisi. All of them were single-minded idealists and individualists often at odds with their society, often driven to confrontations with authority, thus provoking authority to destroy them (Irving, Montalembert, Savonarola, Jeanne), or else aiming to transform it by transforming the religious life of the communities where they found themselves, whether nineteenth century Scotland and France or fifteenth century Florence (Irving, Montalembert, Tulloch, Francis, Chalmers, Savonarola, and in his later years Laurence Oliphant). Montalembert fought for religious and educational liberty and the revival of the spirit of monasticism in the increasingly secularised France of the time of Louis Philippe and Napoleon III. Savonarola imposed a brief regime of stern austerity upon Florence, epitomised by the famous Bonfire of Vanities of 1496, which Mrs Oliphant describes with the picturesqueness of detail in which her biographies are rich, indeed self-indulgently rich. Tulloch, whose biography is the least dramatic and most domestic of the biographies, played his part in the revitalising and humanising of Scottish religious life in the aftermath of the Disruption of 1843, and full detail is given of this in the eighth chapter of Mrs Oliphant's biography, "The Renaissance of the Scotch Church".

I have stressed the domesticity of the Tulloch biography. In any of Mrs Oliphant's biographies the domestic life of her subject is as important as the dramatic events in which he or she is involved. To her the trivialities of everyday life have as important a role to play as the great events of the world outside, since "the narrowest domestic record widens our experience of human nature, which, of all things involved, changes least from one generation to another". She speaks of "that assured and tranquil life in which no great thing happens, but in which all the events of life are developing",[11] and gives as much space as she can to the daily routine of her subjects, their gardens and parlours, their experience as parents, their private relationships. There is little scope for this in *Irving* or the Savonarola chapters, but Irving's affection for children is lightly stressed as a foil to the dramatic events of his life. The biography of Queen Victoria, published in its final form three years after Mrs Oliphant's death, devotes only two of its eight chapters to the Queen's public life, and its title in the body of the book is *The Domestic Life of the Queen*, although on the title page it appears as *Queen Victoria, a Personal Sketch.* And in the historical character studies which I shall examine in the next section political events are treated mainly as a background to the study of mood, motive and human relationships.

Mrs Oliphant's inclination to picturesque and evocative description and commentary sometimes betrays her into overuse of words like "romantic" and "poetic" and of self-conscious imagery; and picturesque detail, especially at the dramatic highlights of her subject's life, for example eloquent, poetic, graphic descriptions of the executions of Savonarola and Jeanne d'Arc. Nevertheless, as I shall later show, she never sensationalises tragic events. She is least interesting when she maintains a reverential tone which cannot allow a sharp enough picture of her subject. This is particularly true of the life of Thomas Chalmers, interesting only as a contribution to the ecclesiastical politics of the nineteenth century Scottish Kirk.

V

The two series of *Historical Sketches*, and the five books of urban history seem to form a different category of books from the biographies; but their main interest is essentially biographical. The *Historical Sketches* were a series of character studies of distinguished figures at the time of George II and of Queen Anne, published respectively in 1869 and December 1894.[12] Mrs Oliphant saw history as the chronicle of individual human beings. If it seems that by titling her chapters, for example, "The Poet", "The Reformer", "The Philosopher", "The Painter", "The Journalist", "The Humourist" (from the George II volume, Pope, Wesley, Berkeley and Hogarth, and, from the Queen Anne volume, Defoe and Addison) Mrs Oliphant is implying that her studies are generic rather than particular, intended to represent each person as characteristic of the age in which he or she lived, the articles themselves prove the contrary. Each one of them is treated purely as an individual, only lightly placed within the context of history, but largely examined for complexities and ambiguities of motivation and for the richness of their personality. Mrs Oliphant's approach is essentially that of her biographies. The final sentence of "The Man of the World", which is a study of Lord Chesterfield, makes her point of view very clear: "[Chesterfield's] Letters are within everybody's reach; but they are not so wonderful, so unique, or so manifold, as was the man"[13]. The words "unique" and "manifold" are significant. Mrs Oliphant was constantly drawn to people who, while seeming to conform to a stereotype, prove on close examination to be sharply individualised, distinguishable by motivation, background and circumstances from other people apparently similar. And in both novels and biographies she responds most readily and creatively to characters who are multifarious, complex, ambiguous or even ambivalent, and quite frequently paradoxical. She is often drawn to the strange, the excessive and the unfathomable. She attempts again, for example, to explain the strange story of Swift's relationship with Stella and Vanessa, and she describes with mixed feelings the extravagant emotional behaviour at Wesley's public meetings, "wild and wonderful scenes, exhibitions of the strangest and most indecorous emotion".[14] (Her view on such events seems to have hardened since *Irving*.)

Between 1876 and 1895 Mrs Oliphant published five books designed as contributions to urban history. She chose three Italian cities, Florence (1876), Venice (1887), and Rome (1895), and also Edinburgh (1890) and Jerusalem (1891). Each book was published for the Christmas season, each was lavishly illustrated and aimed to celebrate the visual scene of each city, with a tribute to the artists and writers, politicians and churchmen who had contributed to the life of the city, each was lyrical and evocative, picturesque and "graphic", a word much favoured by reviewers. The three Italian books, each with the word *Makers* in the title, had much in common; they confine themselves almost entirely to the medieval period, and make serious attempts to assess the historical processes that had moulded these three cities. But Mrs Oliphant cannot be taken seriously as a histor-ian, and in the brief preface to *Makers of Modern Rome* she acknowledges that "original research" cannot be expected from her because she is not "trained in the ways of learning". A similar admission is made at the end of the Introduction to *Jerusalem.* The three Italian city books are notable mainly for eloquent and picturesque description, and for those character studies which give her the opportunity for vivid narrative.

The other two city books are slightly different in struct-ure. *Royal Edinburgh* selectively covers the history of that city from Margaret of Scotland to Sir Walter Scott, with chapters on John Knox and Mary Stuart, and on the poets Allan Ramsay and (unconvincingly included in a book on Edinburgh) Robert Burns. It is more frankly a book of character sketches than its Italian companions, and is highly nostalgic and evocative. The narrative of *Jerusalem* is taken entirely from the Bible, from David to Jesus, and the immediacy and objectivity of the Biblical narra-tive are overlaid by the interpretative comments and biographical rhetoric which by 1891 had become habitual to Mrs Oliphant. Several reviewers complained of this, not unreasonably.[15]

Mrs Oliphant's approach to biography is essentially that of a novelist. She adopts an intimate approach to her biographical subject, inviting the reader to identify with him, speculating on motives and imagining thought processes which her authorities may not necessarily justify. It is certainly legitimate for her to challenge the conclusions of previous biographers and suggest more complex motivation than they allow; less legitimate in a biography is a rhetorical device in which she indulges from time to time, inviting the reader, sometimes with the use of an exclamatory style, to imagine the feelings or unspoken thoughts of her hero or heroine. She treats her subjects like characters in one of her novels, for example interpreting the ambivalent emotional state of Francis of Assisi during a brief crisis of doubt, which the medieval commentator interprets in the simplest way possible, unable to see the inner workings of Francis's mind.[16] And perhaps the most striking passages in her biography of Francis are those in the first two chapters describing his

emotional crisis and complex, unstable state of mind at the time
of his conversion, and the examination in a later chapter of he
strange, compulsive power of asceticism for Francis.

VI

Mrs Oliphant took the art of biography very seriously, and
made many comments on it. She reviewed many biographies during
her career, and in her article "Men and Women" of 1895 (item 475)
she insists that biographers and historians should be trained,
while novelists and poets probably cannot. A good model for
training biographers is suggested:

> Could Lockhart guide the pen, could he show what to leave
> out, what to pile on, - might he teach the learner himself
> to grow in knowledge, gradually, lovingly, with the
> character he expounds, making it also to grow upon the
> reader in natural development, like the unfolding petal by
> petal of a noble flower![17]

This is idealistic and optimistic, but elsewhere when she
reviewed biographies she offers more specific recommendations.
Her most considered analysis of the art of biography was provoked
by her disapproval of what she saw as the indiscretion of
Froude's biography of Thomas Carlyle, and was published in *The
Contemporary Review* in July 1883, "The Ethics of Biography" (item
498). In this article she recommends above all that a biographer
should aim to achieve balance. The biographer should steer a
middle course between the excess of hero-worship and partisanship
on the one hand, and on the other hand cynical denigration,
although denigration is the worse approach since "our defender is
at all times more nearly right than our detractor". He should
avoid an excess of documentation, and over-interpretation of the
problems and mysteries of his subject's life. His aim should to
be to highlight the essential qualities of his subject and to
avoid the accidental. He must "guard himself from superficial
impressions" and aim to discover the real man or woman behind
appearances. But he must scrupulously avoid "that prying
curiosity which loves to investigate circumstances, and thrust
itself into the sanctuaries of individual feeling". And this
entails avoidance of the flood of trivialities and indiscretions
that so often disfigures biographies. The biographer "must use
his imagination only as an adjunct to his sympathies, and as
giving him the power of realizing the position of his hero, and
putting himself in his place; and ... he must violate no law of
testimony, and call no unfair witnesses". He must possess "that
power of penetrating beneath the surface into the character of
another, which is sympathy, imagination, genius, all in one".[18]

It would be interesting to assess Mrs Oliphant's biographies
in the light of her own criteria. But I can give only brief space
to such an assessment here. It is reasonable to give her credit
for achieving the objectivity and detachment that she recommends,
even though reviewers complained of undue hero-worship, especially in *Irving*, where she was less than just to some of the
participants in Irving's tragedy. She usually makes fair attempts
to give a balanced evaluation of the biographical information
that she is using, scrupulously avoiding, for example, a verdict
on the true nature of Jeanne d'Arc's "voices", just as earlier

she had refused to comment on the extraordinary "tongues" (gloss-olalia) which manifested themselves at Irving's services. I have already mentioned her over-indulgence in lyricism, and sometimes she does risk the over-interpretation she deplores; but it can fairly be said that in her best biographical work she does achieve her own ideal of avoiding an excess of the detail which obscures rather than illuminates. She acknowledges, where it is relevant to do so, that there is a mystery which she is unable to explain; and is usually at her best, as I have already said, when discussing complexity and ambiguity. The most interesting passages in her undramatic life of John Tulloch are those describing his periodical bouts of deep depression. Much of this biography concerns ecclesiastical and university politics, which gives no scope to Mrs Oliphant's distinctive gifts as a biographer. But the chapters on Tulloch's depression, interweaving Tulloch's own descriptions of his affliction, in letters and diaries, with sensitive and perceptive analyses of them by Mrs Oliphant, are among the most memorable sequences in her non-fiction. As an examination of the painful phenomenon of clinical depression they are worthy of mention alongside that classic study of the subject, Coleridge's "Dejection: an Ode". What can certainly be said of all her biographies after *Irving* is that they are always lucid and accessible to the reader.

Mrs Oliphant's biographies are at their best when her story becomes tragic, because here the voice of disillusion that appears in her novels is most clearly heard. She treats tragedy with detachment and without inflated rhetoric, because she can reflect her own experience of life. To illustrate this I deliberately choose quotations from minor biographies, mainly from *Jeanne d'Arc*. Although Jeanne faces "the deep distress of having been abandoned in the sight of men, perhaps the profoundest pang of which nature is capable", and discovers that "the most terrible of all despairs is such a pause and horror of doubt lest nothing should be true" as was felt by the followers of Jesus after the Crucifixion, perhaps also by Jeanne, nevertheless she was "no supernatural heroine, but ... a terrified, tormented, and often trembling girl". In her literary biography *Cervantes* Mrs Oliphant speaks of "a tragedy, not so much of gross and fleshly passion, as of that endless human blundering and piteous folly which [is] so much closer to every man's experience", and in these words we hear the voice of the mature Oliphant novels.[19]

Probably of all Mrs Oliphant's biographies the one that most satisfies her own criteria, and is also likely to appeal most to the modern reader, is that of Laurence Oliphant, a man rich in the complexities and the mysteries of motivation that attracted her. She may not unreasonably be considered to have done justice to a man whom Michael Sadleir has described as "double-natured to an extraordinary degree. In his one personality he combined the extremes of adventurous gallantry and mystic unreason."[20] Her most powerful and mature handling of the theme of disillusion in her biographies is found in the treatment of Oliphant's loss of faith in the evangelist Harris: "that most tremendous of moral convulsions, the throwing off of a long and confirmed allegiance, the destruction of a faith that had been for many years the chief thing in his life."[21] A recent biographer of Laurence Oliphant frequently cites Mrs Oliphant's biography, and takes it seriously as an authority, although noting her reticence and evasiveness on some delicate matters.[22]

VII

A little space musts be given to Mrs Oliphant as a literary critic, choosing very selectively from a wealth of material. There is little need to do more than mention two of the three short books she ontributed to the Blackwood series which she herself edited, Foreign Classics for English Readers, studies of Molière and Cervantes, and her book on Sheridan contributed to the English Men of Letters Series. As always she seems to concentrate her energies upon the life of the writer rather than upon his work. For example, the two chapters devoted to *Don Quixote* in the Cervantes volume consist almost entirely of extended plot summary, with occasional brief interpretative comment. And it is not easy to understand why Macmillan offered her Sheridan for the EML series. How much more interesting would have been a book from her on Jane Austen or Sir Walter Scott. Her comments on Sheridan's plays are largely conventional, although there is a convincing analysis of the faulty construction of *The School for Scandal*, based upon study of its textual development from early drafts. (Her information was derived exclusively from Thomas Moore's life of Sheridan.)

The first of her three contributions to the Foreign Classics series, a book on Dante, claims rather more detail than its two successors, since Dante's *Divine Comedy* was a major influence upon her religious views and upon her entire series of Stories of the Seen and Unseen. The first three chapters of *Makers of Florence* are concerned with Dante, but they are purely biographical. The monograph, published a year or two later (1879), devotes most of its 208 pages to *The Divine Comedy*, summarising it with eloquent enthusiasm for its imaginative intensity and the powerful sense of circumstantial reality in its presentation of human suffering in the *Inferno*. Mrs Oliphant finds her attention wandering when allegory or mystification takes priority over human feeling: "even the sometimes sublime strain of the *Paradiso* is impaired by the very large admixture of theology and philosophy to which the denizens of heaven give vent". And she is most deeply moved by Dante's treatment of the suffering of individual human beings: "The fierce human anguish [of Ugolino], so real and close to the spectator, moves us as no vaguer and vaster misery can".[23]

Mrs Oliphant published two literary histories, respectively of the Romantic period (1882) and of the Victorian period (1892). She aimed to be all-inclusive, including chapters on historians, philosophers, theologians and in the Victorian volume scientists (although this particular chapter was probably written by her son and collaborator Francis Romano Oliphant). As a result she is often more superficial than she might have been had she been more selective, thus confining herself to those authors on whom she was well-informed. Characteristically, the history of the Romantic period tends to be a series of character sketches, with incidental comments on the author's works, often very personal, subjective and emotive. Mrs Oliphant was not much more qualified as a literary historian than she was as a general or urban historian; and many reviewers of the earlier history commented unfavourably on her inability to provide a balanced perspective of the historical and cultural events that led to the Romantic Movement.[24] Conceding these undeniable limitations, one may still find much of interest in these histories. And as the history of Victorian literature reduces biographical information to a minimum it is more confined to literary fact and opinion than the earlier history.[25] There is, however, one remarkable exception. In the third chapter of the first volume of *The Victorian Age* there is a sustained tribute to Carlyle, eloquent and slightly extravagant in its imagery. Here character study takes priority over literary criticism, although there is an interesting defence of the notorious Carlyle style.

Mrs Oliphant judges her predecessors and contemporaries from her wide human experience, guided by her intelligence and sensitivities, and by her particular preoccupations, sometimes personal, sometimes aesthetic. Her views of Cowper, Burns, Crabbe, Wordsworth, Tennyson, Browning, Rossetti and other poets are of value, not because we necessarily endorse her verdicts, which are sometimes orthodox, sometimes idiosyncratic, but because they offer us an approach to these poets which is distinctly individual. (Her treatment of Keats is sympathetic but superficial; but although she does her best to give a balanced evaluation of Byron and Shelley she is temperamentally incapable of doing them justice.) Her views of novelists will interest us much more, and her tributes to Sir Walter Scott and to the three women novelists Maria Edgeworth, Jane Austen and Susan Ferrier are among the most valuable chapters of the earlier history, although it is a pity that she is too often content with enthusiasm for the novelists' characters rather than close examination of the individuality of their novels. In the Victorian volume she offers far too many novelists, and can scarcely say much of interest about most of them. But her views of Dickens, George Eliot, Trollope and Charlotte Brontë deserve to be taken seriously by the modern reader, even though her choice of novels to comment on is strangely selective; and the failures of her insights are as remarkable as her successes. For example, she has nothing to say on *The Mill on the Floss*. However, she had already commented upon this novel in 1885 in her review of J.W. Cross's life of George Eliot in *The Edinburgh Review* (item 507), speaking of it with warm admiration. Similarly, her view of Charlotte Brontë can be more extensively studied in her article "The Sisters Brontë", published in 1897 in a Diamond Jubilee volume on the women novelists of Queen Victoria's reign (item 238).

Mrs Oliphant's preference in poetry and novels is for the close observation of the world of human experience, viewed with affection and humour, but not with documentary realism. She admires the feeling for emotional truth which gives us the pleasure of recognition, and she also looks for the particularity of detail which gives individuality and familiarity to universal truth. Her preference for sobriety of tone makes her unsympathetic to poets like Shelley and novelists like Dickens and Emily Brontë. And her preference for novels which give a wide range of human experience, not a limited sector of it, makes her sceptical of novels like *Jane Eyre*, with their inexhaustible obsession with the need to be loved. In poetry she responds to lyricism and to the tender handling of grief and sorrow in poems like *In Memoriam*.

Mrs Oliphant's claims to be taken seriously as a literary critic are to be found mainly in her reviews of novels and biographies, and perhaps also poetry, in *Blackwood's Magazine* and elsewhere; but to illustrate what may be her finest passage of literary criticism I must give some detail of her article in the *George II* volume on Richardson, to whom she was drawn by his sympathy for and understanding of women. Richardson had learned much from constant companionship with women, and "the sisters of the boy upon whom we are spending heaps of money at Eton and Oxford are not only much pleasanter to talk to, but very much more ready and better qualified in many instances to take part in those mild intellectual encounters, those little incursions over the borders of metaphysics, discussions of motives, sentiments, cases of conscience, points of social honour, which are the most prolific subjects of conversation, than - not only their brother, but their brother's tutor, and all the learned community to which he belongs". The benefits of such conversations prove themselves when Richardson comes to create Clarissa, and I must quote at some length Mrs Oliphant's tribute to his heroine. "This conception stands by itself amid all the conceptions of genius"; Clarissa is "... a virgin-martyr, a poetic visionary being, one of the few original types of art"; she "has but a garrulous and pottering expositor, but in her own person she is divine"; "the highest poetic creation of the age is this one matchless figure". "[She] exists by her own right, and is not the fruit of observation, or study, or knowledge of the world". "Not a woman of her generation is half so true to nature". Mrs Oliphant is amazed that such insight into a woman has been achieved by a man, and that no woman writer has yet come near it. And she pays a tribute to Richardson's artistic integrity in holding to his chosen tragic ending for *Clarissa*. "With what an intuitive perception of the best principles of art he kept by his original idea. ... [T]he interests of morality concurred with the highest necessities of art".

Mrs Oliphant goes on to a telling and perceptive analysis of Lovelace, whom she compares with Fielding's Tom Jones, insisting that Lovelace is a far more interesting study of a rake, having more complexity, more depth, more ambivalence. Richardson, she insists, has "that supreme power of natural selection which belongs to genius". She concludes this remarkable article with an analysis of the reasons why *Sir Charles Grandison* is an inferior book, noting, for example, the failure of the idealised and overpraised hero, since "... all the admiration the reader can give is forestalled, and he feels himself limping a world behind the enthusiastic audience in the book itself".[26]

The tribute to Clarissa is very eloquent, but it is more than eloquence. It implies the view that great art transcends the need for "observation, or study, or knowledge of the world", important though these are, and searches for the universal, symbolic poetic truth that underlies the observed reality; a literary character must not only be individualised but also have the universality of myth; it must display the power to recreate and interpret what the writer has experienced.[27]

VIII

Brief reference must be made to Mrs Oliphant's last, and in many ways most enduring, work of non-fiction, *Annals of a Publishing House*, which combines a biography of the publisher William Blackwood, 1775-1834, and of his sons, with a detailed literary history of *Blackwood's Magazine* and its contributors. It was exhaustively, and exhaustingly, researched and has frequently been cited as an authority by historians and scholars, although it needs supplementing and correcting by later research.[28] Of particular value is the first volume, with chapters on the four leading figures of early Blackwood days: John Gibson Lockhart, Christopher North (John Wilson), James Hogg, and William Maginn, and useful biographical information upon Coleridge and De Quincey. Volume II is of less interest, but includes passages about George Eliot and Branwell Brontë not previously available. The two volumes are characteristic of Mrs Oliphant in their many quick vivid sketches of character; she is always ready to enter dramatically into the state of mind of the Blackwoods and their authors, no doubt an inadvisable procedure for a biographer. Nevertheless she always concedes priority to documentation, especially the extended quotation of letters from the Blackwood files, and sometimes she shows considerable skill in summarising long and complex correspondences to extract their gist.

IX

It would be impossible in an introduction like this to do justice to Mrs Oliphant's journalism and book reviewing, which kept her occupied throughout her long career. She was an inexhaustible reviewer of books; not merely novels and biographies and other works of imaginative literature, on which she could speak with authority, but on virtually any subject, whether or not she had the chance to do any background reading on it. She was steering an uneasy course between dilettantism and a wide-ranging curiosity about all human phenomena. And yet at times she is able to speak with a seeming authority which can often carry conviction. Section B of the bibliography lists all books reviewed and briefly annotates some of the specialist articles; and I need not give further detail here.

Late in her life Mrs Oliphant wrote articles in which she made discursive commentary upon a wide range of contemporary topics, political, social, artistic, literary, or whatever of interest had come to her attention. This includes the series "The Looker-on" contributed to *Blackwood's Magazine* and "Things in General" contributed to *Atalanta*, a periodical for young women, and also two series of articles listed in this bibliography for the first time: "A Commentary from/in an Easy Chair" contributed to *The Spectator*; and the recently identified "A Fireside Commentary", contributed to *St.James's Gazette.* In her autobiography Mrs Oliphant refers to an article in this newspaper on her youthful campaigning against the Corn Laws.[29] This was published in the *Gazette* on 11 January 1888, and was the first of 21 articles with this title. Then after a slight gap appeared thirteen articles with the signature "M". These in style and content are clearly the work of Mrs Oliphant. Moreover, *The Spectator* had in 1874 and 1884 published two Letters to the Editor over this signature (items 562 and 573), known from documentation held in the *Spectator* library to be by Mrs Oliphant; and two further Letters to the Editor signed "M" followed in 1894 and 1896 (items 614 and 615).[30]

It is unlikely that Section B is as complete as one would desire. Many of Mrs Oliphant's contributions to periodicals, especially newspapers, have probably still to be identified, as they would certainly have been unsigned. One article which I have been able to trace is a short summary of Laurence Oliphant's career published in *St James's Gazette*. She tells us that she had intended to review Oliphant's last book *Scientific Religion*

(1888) "in a newspaper to which I happened to have access at the moment", but, unable to understand the book, compromised with a study of his career.[31] The newspaper to which she had access in 1888 was *St James's Gazette*; and the article appeared on 22 May of that year. It is unsigned, but is unmistakably the article which Mrs Oliphant describes. There may be other articles to be discovered, identifiable only by recognition of Mrs Oliphant's style and manner.

X

Mrs Oliphant seems to have taken herself seriously as a poet. The second chapter of *Sundays*, "Going up to Jerusalem", consists mainly of a thirteen-page poem in irregular rhymed verse. And *Dante* contains many long translations from the *Vita Nuova* and the *Divine Comedy*. Some of the poems listed in Section C are ambitiously written in complex verse forms (items 621, 623, 626, 631, 632). Near the end of her life she considered a small volume of collected poems.[32] But Mrs Oliphant never allowed herself the time to achieve distinction as a poet, and one cannot dissent from Elisabeth Jay's verdict: "her poetry was utterly unmemorable because the constraints of conventional metrical discipline never allowed her to do more than imitate other poets' rhythms or pad out her verses with line-fillers."[33]

NOTES AND REFERENCES

[1] Mrs Q. D. Leavis, Introduction to Oliphant, *Autobiography and Letters*, Leicester University Press, 1974, <10>.

[2] *Sundays*, 1, 5-6, 8-10.

[3] This is the topic with which Elisabeth Jay deals in her reference to the book (Jay, *Mrs Oliphant: "A Fiction to Herself"*, Oxford, 1995, 209). Mrs Oliphant derived her social philosophy on the promotion of personal charity partly from the Scottish theologian Thomas Chalmers, mentioned later in this Introduction, and she refers to this theme in her biography of Chalmers, and also in her biography of Edward Irving, and even in her history of English literature of the Romantic period. Fuller treatment of the theme is to be found in her article "Social Science" published in *Blackwood's Magazine* in December 1860 (item 289).

[4] *Sundays*, 20. Elisabeth Jay considers *Sundays* to be an "improving book for children" (*Oliphant*, 133 and 320, n. 134); but I find this unconvincing. My quotations suggest a book intended for adults, encouraging a modification of their approach to religion, and a maturer awareness of the world in which they live.

[5] *Irving*, II, 22; II, 64; I, 215; II, 337. Mrs Oliphant is at times at pains to defend Irving against the charge of egotism; but often the biographical information she proceeds to give calls in question the validity of her defence.

[6] *Irving*, II, 136.

[7] Annan is the Dumfriesshire town where Irving was born, and

where in 1822 he was ordained.

[8] *Irving* II, 191; II, 88; II, 108; II, 100.

[9] *Irving*, II, 23.

[10] *Irving*, I, 407.

[11] "Autobiographies, no 1 - Benvenuto Cellini" (item 404), 2; *Annals of a Publishing House*, II, 67.

[12] The month as well as the year is mentioned because December was the date of the British publication, of the full text. The abridged text, published in America earlier in 1894, has no authority. See the bibliography, items 214 and 215.

[13] *Historical Sketches of ... George II*, I, 200.

[14] *George II*, II, 60.

[15] See, for example, "Books of the Week", *The Times*, 17 Dec., 1891, 3; "Books and Book Gossip", *The Sunday Sun*, 20 Dec., 1891, 1; (Sir Charles Wilson), rev. of *Jerusalem, The Athenaeum*, 12 Mar., 1892, 355-6; "Notices", *The Guardian*, 20 Apr., 1892, 587. (*The Guardian* was not *The Manchester Guardian*, but an Anglican newspaper published in London.)

[16] *Francis of Assisi*, 88.

[17] "Men and Women", 621.

[18] "The Ethics of Biography", 83, 84, 87, 89.

[19] *Jeanne d'Arc*, 393, 208, 384; *Cervantes*, 120. In the last quotation Mrs Oliphant is referring to one of Cervantes's "Exemplary Novels", but her words faithfully reflect her approach to the tragedies she describes in her novels and biographies.

[20] Michael Sadleir, Foreword to Laurence Oliphant, *Piccadilly*, reprint, Constable's Miscellany of Original & Selected Publications in Literature (London: Constable and Co., 1928), v. *Piccadilly*, a satirical novel, was originally published in 1870 and was reviewed by Mrs Oliphant in *Blackwood's Magazine* in October 1870 (item 333). This was her first chance to comment upon Oliphant, and her next was her obituary, with a brief biography, published in *Blackwood's Magazine* in February 1889 (item 447).

[21] *Laurence Oliphant*, II, 206.

[22] See Anne Taylor, *Laurence Oliphant 1829-88* (Oxford: Oxford University Press, 1982). References to MOWO's reticence are to be found on pp. 126, 147 and 255-7.

[23] *Dante*, 194, 106.

[24] See, for example, (Theodore Watts [later Watts-Dunton]), *The Athenaeum*, 27 May, 1882, 659-60; *Saturday Review*, 24 Jun., 1882,

603-4; "Contemporary Literature", *The British Quarterly Review* 76 (Jul. 1882), 208-12; *The Guardian*, 11 Oct. 1882, 1421-2. For *The Guardian* see note 15. Similar complaints were made of her lack of historical perspective in reviews of her five books of urban history. See in particular a review of *Makers of Modern Rome* by E. Armstrong, *The English Historical Review* 11 (Oct., 1896), 771-2.

[25] The history of Victorian literature was in some ways an extension of a Golden Jubilee article published in June 1887 in *Blackwood's Magazine*, a survey of the literature of the previous fifty years under the general title of "The Old Saloon" (item 437).

[26] *George II*, II, 219, 236-238, 243, 254, 255. The full analysis of Clarissa is 233-239 and of Lovelace 243-46.

[27] Another novel which Mrs Oliphant greatly admired was Defoe's *Journal of the Plague Year.* Her praise of the book highlights its poetic concentration, which transcends the accurate communication of fact. (The word "poetic", here as in the Clarissa passage, is Mrs Oliphant's own.) See *Queen Anne* (British ed.), 327-30.

[28] See, for example, Alan Lang Strout, "Walter Scott and *Maga*", *The Times Literary Supplement*, 5 Feb., 1938, 92; and Frank D. Tredrey, *The House of Blackwood 1804-1954* (London and Edinburgh: Blackwood, 1954).

[29] Oliphant, *Autobiography*, ed. Jay. (See item 730 in the Addenda to this bibliography), 25.

[30] Elisabeth Jay makes use of the *St James's Gazette* articles in her 1995 biography of Mrs Oliphant (see note 3 above).

[31] *Laurence Oliphant,* II, 356.

[32] Letter to Mr [William] Blackwood, 15 September, 1892, *A&L*, 391.

[33] Jay, *Oliphant*, 298.

BIBLIOGRAPHY

This bibliography completes the work of my previous bibliography
of Mrs Oliphant's fiction and also her autobiography (Victorian
Fiction Research Guides XI, 1986), extended by Addenda 2,
published in 1990. It aims to be as complete as possible,
including all information available about Mrs Oliphant's non-
fiction and manuscripts. All first editions have been examined,
and many later British editions. Other information about British
editions has been taken from the English Catalogue of Books.
Regrettably almost all information about American editions,
except where otherwise stated, has had to be taken from the
National Union Catalogue and the American Catalogue. Three of Mrs
Oliphant's urban histories, *Makers of Florence*, *Makers of Venice*
and *Royal Edinburgh*, were extremely popular with American
publishers, and it has not been possible to identify the dates of
many editions published by others than Macmillan, the original
publisher. No doubt an American scholar may wish to research the
publishing history of these three books, and can thus disentangle
the complexities revealed in this bibliography.

Section B aims to be as complete as possible, listing all Mrs
Oliphant's articles and minor journalism. But it is likely that
some articles contributed to newspapers and lesser known periodicals remain to be discovered. The Wellesley indexes have been
consulted widely; but this bibliography supplies information not
available in Wellesley, details of books reviewed and brief
annotation of some articles.

Abbreviations

A Cat	The American Catalogue.
A&L	*Autobiography and Letters of Mrs Margaret Oliphant*, ed. Mrs Harry Coghill (Edinburgh and London: Blackwood, 1899). (See VFRG XI, item 724.)
BL	The British Library.
E Cat	The English Catalogue of Books.
LL Cat	The London Library Catalogue.
MOWO	Mrs Oliphant (Margaret Oliphant Wilson Oliphant).
NLS	The National Library of Scotland.
NU Cat	The National Union Catalogue.
NY	New York.
ULL	The University Library, London.
VFRG XI	Victorian Fiction Research Guides XI (see above).

Other abbreviations, of periodical titles, are self-explanatory.

Acknowledgements

The library of *The Spectator* owns a set of ledgers, containing
handwritten lists of contributions with named authors, covering
the years November 1874 to November 1877 and November 1880
onwards. I am grateful to Charles Seaton, librarian at *The
Spectator*, for permission to consult these ledgers on various
occasions, and thus to identify Mrs Oliphant's contributions to
the magazine. I also acknowledge with gratitude the assistance of
the ongoing Athenaeum Project in identifying her contribution to
that periodical. The Project is a joint venture of the City
University, London, the State University of Ghent, Belgium, and

the Free University of Brussels, led by Professor Oskar Wellens
of the University of Brussels. The City University holds in its
library the complete sequence of bound volumes of *The Athenaeum*,
each article marked in a contemporary hand with its author's
name, usually in an abbreviated form. (These volumes were
previously owned by *The New Statesman*.) Information on *The
Spectator* has also been obtained from William Beach Thomas, *The
Story of The Spectator 1828 - 1928* (London: Methuen, 1928).

I should also like to express my gratitude to the staff at The
British Library, the British Newspaper Library, The Bodleian
Library, Cambridge University Library, The National Library of
Scotland, The University Library of London and the John Rylands
University Library of Manchester, who at different times gave me
great assistance and guidance in my researches. I should also
like to express a personal debt of gratitude to Jeremy Pritchard,
owner of the computer on which I learned the use of that instru-
ment and prepared the greater part of this bibliography. (Sadly,
he died in December 1993.)

A Non-Fiction

Sundays

1   First ed. *Sundays/* by Mrs Oliphant.
Quotation from Herbert on title page ("This day my Saviour rose
...")
London: James Nisbet and Co. 1858. 1 vol. (In fact published Dec
1857.) 222 pp.

2   Second (?) ed. London: Griffin (Richard) & Co, 1861.

Translation of The Monks of the West

3   *The/ Monks of the West/ from St Benedict to St. Bernard/* by/
the Count de Montalembert, / Member of the French Academy./
Authorised Translation.
Edinburgh and London: William Blackwood and Sons, 1861-79. 7
vols. (Vols I, II, 1861; vols III, IV, V, 1867; vols VI, VII,
1879.)
MOWO not named as translator.

The Life of Edward Irving

4   First ed. *The Life/ of/ Edward Irving,/ Minister of/ The
National Scotch Church, London./* Illustrated by his Journals and
Correspondence. (black letter)/ by/ Mrs. Oliphant. / Quotation of
a prayer of Irving's ("Whether I live ... I am the Lord's."
Amen.).
Dedicated "to all who love the memory of Edward Irving".
London: Hurst and Blackett. 1862 (May). 2 vols.
Portrait frontispiece to vol. 1. I: xiv + 420 pp. II: 503 pp.
Includes three appendices not subsequently reprinted.

5   American ed. NY: Harper and Brothers, 1862. 1 vol.

6   Second British ed. Hurst and Blackett, 1862 (Oct). 2 vols.
Preface to the Second Edition. Text revised, slightly cut, and
corrected, esp. Vol. II, inc. two footnotes referring to
criticisms made of the first ed.
Two appendices, different from those in first ed.

7   Three rpts of second ed., 1862. NU Cat records "5th ed." in
1 vol. This cannot be the fifth *edition*, if published in 1862.
But if in 1 vol, it should be the 1864 ed, item 8. (Cf also 9 and
10.)

8   Third British ed. Hurst and Blackett, 1864. 1 vol.
"Carefully revised". Index included. No appendices. Some cuts
from Chapter 16. ix + 442 pp.

9   Fourth British ed. Hurst and Blackett, n.d. (1865). 1 vol.
Text unchanged from 1864.
Hurst and Blackett Standard Library 30.

10   Fifth British ed. Hurst and Blackett, n.d. (1873). 1 vol.
Hurst and Blackett's Standard Library.

Apparently a simple rpt of Fourth Edn.

11   Rpt of fifth ed., 1880s.

12   Sixth British ed. Hurst and Blackett, Jul 1897. 1 vol.

Historical Sketches of the Reign of George II

All chapters first printed in *Blackwood's Magazine* as follows:

13   "The Queen", *BM* 103 (Feb 1868), 195-221.
Queen Caroline.

14   "The Minister", *BM* 103 (Apr 1868), 412-40.
Sir Robert Walpole.

15   "The Man of the World", *BM* 103 (May 1868), 511-33.
Lord Chesterfield.

16   "Lady Mary Wortley Montagu", *BM* 104 (Jul 1868), 1-25.

17   "The Poet", *BM* 104 (Aug 1868), 226-51.
Alexander Pope.

18   "The Young Chevalier", *BM* 104 (Sep 1868), 259-85.
Prince Charles Edward Stuart.

19   "The Reformer", *BM* 104 (Oct 1868), 428-56.
John Wesley.

20   "The Sailor", *BM* 104 (Dec 1868), 678-98.
Commodore Anson.

21   "The Philosopher", *BM* 105 (Jan 1869), 1-29.
Bishop Berkeley.

22   "The Novelist", *BM* 105 (Mar 1869), 252-76.
Samuel Richardson.

23   "The Sceptic", *BM* 105 (Jun 1869), 665-91.
David Hume.

24   "The Painter", *BM* 106 (Aug 1869), 140-68.
William Hogarth.

25   Serialization in *Littell's Living Age*, Boston, Mass.

1868

"Queen Caroline, Wife of George II", 7 Mar.
"Sir Robert Walpole", 9 May.
"Lord Chesterfield", 6 Jun.
"Lady Mary Wortley Montagu", 8 Aug.
"Alexander Pope", 12 Sep.
"The Young Chevalier", 3 Oct.
"The Reformer (John Wesley)", 7 Nov.

1869

"The Sailor - Commodore Anson", 9 Jan.
"The Philosopher - Bishop Berkeley", 13 Feb.
"The Novelist - Richardson", 10 Apr.
"The Sceptic - David Hume", 3 Jul.
"The Painter - Hogarth", 18 Sep.

26   First ed. *Historical Sketches/ of the/ Reign of George Second/* by/ Mrs Oliphant./ Quotation from *Alls Well that Ends Well.*
Dedicated to Leila Macdonald.
Edinburgh and London: William Blackwood and Sons, 1869 (Nov). 2 vols. I: 389 pp. II: 404 pp.

27   American ed. Boston, Littell and Gay, n.d. (1869). 1 vol. "First published in *Littell's Living Age*".

28   Second British ed. Blackwood, 1870 (May). 1 vol. 504 pp.

29   Third British ed. Blackwood, 1875 (Nov). 1 vol. 504 pp.
Title simply *Historical Sketches*. Minor changes of text.

Francis of Assisi

30   First ed. *Francis of Assisi/* by/ Mrs Oliphant./ Drawing of head and shoulders of Francis with halo.
Quotation from Dante on back of title page. Dedicated in Italian to "Franceschi miei" (her two sons Cyril Francis and Francis Romano). xxiv + 304 pp.
London: Macmillan, 1870 (Nov or Dec).
The Sunday Library for Household Reading.
Frontispiece. Portrait of Saint Francis on title page.

31   Second ed. (or reissue of first?) Macmillan, 1871.

Later eds - or reissues (E Cat or NU Cat)

32   Macmillan, 1877.

33   Macmillan, n.d. (1885).

34   London and NY: Macmillan, 1888.

35   London and NY: Macmillan, 1889.

36   London and NY: Macmillan, 1892.
Reduced in size?

37   Macmillan, 1894.

38   London and NY: Macmillan, 1898.

39   London: Macmillan, 1902.

40   London: Macmillan, 1907.

Memoir of Count de Montalembert

41   First ed. *Memoir/ of/ Count de Montalembert/ Peer of France/ Deputy for the Department of Doubs/ A Chapter of Recent French History/ by/ Mrs Oliphant/ Author of the Life of Edward Irving/ S. Francis of Assisi,* etc.
Quotation from Spenser facing title page.
Dedicated to the Comtesse de Montalembert.
Edinburgh and London: William Blackwood and Sons, 1872 (Aug). 2 vols. I: xi + 352 pp; II: v + 409 pp.

42   Tauchnitz ed. Leipzig: Bernhard Tauchnitz, 1872. 2 vols.

43   French adaptation. *Le Comte de Montalembert,* étude d'après l'ouvrage de Madame Oliphant (*Memoir of Count de Montalembert*), par Mme August Craven.
Paris: Librairie Académique, Didier et Cie, 1875.
Largely a paraphrase of MOWO, with frequent translations.

The Makers of Florence

Some chapters published in periodicals as follows:

44   "The Painter", *Macmillan's Magazine* 30 (Jul 1874), 229-50.
Fra Angelico.
Subsequently Chapter VII.

45   "The Frate", *MM* 30 (Aug 1874), 323-33.
Sant' Antonio, Bishop of Florence; Girolamo Savonarola.
Subsequently Chapters VIII and IX.

46   "Preacher and Prior", *MM* 30 (Sep 1874), 418-28.
Girolamo Savonarola, continued.
Subsequently Chapter X.

47   "Savonarola as a Politician", *MM* 31 (Jan 1875), 223-35.
Subsequently Chapter XI.

(All of these published anonymously.)

48   "The Sperimento", *MM* 32 (Jun 1875), (Jun 1875).
Continuation of the story of Savonarola.
Subsequently Chapter XII.

49   "The Prophet's End", *MM* 32 (Sep 1875), 424-33.
The execution of Savonarola.
Subsequently Chapter XIII.

(These two attributed to MOWO on contents page.)

50   "The Early Years of Dante", *The Cornhill Magazine* 32 (Oct 1875), 471-89.
Unsigned.
Subsequently Chapter I.

51   "Dante in Exile", *MM* 32 (Dec 1875), 670-90.

Unsigned.
Revised as Chapter III, with the early paragraphs extended as Chapter II.

52 "Michael Angelo", *Blackwood's Magazine* 120 (Oct 1876), 461-82.
Unsigned.
Revised as Chapter XV.

53 First ed. *The/ Makers of Florence/ Dante Giotto Savonarola/ and Their City/ by/ Mrs Oliphant.*
London: Macmillan and Co., 1876 (Dec) 1 vol.
Frontispiece and fifty-three illustrations, from drawings by Professor Delamotte. xviii + 395.
The periodical articles revised, and the following new chapters added: IV, V, VI, XIV.

54 Second ed. (or rpt). Macmillan, 1877. "Reprinted".
Preface to Second Edition - not retained in later eds. Textually identical with first ed.

55 New ed. "Third and Cheaper Edition". Macmillan, 1881.
Repaginated: xx + 422.

56 Rpt, 1883.

57 Rpt, 1885.

58 Rpt, Jan 1888.

59 Rpt, Nov 1888.

60 Rpt, 1889.

61 American ed. NY: H.M. Caldwell, n.d. (1880s). 338 pp.
NU Cat lists this twice, once with no date suggested. Probably the two entries represent one ed.

62 Extra illustrated edition, Dec 1891.

63 Rpt, 1892.

64 American ed. NY: Macmillan, 1894. 4 vols. ("New miniature ed." A Cat.)

65 American ed. NY: Merrill and Baker, 1896.
The Gentleman's Library. 338 pp.

66 American ed. NY: H.M. Caldwell, 1896. Illustrated Library of Famous Books, no 141.

66a NY: H.M. Caldwell, 1896. Illustrated Library of Famous Books, "new escutcheon series", no 34.

67 NY: H.M. Caldwell, 1896. "Artist ed."

(The last three A Cat.)

68   NY: A.L. Burt, 1890s (1897?) The Home Library. 436 pp.

69   British ed. Rpt, 1897.

70   Rpt, 1901.

71   American ed. NY: the Macmillan Company, 1901. 422 pp.
No doubt identical with previous British eds, 1881-1901.

72   American ed. NY: H.M. Caldwell, 1901. Berkeley Library. (A
Cat.) Cf 61, 66, 66a, 67.

73   American ed. NY: A.L. Burt Company, 1901 (?) The Home
Library. 436 pp. Reprint of 68?

74   British ed. rpt, 1903.

75   American ed. NY: The Macmillan Company, 1904. "Four vols in
one".

76   American ed. NY: The Macmillan Company, 1906. "Two vols in
one".

77   British ed. Rpt, 1908. (Copy at ULL. All details as 1881.)

78   New ed? London and NY: Macmillan, 1914. described as "4th
ed.". (In NU Cat: "1881. 1914".)

*****

American eds, undated or incompletely dated (NU Cat)

79   NY: Morris, n.d. Philobiblion ed. 436 pp.

80   NY: Merrill and Baker, 1890s. The Levant ed. 338 pp.

81   NY: T.Y. Crowell, 1900s. 338 pp.

82   NY: The Mershon Company, 1900s.

83   Philadelphia: H.T. Coates, 1900s? 338 pp.

Dante

84   First ed. *Dante*/ by/ Mrs Oliphant.
Edinburgh and London: William Blackwood and Sons, 1877.
Foreign Classics for English Readers I. 208 pp.

85   American ed. Philadelphia: J.B. Lippincott and Co, 1877.
Foreign Classics for English Readers.

86   Rpt of 84, 1879.

87   Rpt, 1887.

88   Cheap rpt, Jun 1898.

89   Rpt, 1906.

Dress

90   First ed. *Dress*/ by/ Mrs Oliphant./ A design of a fruit tree
in a jar with ART AT HOME on tree trunk.
London: Macmillan and Company, 1878 (Nov or Dec)
Art at Home Series, 7.
Frontispiece. Eight drawings by R.H. 103 pp.

91   American ed. Philadelphia: Porter and Coates, 1879.
Art at Home Series. 103 pp.

Molière

92   First ed. *Molière*/ by/ Mrs Oliphant/ and/ F. Tarver MA.
Edinburgh and London: William Blackwood and Sons, 1879 (Feb)
Foreign Classics for English Readers VI. x + 192 pp.

93   American ed. Philadelphia: J.B. Lippincott and Co. [1879].
Foreign Classics for English Readers.

94   Rpt of 92, 1887 (?).

95   Cheap rpt, Sep 1898.

96   Rpt, 1902.

Queen Victoria

97   First version. *The Life of the Queen. The Graphic* Summer
Number, 28 Jun 1880, 1-36.
Six chapters, illustrated.

98   Second version. "Queen Victoria", *Harper's New Monthly
Magazine* 61 (Jul. 1880), 221-39.
Four chapters, illustrated. This is the *Graphic* text abridged,
Chapters 4 to 6 reduced to one chapter. Chapter 5, "Public Life",
in *The Graphic* is almost entirely omitted; other omissions made.

99   Rpt of 97. Apparently published by Messrs Low, Sep/ Oct
1880, without MOWO's permission. See *A&L*, 288. No copy seen;
possibly the book was withdrawn.

100   American ed. *The Queen*. NY: Harper and Brothers, 1880.
Franklin Square Library 127. 40 pp. 44 engravings.
Not seen. Presumably a rpt of either 97 or 98.

101   Third version. *The Queen's Record Reign*. (Heading of page 1:
The Life of Queen Victoria). *The Graphic* Diamond Jubilee number,
1 Jun 1897. Six chapters. 33 pp. Lavishly illustrated.
97 rewritten, and its last pages extended to bring events from
1880 to 1897.

102   Fourth version; first ed. *Queen Victoria/ A Personal*

Sketch/ by/ Mrs Oliphant/ Illustrated.
London, Paris, NY and Melbourne: Cassell and Company Limited,
1900 (Sep)
Text headed *The/ Domestic Life of the Queen*/ by/ Margaret
Oliphant,/ Author of *Royal Edinburgh*, *The Makers of Venice* etc.
etc. Eight chapters and endnote written after MOWO's death. 160
pp.
Frontispiece and many illustrations, different from those in
1897.
Chapters I-V of 1897, rewritten; chapter VI of 1897, extended to
four chapters.

103 Rpt of 102, probably simultaneously.
Separately paginated prologue to *The Life and Times of Queen Victoria*, by Robert Wilson. Cassell, 1900 (Sep). 2 vols. (A revised
edition of a book originally published in 1887, 1888, 1891-93.)
This ed. originally published in 29 weekly parts from 30 May
1900. MOWO's prologue presumably not included until September.

104 Rpt of 102, Jan. or Feb. 1901. With a revised and extended
endnote after the Queen's death.

105 Rpt of 103, 1901 (Apr.), 4 vols.
"Brought down to the date of Her Majesty's lamented death". Cf
previous item.

Cervantes

106 First ed. *Cervantes*/ by/ Mrs Oliphant.
Edinburgh and London: William Blackwood and Sons, 1880 (Nov or
Dec) Foreign Classics for English Readers XI. x + 212 pp.

107 American ed. Philadelphia: J.B. Lippincott and Co [1881].
Foreign Classics for English Readers.

108 Rpt of 106, 1887 (?)

109 Cheap rpt, Dec 1898.

The Literary History of England

110 First ed. *The/ Literary History/ of/ England/ in the End of
the Eighteenth and Beginning of the Nineteenth Century*/ by Mrs
Oliphant/ Author of *Makers of Florence* etc./ Quotations from
Bacon, Milton, Montaigne and Addison.
London: Macmillan and Company, 1882 (May). 3 vols.
I: viii + 395 pp; II: 392 pp; III: 406 pp.

111 Reissue. Macmillan, 1882. 3 vols.
Reduced in price. Identical in text, except for a new preface
responding to critics.

112 American ed. NY: Macmillan and Company, 1882. 3 vols.
Identical with 110 or 111?

113 American rpt, 1883. Possibly 2 vols. Cf next item.

114   New ed. Macmillan, 1886. "New ed., in 2 volumes" (NU Cat).
Probably NY and London.

115   London: Macmillan, 1888.

116   NY and London: Macmillan, 1889. 3 vols.

117   Rpt 1895. 3 vols.

118   Rpt, NY and London, 1897. 3 vols.

Sheridan

119   First ed. *Sheridan*/ by/ Mrs Oliphant.
London: Macmillan and Co, 1883 (Aug).
English Men of Letters Series, edited by John Morley. 1 vol. vii
+ 210 pp.

120   American ed. NY: Harper and Brothers, 1883. English Men of
Letters. 199 pp.

121   American rpt. Harper, [1887]

122   British rpt. Macmillan, 1889. Reprinted bound in one volume
with *Sidney* by J.A. Symonds, and *De Quincey* by David Masson. Vol
II in a new series of EML.

123   Rpt. Harper (?), 1894. Portrait ed. of EML. 199 pp.

124   Rpt. London: Macmillan, Oct 1895 (?).

125   Rpt. London, Jan 1896.

126   Rpt. NY, Harper, 1900 (?).

127   Rpt. NY, Harper, 1901. 199 pp.

128   Rpt. London, 1902. Index added.

129   Rpt. NY, Harper, 1902.

130   Rpt. London and NY: Macmillan, 1906. Index.

131   Rpt. London, 1909. Pocket ed.

132   American ed. NY: A.L. Fowle, 1900s.
Makers of Literature. Portrait.
(NU Cat lists an undated ed. by Fowle, 199 pp. Probably this is
the same ed.)

133   New ed. Macmillan, Jul. 1925. (E. Cat.)

Selections from Cowper's Poems

134   First ed. *Selections from Cowper's Poems*. Golden Treasury

Series. London: Macmillan and Co, 1883 (Oct).
Preface by MOWO, v-xxiii. Selection from poems, 1-230.

135   Rpt Dec 1892.

136   Rpt Aug 1905.

Makers of Venice

Three chapters printed in periodicals as follows:

137   "A Soldier of Fortune", *Blackwood's Magazine* 137 (Apr 1885).
Francesco Carmagnola.
Heavily rewritten as Part II, chapter III.

138   "A Venetian Dynasty", *The Contemporary Review* 50 (Aug 1886),
188-208.
The Orseoli.
Slightly rewritten as Part 1, Chapter I.

139   "Marco Polo", *BM* 142 (Sep 1887), 373-86.
Reprinted as Part II, Chapter I.

140   First ed. *The/ Makers of Venice/ Doges, Conquerors,
Painters/ and/ Men of Letters/ by/ Mrs Oliphant/ author of *The
Makers of Florence.*/ Italian quotation, from the poet Sarfatti.
Dedicated to Elizabeth Lady Cloncurry and Emma Fitzmaurice.
London: Macmillan and Co, 1887 (Dec). 1 vol.
Frontispiece and 47 illustrations by R.R. Holmes, F.S.A. xii +
390 pp.
Fifteen chapters in four Parts. Twelve chapters not published
before.

141   Second ed. (?). Macmillan, Feb 1888.
This may be a rpt of 140, and the next item will then be the new
ed.

142   Rpt of 140 - or Second Edn, May 1888.
Repaginated: xii + 410 pp.

143   American ed. NY: H.M. Caldwell, 1888 (?).

144   Rpt of 142, Nov 1888.

145   Rpt Jul 1889.

146   Rpt 1891.

147   Extra Illustrated Edn., 1892.

148   Rpt 1893. 18 extra illustrations from photographs.
Evidently a rpt of 147.

149   American ed. NY: H.M. Caldwell, 1896. Illustrated Library of
Famous Books, no 142.

149a NY: H.M. Caldwell, 1896. Illustrated Library of Famous

Books, "new escutcheon series", no 35.

150 NY: H.M. Caldwell, 1896. "Artist ed."

(The last three A Cat.)

151 British ed. Rpt 1898.

152 American ed. NY: H.L. Bart, 1898. 383 pp.

153 British rpt, 1905.

****

American eds, undated or incompletely dated (NU Cat)

154 Chicago: W.B. Conkey Co, n.d. 418 pp.

155 NY: A,L. Burt, n.d. 382 pp.

156 NY: New York Publishing Co, n.d. 346 pp.

157 NY: Burt, n.d. Burt's Library of the World's Best Books.

158 NY: Merrill and Baker, 1890s. 346 pp.

159 Philadelphia: H.T. Coates and Co, 1890s.

160 Chicago: Homewood Publishing Co, 1900s. 383 pp.

161 NY: The Mershon Company, 1900s. 346 pp.

162 Springfield, Ohio: Crowell Publishing Co, 1900s. My Lady's
Library.

163 NY: A.L. Burt Co, 1900s. 382 pp. Identical with 155?

164 NY and Boston: Thomas Y. Crowell & Co, n.d. xii + 346 pp.
Frontispiece of the Grand Canal; no other illustrations. Text
slightly modified from British eds.
(Copy at BL; spokesman suggests a date between 1890 and 1902.)

Memoir of John Tulloch

165 First ed. *A Memoir/ of the/ Life of John Tulloch, D.D., LLD
/ Principal and Primarius Professor of St Mary's College/ St.
Andrews/ Dean of the Most Ancient and Honourable Order/ of the
Thistle; one of Her Majesty's/ Chaplains in Scotland/ etc. etc./
by/ Mrs Oliphant/ Author of The Life of Edward Irving, etc etc.*
Dedicated to Queen Victoria.
Edinburgh and London: William Blackwood and Son, 1888 (Oct). 1
vol. Frontispiece and one illustration. ix + 502 pp.

166 Second ed. Blackwood, 1889.

167 Third ed. Blackwood, 1889. Little changed from first ed.

Royal Edinburgh

168 One chapter published in advance of first edition: "Margaret of Scotland", in *English Illustrated Magazine* 7 (Nov 1889), 77-91. Eleven illustrations by George Reid RSA. Reprinted as Part I of *Royal Edinburgh*.

169 First ed. *Royal Edinburgh/ Her Saints, Kings, Prophets/ and Poets/* "Mine own romantic town." MARMION / by/ Mrs Oliphant / Author of *Makers of Florence, Makers of Venice*,etc. / With Illustrations / by / George Reid, R.S.A.
Dedicated to Alexander Macmillan.
London: Macmillan and Co., 1890 (Dec) 1 vol.
Frontispiece and 58 illustrations, by George Reid, RSA. Twelve chapters, in addition to item 168. xiii + 486 pp.

170 Simultaneously a fine-paper edition in larger format, Dec 1890.

171 American ed. NY: Mershon Co, 1890?

172 Second British ed. Macmillan, 1891 (Apr)
Repaginated: xiii + 520 pp.

(*Note*: NU Cat lists 1890 eds with respectively 456 and 520 pages. Possibly the 520-page ed. should read 1891.)

173 Third (?) ed. (Rpt?) Macmillan, 1893. 535 pp. (NU Cat.)

174 American ed. NY: H.M. Caldwell, 1896. Illustrated Library of Famous Books, no 198.

174a NY: H.M. Caldwell, 1896. Illustrated Library of Famous Books, "new escutcheon series", no 35.

175 NY: H.M. Caldwell, 1896. "Artist ed."

   (The last three A Cat.)

176 American ed. NY: A.L. Burt, (1900). The Home Library. 495 pp.
(NU Cat also lists an undated edition, 495 pp, no doubt identical with this.)

****

   American eds, undated or incompletely dated (NU Cat)

177 NY: H.M. Caldwell, n.d. 408 pp.

178 NY: H.M. Caldwell, n.d. 337 pp.

   (These eds perhaps connected with 174, 174a or 175.)

179 NY: New York Publishing Co., 1890s. 408 pp.

180 Rahway, N.J.: Mershon Co., 1890s. 408 pp.

181   NY: H.M. Caldwell, 1900s. 408 pp.
Rpt of 177? Or identical with it?

182   NY: Merrill and Baker, 1900s. The Gentleman's Library.
408 pp.

A House of Peace

183   *A House of Peace* by Mrs Oliphant. London: Printed at the
Office of The Art Journal, City Road, 1890. 29 pp., one plate.
Copies at NLS.
A short monograph on the Royal Hospital for Incurables, Putney.

Memoir of Laurence Oliphant

184   First ed. *Memoir/ of the/ Life of Laurence Oliphant/ and of/
Alice Oliphant, His Wife/ by/* Margaret Oliphant W. Oliphant,/
Author of *Life of Edward Irving, Life of/ Principal Tulloch* etc.
Edinburgh and London: William Blackwood and Son, 1891 (May). 2
vols. I: ix + 314 pp. II: vii + 386 pp. Frontispiece to each
volume. Front covers of each volume inscribed with Laurence
Oliphant's signature and his crest and motto "Altiora Peto".

185   American ed. NY: Harper and Brothers, 1891. 2 vols.

186   Tauchnitz ed. Leipzig: Bernhard Tauchnitz, 1891. 2 vols.
Distribution of chapters between volumes different from Blackwood
ed. (Chapter VIII in Blackwood moved from vol. II to Vol. I.)

187   Blackwood ed. rpt, 1891 (May?). 2 vols. (Described as 2nd ed.
in LL Cat.)

188   Second rpt, 1891. 2 vols.

189   Third rpt, 1891. 2 vols.

190   Fourth rpt, Jul 1891. 2 vols.

191   Fifth rpt, 1891, 2 vols.

192   Sixth rpt, Sep 1891. 2 vols.

(*Note*: These six reprints were called the second to seventh
editions. But this is impossible. They are simple reissues.)

193   Second (third?) ed. Blackwood, 1892. 1 vol. xv + 420 pp.
Preface to the New Edition, ix - x. No changes seem to have been
made to the text.

Jerusalem

194   Preliminary to first ed. *The House of David*. NY and London:
Macmillan and Co, 1891. 224 pp, inc. illustrations.
Running title: *Jerusalem*.
Forms Part 1 of *Jerusalem, Its History and Hope*.

195 First ed. *Jerusalem/ Its History and Hope/* by/ Mrs Oliphant/
Author of *Makers of Florence, Makers of Venice* etc./ Unattributed
quotation ("Mount Zion ...") on title page.
London and NY: Macmillan, 1891 (Dec) 1 vol.
On spine: *Jerusalem / the / Holy City.*
Frontispiece and 51 illustrations by Hamilton Aidé and F.M. Good.
xxiii + 515 pp.

196 Rpt 1892.

197 Second ed. (Or rpt?) Macmillan, Oct 1893.

198 Rpt. London: Darf Publishers Ltd, 1985. xxv + 576 pp.
Title page: *Jerusalem/ The Holy City/ Its History and Hope.* 576
pp.
Illustrations as in early eds, but with minor differences.
Includes a dedication to her son and niece, and to her dead son
Cyril - not included in any 1891 ed. Perhaps this reprints 1893
(item 197).

The Victorian Age of English Literature

199 First ed. *The Victorian Age/ of/ English Literature/* by/ Mrs
Oliphant/ and F.R. Oliphant, BA. / "The spacious times of great
Victoria".
London: Percival and Co, 1892 (Dec). 2 vols. I: viii + 335 pp. II:
viii + 351 pp.
Identical prefaces to the two volumes, which were intended to be
sold separately. The two volumes separately indexed.

200 American ed. NY: Lovell, n.d. (1892?) 647 pp.

201 American ed. NY: Dodd, Mead, [1892]. 2 vols. 647 pp.

202 Also Dodd, Mead ed. in the Ajax Series, [1892]. 1 vol.

203 American ed. NY: Tait, Sons and Co. [1892].

204 Leipzig ed. Leipzig: Heinemann and Balestier, 1893. 2 vols.
The English Library 171 and 172.

205 Second British ed. (Or rpt?) Percival, Jan 1897. 2 vols.
Reduced in price.

206 American ed. NY: T.Y. Crowell, 1900. Popular Library of
Notable Books. (A Cat.)

207 American ed. NY: International Association of Newspapers and
Authors, 1901. 2 vols. (Information from D.J. Trela.)

208 American ed. NY: International Association of Newspapers and
Authors, 1901. Ajax Series. 1 vol. (Information from D.J. Trela.)

The Reign of Queen Anne

Some chapters published in *The Century* (NY) as follows:

209   "The Princess Anne", in *Cent* 45 (n.s. 23) (Apr 1893), 904-22.
Represents the first chapter of the London ed.

210   "The Queen and the Duchess", in *Cent* 46 (n.s. 24) (May 1893), 101-19.
Represents the second chapter of the London ed.

211   "The Author of *Gulliver*", in *Cent* 46 (n.s. 24) (Jul 1893), 401-18.
Represents the fifth chapter of the London ed.

212   "The Author of *Robinson Crusoe*", in *Cent* 46 (n.s. 24) (Sep 1893), 740-53.
Represents the sixth chapter of the London ed.

213   "Addison the Humorist", in *Cent* 48 (n.s. 26) (Sep 1894), 702-09.
Represents the seventh chapter of the London ed.

These are abridged, and at times rewritten, versions of MOWO's text. The overall title is *The Reign of Queen Anne*, and each instalment is fully illustrated (except that 213 has only two portraits.)

214   American ed. *Historical Characters of the Reign of Queen Anne*, by Mrs M.O.W. Oliphant. NY: The Century Co, 1894.
Frontispiece, 8 plates, 25 portraits. 207 pp.
A rpt of the abridged text from *The Century*.

215   British ed. *Historical Sketches/ of the/ Reign of Queen Anne/ by/ Mrs Oliphant*.
London: Macmillan and Co., 1894 (Dec).
Frontispiece and 16 other illustrations. 381 pp.
Restores MOWO's original text, and includes two chapters (third and fourth) on "The Quaker" (William Penn). The other chapters appear as "The Queen and the Duchess", two chapters, "The Dean", "The Journalist", and "The Humourist" (sic).

Thomas Chalmers

216   First ed. *Thomas Chalmers/ Preacher Philosopher/ and Statesman/ by/ Mrs Oliphant*.
London: Methuen and Co., 1893 (May).
255 pp. English Leaders of Religion Series, edited by A.M.M. Stedman MA. Frontispiece.

217   American ed. Boston and NY: Houghton, Mifflin and Company, 1893.

218   Second British ed. (Rpt?) Methuen, Nov 1896.

219   Third ed. (Rpt?) Methuen, 1905. "New and cheaper issue".

220   "New and cheaper ed." (The fourth?) Methuen, 1912. 255 pp.

The Makers of Modern Rome

221 First ed. *The Makers/ of/ Modern Rome/ In Four Books/ I. Honourable Women Not a Few/ II. The Popes who Made the Papacy/ III. Lo Popolo: and the Tribune of the People/ IV. The Popes Who Made the City/ by/* Mrs Oliphant/ Author of *The Makers of Florence.*
Dedicated to the memories of her husband, daughter Maggie and son Francis Romano.
London: Macmillan and Co., 1895 (Dec) 1 vol. Frontispiece and 70 illustrations by Henry P. Riviere, A.R.W.S. and Joseph Pennell. xvii + 618 pp.

222 Simultaneously a fine-paper, larger-format ed. Cf 170.

223 Rpt Jan 1896.

224 American ed. NY and London: Macmillan, 1896.
"Set up and electrotyped November 1895. Reprinted January 1896." No doubt identical with 221.

225 Second British ed. Macmillan, 1897. Smaller format on the model of previous volumes in the series (*Florence, Venice, Edinburgh, Jerusalem*). xvii + 618 pp.

226 Second American ed. NY and London: Macmillan, 1897. No doubt identical with 225.

A Child's History of Scotland

227 First ed. *A Child's/ History of/ Scotland/ by/* Mrs Oliphant. Two drawings on title page. Dedicated to MOWO's great-niece Margaret Valentine.
(On front cover: *The Childrens Study, / Scotland.*)
London: T. Fisher Unwin, 1895. (In fact published Feb 1896.) The Children's Study I. Frontispiece, and decorations at head of each chapter. 233 pp.

228 Second ed. Re-titled: *A History of Scotland for the Young.* Revised and enlarged and "issued in a larger form and type". 307 pp.

229 American ed. Title: *A History of Scotland for the Young.* NY: M.F. Mansfield, (1898). 307 pp.

230 Rpt of 228, 1899.

231 Rpt of 229, 1901.

232 Rpt of 228, 1909. 240 pp. Possibly this is in fact a new ed. (NU Cat)

Jeanne D'Arc

233 First ed. *Jeanne D'Arc/ Her Life and Death/* by/ Mrs
Oliphant/ Author of *Makers of Florence, Makers/ of Venice*, etc.
Dedicated to "Cousin Annie (Mrs Harry Coghill)".
NY and London: G.P. Putnam's Sons. The Knickerbocker Press
(Jun). Heroes of the Nations Series. Frontispiece, and 23
illustrations and maps. x + 407 pp.
There may also have been an ed. published only in New York.

234 Rpt or new ed. NY and London, Putnam, 1899.

235 NY and London, Putnam, 1905.

236 Putnam, 1908. (NY only?)

237 New Edn. Garden City, NY, Garden City Publishing Co, 1926.

Women Novelists of Queen Victoria's Reign

238 *Women Novelists/ of/ Queen Victoria's Reign/ A Book of App-
reciations/* by/ Mrs Oliphant, Mrs Lynn Linton,/ Mrs Alexander,
Mrs Macquoid, Mrs Parr,/ Mrs Marshall, Charlotte M. Yonge,/
Adeline Sergeant and Edna Lyall.
London: Hurst and Blackett, Ltd, 1897 (Jun).
Contribution by MOWO: "The Sisters Brontë", 1-60.

Annals of a Publishing House

239 First ed. *Annals of a Publishing House/ William Blackwood/
and/ his Sons/ Their Magazine and Friends/* by/ Mrs Oliphant.
Dedicated by William Blackwood to the memory of MOWO.
Edinburgh and London: William Blackwood and Sons, 1897 (Oct). 2
vols. I: xv + 522 pp; II: ix + 514 pp. Prefatory note in Vol I by
William Blackwood. Frontispiece to each volume, and two portraits
in Vol II.
NB Some copies replace II, 185-92 (a letter by John Sterling and
other passages by him), with more generalised comment.

240 Rpt, 1897. 2 vols. New ed?

241 Rpt, 1898. 2 vols. Third ed? Uniform with *Annals*, vol
III: *John Blackwood*, by his daughter Mrs Gerald Porter. Newly
published by Blackwood, 1898.

242 American ed. NY: C. Scribner's Sons, 1897-98. (Printed in
Edinburgh.) 1898 includes Vol III.

B Articles

Excluding the periodical versions of *Historical Sketches of the Reign of George II, The Makers of Florence, The Makers of Venice, Royal Edinburgh, Historical Sketches of the Reign of Queen Anne,* and *Queen Victoria.*

I Periodicals and Encyclopedias

Atalanta

243 "Things in General" 1, *At* 7 (Oct 1893), 56-9.
The first of a series of discursive topical articles. The present political crisis; Kipling and E. F. Benson, etc.

244 "Things in General" 2, *At* 7 (Nov 1893), 122-3.
The coal strike; labour and wages, etc.

245 "Things in General" 3, *At* 7 (Dec 1893), 220-3.
The price of coal; the stereotyping of women, etc.

246 "Things in General" 4, *At* 7 (Jan 1894), 286-8.
A plea for personal charity, etc.

247 "Things in General" 5, *At* 7 (Mar 1894), 415-7.
Disillusion; the higher education of women; the Music Hall, etc.

248 "Things in General" 6, *At* 7 (Apr 1894), 478-81.
Foreign travel, etc.

249 "Things in General" 7, *At* 7 (May 1894), 543-5.
Marcella, by Mrs Humphry Ward; poverty; prejudice, etc.

250 "Things in General" 8, *At* 7 (Jun 1894), 603-5.
The London scene; the poetry of Leopardi, etc.

251 "Things in General" 9, *At* 7 (Aug 1894), 732-4.
The increasing assertiveness of feminists, etc.

252 "Things in General" 10, *At* 7 (Sep 1894), 800-1.
Weather; the experience of disillusion, etc.

The Athenaeum

253 "The Complaints of Authors" (editorial title), 7 Feb 1891, 187.
A complaint of the republication by Messrs Tillotson of Bolton, without permission, of a story by MOWO (i.e. *The Heir Presumptive ... in London Society*). Unsigned.
An answer by Messrs Tillotson was published, *The Athenaeum*, 14 Feb 1891, 219.

Blackwood's Magazine

254 "Mary Russell Mitford", *BM* 75 (Jun 1854), 658-70.
Our Village, *Belford Regis*, *Atherton*, etc. Childhood memories of first reading Mitford.

255 "Evelyn and Pepys", *BM* 76 (Jul 1854), 35-52.
The two diarists seen against the background of Restoration society.

256 "The Holy Land", *BM* 76 (Sep 1854), 243-55.
Rev. of *Narrative of a Journey through Syria and Palestine in 1851 and 1852,* by Lieut. Van de Velde.

257 "Mr. Thackeray and his Novels", *BM* 77 (Jan 1855), 86-96.
The Rose and the Ring, *Vanity Fair*, *Pendennis*, *Henry Esmond*, *The Newcomes*.

258 "Bulwer", *BM* 77 (Feb 1855), 221-33.
Pelham, *The Caxtons*, *My Novel*; Bulwer (Lytton)'s reputation.

259 "Charles Dickens", *BM* 77 (Apr 1855), 451-66.
Hard Times; Dickens's career from *Pickwick Papers* to *Bleak House*.

260 "Modern Novelists Great and Small", *BM* 77 (May 1855), 554-68.
Mrs Gore, Mrs Trollope. Mrs Marsh; *Jane Eyre*; Miss Kavanagh, Mrs Gaskell, Mrs Craik, Geraldine Jewsbury, Charlotte Yonge, etc.; Nathaniel Hawthorne, Charles Lever, Wilkie Collins, Charles Reade, G. P. R. James, Harrison Ainsworth, etc. Also *Mathew Paxton* by MOWO's brother William Wilson.

261 "Modern Light Literature - Theology", *BM* 78 (Jul 1855), 72-86.
The Broad Church. F. D. Maurice.

262 "Modern Light Literature - Science", *BM* 78 (Aug 1855), 215-30.
Rev. of *Glaucus*, by Charles Kingsley; *The Aquarium*, by Philip Gosse; *Drops of Water*, by Agnes Catlew; *Episodes of Insect Life* (and other books) by Acheta; *Food, and its Adulterations*.)

263 "Modern Light Literature - History", *BM* 78 (Oct 1855), 437-51.
The histories of Agnes Strickland. Rev. of *Queens Before the Conquest*, by Mrs Matthew Hale; *Lives of the Queens of the House of Hanover*, by Dr Doran; *Anne of Brittany*, by Miss Costello; *Life of Mary de Medici* by Miss Pardo; *The Old Court Suburb*, by Leigh Hunt.

264 "Modern Light Literature - Travellers' Tales", *BM* 78 (Nov 1855), 586-99.
Rev. of *Pilgrimage to El Medinah*, by Richard F. Burton; *Rambles Beyond Railways*, by Wilkie Collins; *The Wabash*, by J. R. Bester; *Purple Tints of Paris*, by Bayle St.John.

265 "Modern Light Literature - Art", *BM* 78 (Dec 1855), 702-17.
Ruskin; rev. of *Sacred and Legendary Art*, by Mrs Jameson;

Handbook for Young Painters, by Mr (C. R.) Leslie; *Modern Painting at Naples*, by Lord Napier; *Brick and Marble Architecture in Italy*, by George Edmund Street.

266 "Modern Light Literature - Poetry", *BM* 79 (Feb 1856), 125-38.
Tennyson, Mrs Browning, Dobell, Alexander Smith, Longfellow's *Hiawatha*, etc.

267 "Religion in Common Life", *BM* 79 (Feb 1856), 243-6.
Rev. of *A sermon Preached in Crathie Church before the Queen and Prince Albert*, by the Rev. John Caird.

268 "Sydney Smith", *BM* 79 (Mar 1856), 350-61.
Rev. of *Memoir* by Sydney Smith's daughter Lady Holland.

269 "The Laws Concerning Women", *BM* 79 (Apr 1856), 379-87.
Ostensibly a review of *A Brief Summary, in Plain Language, of the Most Important Laws Concerning Women, Together with a Few Observations Thereon* (by Barbara Leigh-Smith).

270 "Macaulay", *BM* 80 (Aug 1856), 127-41.
Rev. of *The History of England*.

271 "Macaulay" 2, *BM* 80 (Sep 1856), 365-78.
The same subject continued, concentrating on Macaulay's view on Scotland.

272 "Family History", *BM* 80 (Oct 1856), 456-71.
Rev. of *Lives of the Lindsays*; *Memoir of ... George Baillie of Jerviswood and of Lady Grisell Baillie by their Daughter Lady Murray of Stanhope*.

273 "A New Una", *BM* 80 (Oct 1856), 485-9.
The exiled Queen of Oude (sic) in a London house near Regent's Park.

274 "The Art of Cavilling", *BM* 80 (Nov 1856), 613-28.
The Baconian heresy, and similar attempts to undermine greatness.

275 "Picture-Books", *BM* 81 (Mar 1857), 309-18.
Rev. of *The Book of Job*, with illustrations by John Gilbert; *Evangeline* by Longfellow, with illustrations by John Gilbert; *The Task* by Cowper, illustrated by Birket Foster; Grahame's *Sabbath*, illustrated by Birket Foster; Pollok's *Course of Time*; *Rhymes and Roundelayes in Praise of a Country Life*; *The Poets of the Nineteenth Century*, selected and arranged by rev. R. A. Wilmott; *Pictures of Life and Character*, by John Leech.

276 "Charles the Fifth", *BM* 82 (Jul 1857), 40-55.
Rev. of *The Cloister Life of Charles V*, by W. Stirling.

277 "Modern Light Literature - Society", *BM* 82 (Oct 1857), 423-37.
Diaries, etc; rev. of *The Two Aristocracies*, by Mrs Gore; *Pendennis*, by Thackeray; *A Woman's Story*, by Mrs S. C. Hall; *Heartsease*, by Charlotte Yonge; *The Young Lord*, by Lady Emily Ponsonby; *Woman's Devotion*, by the author of *Margaret and her*

Bridesmaids; Scottish society.

278 "Béranger", *BM* 83 (Jan 1858), 102-20.
Rev. of *Ma Biographie*, by Béranger, English copyright translation.

279 "The Condition of Women", *BM* 83 (Feb 1858), 139-54.
An examination of the legal position of women, from a fairly conservative standpoint.

280 "The Missionary Explorer", *BM* 83 (Apr 1858), 385-401.
Dr Livingstone and others.

281 "Religious Memoirs", *BM* 83 (Jun 1858), 703-718.
Rev. of *Biographical Sketch of Sir Henry Havelock*, by Rev. W. Brock; *Memorials of Hedley Vicars*.

282 "The Byways of Literature", *BM* 84 (Aug 1858), 200-16.
"Reading for the Million" - a study of popular literature.

283 "Edward Irving", *BM* 84 (Nov 1858), 567-86.
A brief biography.   Preliminary sketch for the 1862 biography.

284 "Sermons", *BM* 84 (Dec 1858), 728-42.
Rev. of *Sermons*, by the Rev. John Caird, minister of the Park Church, Glasgow.

285 "The Seaside in the Papal States", *BM* 86 (Oct 1859), 471-88.
A travelogue; scenery, towns, a party of travellers, a speech by a holy friar.

286 "A Week in Florence", *BM* 86 (Nov 1859), 583-607.
Six separate days described.

287 "Scottish National Character", *BM* 87 (Jun 1860), 715-31.
Rev. of *Reminiscences of Scottish Life and Character*, by E. B. Ramsay, Dean of Edinburgh.

288 "Poetry", *BM* 88 (Jul 1860), 37-53.
Preamble of about eight pages. Tennyson. Owen Meredith, *The Wanderer, Lucile*.

289 "Social Science", *BM* 88 (Dec 1860), 698-715.
Public and private charity, sociology, hygiene, work for women, etc.

290 "A Merry Christmas!", *BM* 89 (Jan 1861), 106-14.
Rev. of various Christmas books, inc. Tennyson's *May Queen*. Christmas numbers, etc.

291 "The Monks of the West", *BM* 89 (Jun 1861), 665-81.
Rev. of the book by Montalembert, the authorised translation - i.e. MOWO's own. The first two volumes.

292 "Joseph Wolff", *BM* 90 (Aug 1861), 135-53.
Rev. of *Travels and Adventures of the Rev. Joseph Wolff D.D., LLD, Vicar of Ile Brewers, near Taunton, and late Missionary to the Jews and Mahommedans in Persia*.

293 "Scotland and her Accusers", *BM* 90 (Sep 1861), 267-83.
A protest against stereotyped views of the Scots, especially as
expressed by Henry Thomas Buckle.

294 "Augustus Welby Pugin", *BM* 90 (Dec 1861), 670-89.
Rev. of *Recollections of A. N. Welby Pugin and of his father
Augustus Pugin ....* by Benjamin Ferrey.

295 "J. M. W. Turner R. A.", *BM* 91 (Jan 1862). 17-34.
Rev. of *The Life of J. M. W. Turner R. A.*, by Walter Thornbury.

296 "The Lives of Two Ladies", *BM* 91 (Apr 1862), 401-23.
Rev. of *Autobiography and Correspondence of Mary Grenville, Mrs
Delany*, edited by the Right Hon. Lady Llanover; *Autobiography and
Literary Remains of Mrs Piozzi*, edited by A. Hayward QC.

297 "Sensation Novels", *BM* 91 (May 1862), 564-84.
Rev. of *The Woman in White*, by Wilkie Collins; *Great Expecta-
tions*, by Charles Dickens; *Owen, a Waif*, by the author of *No
Church* (F. W. Robinson).

298 "The New Exhibition", *BM* 91 (Jun 1862), 663-72.
Reminiscences of 1851. The second Great Exhibition newly opened.

299 "David Wingate", *BM* 92 (Jul 1862), 48-61.
Rev. of *Poems and Songs*, by David Wingate, a Scottish collier
poet.

300 "Sermons", *BM* 92 (Aug 1862), 202-20.
The value and use of sermons. Reference to Macphail's *Edinburgh
Ecclesiastical Journal*, etc.

301 "John Wilson", *BM* 92 (Dec 1862), 751-67.
Rev. of *Christopher North, a memoir by his daughter, Mrs Gordon*;
Recreations of Christopher North. The foundation of *Blackwood's
Magazine*.

302 "Henri Lacordaire", *BM* 93 (Feb 1863), 169-87.
Rev. of *Le Père Lacordaire*, par le Comte de Montalembert.

303 "Marriage Bells", *BM* 93 (Apr 1863), 251-4.
The wedding of the Prince of Wales.

304 "Girolamo Savonarola", *BM* 93 (Jun 1863), 690-713.
Rev. of *Savonarola and his Times*, by Pasquale Villari, translated
by Leonard Horner.

305 "Novels", *BM* 94 (Aug 1863), 168-83.
Rev. of *The Story of Elizabeth*, anon. (by Annie Thackeray);
Church and Chapel, by the Author of *No Church* (F. W. Robinson).

306 "Tara", *BM* 94 (Nov 1863), 624-34.
Rev. of *Tara: a Mahratta Tale*, by Captain Meadows Taylor, author
of *Confessions of a Thug*, etc.

307 "The Life of Jesus", *BM* 96 (Oct 1864), 417-31.
Rev. of *Lectures on M. Renan's Vie de Jésus*, by John Tulloch,

Principal of St Mary's College, St. Andrews.

308 "Life in an Island", *BM* 97 (Jan 1865), 72-88.
Autobiographical - life on Capri. Reference to *A Winter in the
Two Sicilies*, by Julia Kavanagh.

309 "Josiah Wedgwood", *BM* 98 (Aug 1865), 154-70.
Rev. of *The Life of Josiah Wedgwood; with an Introductory Sketch
of the Art of Pottery in England*, vol 1, by Eliza Meteyard.

310 "Giacomo Leopardi", *BM* 98 (Oct 1865), 459-80.
A study of Leopardi as poet and writer of prose and *pensieri*,
etc.

311 "French Periodical Literature", *BM* 98 (Nov 1865), 603-21.
A series of articles in French magazines, esp. *La Revue des Deux
Mondes* and *Le Correspondant*. English and American themes.

312 "General Lamoricière", *BM* 99 (Feb 1866), 224-35.
Rev. of *Le General de la Moricière*, par le Comte de Montalembert.

313 "The Nile", *BM* 100 (Aug 1866), 205-24.
Rev. of *The Albert Nyanza, Great Basin of the Nile*, by Samuel
White Baker.

314 "The Great Unrepresented", *BM* 100 (Sep 1866), 367-79.
A discussion of the views of John Stuart Mill concerning the
claim of women householders to the vote.   Ironic treatment.

315 "Victor Hugo", *BM* 100 (Dec 1866), 744-69.
Les Travailleurs de la Mer; also *Les Misérables* and *Notre Dame de
Paris*.

316 "The History of Scotland", *BM* 101 (Mar 1867), 317-38.
Rev. of *The History of Scotland, from Agricola's Invasion to the
Revolution of 1688*, by John Hill Burton, vols I - IV.

317 "Elizabeth and Mary", *BM* 101 (Apr 1867), 289-414.
Biographical. A follow-up to "The History of Scotland".

318 "Novels", *BM* 102 (Sep 1867), 257-80.
Sensation novels.   Miss Braddon, Miss Broughton, Ouida, Edmund
Yates, Annie Thomas, etc.   By contrast Trollope's *The Claverings*
and *The Last Chronicle of Barset*, and Miss Thackeray's *The
Village on the Cliff*.

319 "A Royal Idyll", *BM* 102 (Sep 1867), 375-84.
Rev. of *The Early Years of His Royal Highness the Prince Consort*.

320 "A City of the Plague", *BM* 102 (Oct 1867), 452-61.
The plague in Albano. Mainly one long quotation from a lady to a
correspondent of *The Times*.

321 "The Conversion of England", *BM* 102 (Dec 1867), 702-24.
Rev. of *The Monks of the West*, vols III, IV, V, by Montalembert
- MOWO's own translation. Cf 291.

322 "The Queen of the Highlands", *BM* 103 (Feb 1868), 242-50.

Rev. of *Leaves from the Journal of our Life in the Highlands* (by Queen Victoria).

323 "The Latest Lawgiver", *BM* 103 (Jun 1868), 675-91.
Rev. of *Time and Tide by Weare and Tyne*, by John Ruskin.

324 "Bunsen", *BM* 104 (Sep 1868), 285-308.
Rev. of *A Memoir of Baron Bunsen, late Minister Plenipotentiary and Envoy Extraordinary of His Majesty Frederick William IV, at the Court of St. James*, by his widow Frances Baroness Bunsen.

325 "Charles Reade's Novels", *BM* 106 (Oct 1869), 488-514.
Peg Woffington, Christie Jonnston, Griffith Gaunt, the David Dodd series, *The Cloister and the Hearth, Foul Play*.

326 "Saint-Eloy-sur-les-Dunes", *BM* 106 (Nov 1869), 600-17.
Description of a French town.

327 "Mr Froude and Queen Mary", *BM* 107 (Jan 1870), 105-22.
Rev. of *History of England - Reign of Elizabeth*, by James Anthony Froude. Critical examination of the treatment of Queen Elizabeth and Mary Stuart.

328 "Miss Austen and Miss Mitford", *BM* 107 (Mar 1870), 290-313.
Rev. of *A Memoir of Jane Austen*, by J.E. Austen-Leigh; the letters of Mary Russell Mitford (*The Life of Mary Russell Mitford ... related in a selection from her letters to her friends*, edited by the Rev. A.G.L'Estrange).

329 "Chatterton", *BM* 107 (Apr 1870), 453-76.
Rev. of *Chatterton: a Biographical Study*, by Daniel Wilson LLD.

330 "Count Charles de Montalembert", *BM* (Apr 1870), 522-30.
Obituary.

331 "New Books" 1, *BM* 107 (May, 1870), 628-51.
Rev. of *Life, Letters, and Journal of Albrecht Dürer*, by Mrs Heaton; *Life and Works of Albrecht Dürer*, by W.B. Scott; *Memoirs of the Marquis de Montagu*, by the Baroness de Noailles; *Poems* (and plays), by Menella Bute Smedley; *The Earthly Paradise*. Part 3, by William Morris; *Annals of an Eventful Life*, by George Dasent; Trollope's new style of heroine; *Wenderholme*, an anonymous novel.

332 "New Books" 2, *BM* 108 (Aug 1870), 166-88.
Rev. of *Free Russia*, by William Hepworth Dixon; *Ourselves: Essays on Women*, by E. Lynne (sic) Linton; *Poems*, by Dante Gabriel Rossetti; *Poems*, by Frederic W.H. Myers; *Put Yourself in his Place*, by Charles Reade; *Kilmeny*, by William Black; *The Heir Expectant* (an anonymous novel).

333 "*Piccadilly*", *BM* 108 (Oct 1870), 401-22.
Rev. of *Piccadilly*, by Laurence Oliphant.

334 "Boating on the Thames", *BM* 108 (Oct 1870), 460-77.
The Thames from Oxford to Eton and Windsor.

335 "New Books" 3, *BM* 108 (Nov 1870), 607-31.

Rev. of *Lay Sermons, Addresses and Reviews*, by T.H. Huxley; *Saint Anselm*, by Rev. R.W. Church; *The Jacobite Lairds of Gask*, by T.L. Kington Oliphant; *Ginx's Baby: his Birth and Other Misfortunes* (by John Edward Jenkins); *Peasant Life in the North* (anonymous stories of Scotland); *Man and Wife*, by Wilkie Collins.

336   "New Books" 4, *BM* 109 (Jan 1871), 22-47.
Rev. of *Lectures and Essays*, by J.R. Seeley; *Christus Consolator*, by Alexander Macleod; *The Life of Madame de Miramion*, edited by Lady Herbert; *The Life of R.H. Barham*; *Lorna Doone*, by R.D. Blackmore.

337   "New Books" 5, *BM* 109 (Apr 1871), 440-64.
Rev. of *Essays Theological and Literary*, by R.H. Hutton; *Life and Letters of Hugh Miller*, by Peter Bayne MA; *Iona*, by the Duke of Argyll; *Walks in Rome*, by Augustus J.C. Hare; *Friendship's Garland*, by Matthew Arnold; *Tales of Old Japan*, by A.R. Mitford; *Esther Hill's Secret* and *Six Months Hence*, two anonymous novels; *The Siren*, by T. Adolphus Trollope; *The Florentines*, by the Countess de Montemerli.

338   "Charles Dickens", *BM* 109 (Jun 1871), 673-95.
A late obituary; final verdict on his reputation and status.

339   "A Century of Great Poets, from 1750 Downwards I: William Cowper", *BM* 109 (Jun 1871), 763-93.
Largely biographical.

340   "New Books" 6, *BM* 110 (Jul 1871), 62-80.
Rev. of *Fragments of Science for Unscientific People*, by John Tyndall; *Short Studies on Great Subjects*, by J.A. Froude; *Freedom in the Church of England*, by Rev. Stopford A. Brooke; *Episodes in an Obscure Life*, (by the vicar of an East End parish); *Robin Gray* and *For Lack of Gold*, by Charles Gibbons.

341   "A Century of Great Poets ... II: Walter Scott", *BM* 110 (Aug 1871), 229-256.
Poetry and novels.

342   "A Century of Great Poets ... III: William Wordsworth", *BM* 110 (Sep 1871), 299-326.
Biography and close literary analysis.

343   "American Books", *BM* 110 (Oct 1871), 422-42.
Rev. of *The Luck of Roaring Camp, and other Sketches*, by Bret Harte; *Songs of the Sierras*, by Joaquin Miller; *The Breitmann Ballads*; *Gates Ajar*, by Elizabeth Stuart Phelps; *Hitherto: A Story of Yesterday*, by Mrs Whitney; *The Silent Partner* and *Hedged In*, by Elizabeth Stuart Phelps.

344   "New Books" 7, *BM* 110 (Oct 1871), 458-80.
Rev. of *Scrambles Among the Alps*, by Edward Whymper; *The Playgrounds of Europe*, by Leslie Stephen; *Hours of Exercise in the Alps*, by Professor (John) Tyndall; *Julian Fane, a Memoir*, by Robert Lytton; *Memoir of Charles Mayne Young*; *Life and Letters of William Bewick, Artist*, by Thomas Landseer; *A Daughter of Heth*, by William Black.

345   "A Century of Great Poets ... IV: Samuel Taylor Coleridge",
BM 110 (Nov 1871), 552-76.
Biography; *The Ancient Mariner, Christabel*, "Love".

346   "A Century of Great Poets ... V: Robert Burns", *BM* 111 (Feb
1872), 140-68.
Largely biographical.

347   "Voltaire", *BM* (Mar 1872), 270-90.
Rev. of *Voltaire*, by John Morley.

348   "A Century of Great Poets ... VI: Percy Bysshe Shelley", *BM*
111 (Apr 1872), 415-40.
Biographical; plays; Shelley's special quality as a poet.

349   "New Books" 8, *BM* 111 (Apr 1872), 478-99.
Rev. of *Letters and other Writings of the late Edward Denison MP
for Newark*, edited by Sir Baldwin Leighton; *Recollections of Past
Life*, by Sir Henry Holland; *Memoir of Robert Chambers, with
Autobiographic Reminiscences by William Chambers*; *The Songs of
the Russian People*, by W.R.S. Ralston.

350   "New Books" 9, *BM* 111 (Jun 1872), 735-56.
Rev. of *Royal and Republican France*, by Henry Reeve; *Notes on
England*, by H. Taine; *South Sea Bubbles*, by The Earl and The
Doctor; *Shooting the Rapids*, by Alexander Innes Shand; *The
Adventures of Harry Richmond*, by George Meredith; *Lord Kilgobbin*,
by Charles Lever.

351   "A Century of Great Poets ... VII: Lord Byron", *BM* 112 (Jul
1872), 49-72.
Biography, critical analysis, *Childe Harold*.

352   "New Books" 10, *BM* 112 (Aug 1872), 196-217.
Rev. of *Orissa*, by W.W. Hunter; *Lectures on the History of the
Church of Scotland* (by Dean Stanley); *Miscellaneous Writings of
J. Conington MA with Memoir by H.J.S. Smith*; *Goethe and
Mendelssohn*, translated from the German of Dr Karl Mendelssohn-
Bartholdy; *Olrig Grange* (by Walter C. Smith).

353   "William Smith", *BM* 112 (Oct 1872), 429-38.
Obituary for a contributor to *Blackwood's Magazine*.

354   "A Century of Great Poets ... VIII: Johann Wolfgang Goethe",
BM 112 (Dec 1872), 675-97.
Character study and biography; novels and *Faust*.

355   "New Books" 11, *BM* 113 (Dec 1872), 746-65.
Rev. of *The Life of Sir Henry Lawrence*, by the late Major General
Sir Herbert Benjamin Edwards and Herman Merivale; *The Life and
Labours of the late Mr Brassey*, by Sir Arthur Helps; *Memorials of
a Quiet Life*, by Augustus J.C. Hare; *Gareth and Lynette* etc, by
Tennyson; *The Strange Adventures of a Phaeton*, by William Black.

356   "New Books" 12, *BM* 113 (Feb 1873), 206-21.
Rev. of *Enigmas of Life*, by W.R. Greg; *Madame de Sévigné, her
Correspondents and Contemporaries*, by the Comtesse de Puliga; *A
Lady of the Last Century* (Mrs Montagu), by Dr Doran; *Fleurange*,

by Madame Auguste Craven, translated by Emily Bowles.

357 "In London", *BM* 113 (Feb 1873), 222-34.
"Theatres and Shop-windows!" Streets, paintings, plays.

358 "Lord Lytton", *BM* 113 (Mar 1873), 356-78.
Obituary and analysis of Lytton's work. *Pelham*, romances of
crime, *Zanoni, A Strange Story, The Last Days of Pompeii, The
Caxtons, My Novel,* etc.

359 *"Kenelm Chillingly"*, *BM* 113 (May 1873), 615-30.
Lord Lytton's posthumous novel.

360 "Alexandre Dumas", *BM* 114 (Jul 1873), 111-30.
Rev. of *The Life and Adventures of Alexandre Dumas*, by Percy
Fitzgerald; *The Three Musketeers, Twenty Years After, The Vicomte
de Bragelonne, The Count of Monte Christo,* etc.

361 "A Century of Great Poets ... IX: Johann Friedrich
Schiller", *BM* 114 (Aug 1873), 183-206.
Biography; comparison with Goethe and Shakespeare; plays.

362 "New Books" 13, *BM* 114 (Sep 1873), 368-90.
Rev. of *Memoirs and Letters of Sara Coleridge; The Life of George
Grote* (by his widow); *Miscellaneous and Posthumous Works of Henry
Thomas Buckle*, edited with a Biographical Notice, by Helen
Taylor; *Monographs*, by Lord Houghton.

363 "New Books" 14, *BM* 114 (Nov 1873), 596-617.
A preamble about poetry, painting and music. Rev. of *Children in
Italian and English Design*, by Sidney Colvin; Studies in the
History of the Renaissance, by W(alter) H. Pater; *Music and
Morals*, by Rev. H.K. Haweis; Alcestis (anonymous novel); *Sketches
and Essays from The Saturday Review.*

364 "The Indian Mutiny: Sir Hope Grant", *BM* 115 (Jan 1874), 102-
20. Rev. of *Incidents in the Sepoy War of 1857-58, compiled from th
Private Journals of Sir Hope Grant* ...

365 "Fables in Song" *BM* 115 (Feb 1874), 248-66.
Rev. of *Fables in Song*, by Robert Lord Lytton (Owen Meredith).

366 "New Books" 15, BM 115 (Apr 1874), 443-65.
Rev. of *Personal Recollections from Early Life to Old Age of Mary
Somerville with Selections from her Correspondence*, by her
daughter Martha Somerville; *Journal et Correspondance de André-
Marie Ampère; Lettres à une Inconnue*, par Prosper Mérimée;
Autobiography of Dr (Thomas) Guthrie.

367 "New Books" 16, *BM* 115 (Jun 1874), 750-69.
Rev. of *Quatre-vingt-treize, Premier Récit: La Guerre Civile*, by
Victor Hugo.

368 "Two Cities - Two Books", *BM* 116 (Jul 1874), 72-91. Venice and
Florence. *Consuelo*, by George Sand; *Romola*, by George Eliot.

369   "New Books" 17, *BM* 116 (Aug 1874), 166-83.
Rev. of *Essays, Political, Social and Religious*, by Richard
Congreve; *Threading my Way*, by Robert Dale Owen; *Memoirs of Mrs
Barbauld*, by her great-niece Anna Letitia Le Breton; *Songs of Two
Worlds*, by A New Writer (Lewis Morris).

370   "The Ancient Classics", *BM* 116 (Sep 1874), 365-86.
Ancient Classics for English Readers, edited by Rev. W. Lucas
Collins. Homer, Aeschylus, Sophocles, Euripides, Aristophanes,
Plato etc.

371   "Ancient Classics - Latin Literature", *BM* 116 (Nov 1874),
599-620.
Continuation of 370. Virgil, Horace, Cicero, Pliny, Tacitus,
Juvenal etc.

372   "The Life of the Prince Consort", *BM* 117 (Jan 1875), 114-31.
Rev. of *The Life of His Royal Highness the Prince Consort*, by
Theodore Martin.

373   "New Books" 18, *BM* 117 (May 1875), 616-37.
Rev. of *Isaac Casaubon*, by Mark Pattison; *Reminiscences*, by
William Charles Macready; *Untrodden Spain*, by Rev. Hugh James
Rose; *Malcolm*, by George Macdonald,

374   "Art in May", *BM* 117 (Jun 1875), 747-64.
The Royal Academy and other art galleries.

375   "New Books" 19, *BM* 118 (Jul 1875), 82-99.
Rev. of *Renaissance in Italy: Age of the Despots*, by J.A.
Symonds; *A Short History of the English People*, by J.R. Green;
Aristophanes' Apology, by Robert Browning; *Pilgrim Memories,
Travels ... with Henry Thomas Buckle*, by John L. Stuart Glennie;
Miss Angel, by Annie Thackeray.

376   "Rivers", *BM* 118 (Aug 1875), 167-88.
The Thames etc. Rev. of *Our Autumn Holiday on French Rivers*, by
J.L. Molloy; *Etchings on the Loire*, and *Etchings on the Moselle*,
by Ernest George; *Life on the Upper Thames*, by H.R. Robertson;
Taunt's Map and Guide to the Thames.

377   "Lace and Bric-a-Brac", *BM* 119 (Jan 1876), 59-78.
Rev. of *La Dentelle*, par M. Joseph Sequin; *The Bric-a-Brac
Hunter*, by Major H. Byng Hall.

378   "A Century of Great Poets ... X: Alphonse de Lamartine", *BM*
119 (Feb 1876), 207-31.
Anglo-French literary relations. Career of Lamartine with his
most important poems.

379   "Mr Thackeray's Sketches", *BM* 119 (Feb 1876), 232-43.
Rev. of *The Orphan of Pimlico; and other Sketches, Fragments and
Drawings*, by W.M. Thackeray. General discussion of Thackeray's
work.

380   "Eton College", *BM* 119 (Mar 1876), 314-31.
Rev. of *A History of Eton College*, by H.C. Maxwell Lyte,
illustrated by P.H. Delamotte; and a tribute to contemporary

Eton.

381   "Norman Macleod", *BM* 119 (Apr 1876), 507-26.
Rev. of *Memoir of Norman Macleod D.D.*, by his brother, the Rev.
Donald Macleod BA.

382   "Macaulay", *BM* 119 (May 1876), 614-37.
Rev. of *Life and Letters of Lord Macaulay*, by his nephew George
Otto Trevelyan.

383   "The Royal Academy", *BM* 119 (Jun 1876), 753-69.
Detailed criticism of the new Royal Academy exhibition.

384   "Molière", *BM* 120 (Aug 1876), 172-90.
The Dramatic Works of Molière, rendered into English by Henri van
Laun.

385   "Alfred de Musset", *BM* 120 (Sep 1876), 361-82.
Biography, and analysis of poems and plays.

386   "New Books" 20, *BM* 121 (Feb 1877), 175-95.
"Biographies". Rev. of *Life of a Scotch Naturalist* (Thomas
Edward), by Samuel Smiles; *Charles Kingsley: his Letters, and
Memorials of his Life*; *Rahel: her Life and Letters*, by Mrs
Jennings; *Letters of Elizabeth Barrett Browning, addressed to
R.H. Horne*.

387   "Lord Neaves", *BM* 121 (Mar 1877), 380-90.
Obituary for a contributor to *Blackwood's Magazine*.

388   "Harriet Martineau", *BM* 121 (Apr 1877), 472-96.
Rev. of Harriet Martineau's *Autobiography*, with *Memorials* by M.W.
Chapman.

389   "A School of the Prophets", *BM* 122 (Sep 1877), 283-302.
Rev. of *Letters of Thomas Erskine of Linlathen*; *Memorials* of John
Macleod Campbell; *Present-day Papers*, edited by the Bishop of
Argyll. Religious movements in Scotland.

390   "The Opium-Eater", *BM* 122 (Dec 1877), 717-41.
Rev. of *De Quincey's Life and Writings*, by H.A. Page.

391   "New Books" 21, *BM* 123 (Mar 1878), 305-27.
Rev. of *Lessing: his Life and Writings*, by J. Sime; *Charles
Bianconi: A Biography*, by Mrs Morgan John O'Connell; *North
Italian Folks*, by Mrs Comyns Carr; *Marmorne...* (an anonymous
novel); *The City of Sunshine, a Novel*, by Alexander Allardyce.

392   "New Books" 22, *BM* 123 (Jun 1878), 681-702.
Rev. of *Life and Letters of James Hinton*, by Ellice Hopkins; *A
Legacy: being the Life and Remains of John Martin*, edited by Mrs
Craik; *Life in the Mofussil*, by a Bengal Civilian; *My Indian
Garden*, by Phil Robinson; *Medusa and other Poems*, by Lady
Charlotte Elliot; *Round About the Carpathians*, by A.F. Crosse.

393   "Englishmen and Frenchmen", *BM* 124 (Aug 1878), 219-37.
Rev. of *George Moore, Merchant and Philanthropist*, by S. Smiles;
Modern Frenchmen. Five Biographies, by P.G. Hamerton.

394   "Three Days in Paris", *BM* 124 (Oct 1878), 455-74.
Paris; its talk, artists, streets, theatres.

395   "The Novels of Alphonse Daudet", *BM* 125 (Jan 1879), 93-111.
Fromont Jeune et Risler Ainé; The Nabob; Jack.

396   "Two Ladies", *BM* 125 (Feb 1879), 206-24.
Rev. of *Memoirs of the Life of Anna Jameson*, by her niece
Gerardine Macpherson; *Records of a Girlhood*, by Fanny Kemble.

397   "Hamlet", *BM* 125 (Apr 1879), 462-81.
Henry Irving and Ellen Terry; other performances of *Hamlet*;
analysis of the play.

398   "New Books" 23, *BM* 126 (Jul 1879), 88-107.
Rev. of *Hours in a Library*, by Leslie Stephen; *Mixed Essays*, by
Matthew Arnold; *The American, The Europeans: a Sketch*, and *Daisy
Miller and other Stories*, by Henry James.

399   "An American Princess", *BM* 126 (Nov 1879), 543-61.
Rev. of *The Life and Letters of Madame Bonaparte*, by Eugene
Didier; Elizabeth Patterson, an American who married Jerome
Bonaparte.

400   "The Reign of Queen Anne", *BM* 127 (Feb 1880), 139-62.
Rev. of *A History of the Reign of Queen Anne*, by John Hill
Burton.

401   "Russia and Nihilism in the Novels of M. Tourgenieff", *BM*
128 (May 1880), 623-47.
A Sportsman's Tales; Fathers and Sons; Fumée (compared with Henry
James's *Confidence*); *Virgin Soil*.

402   "School and College", *BM* 128 (Jul 1880), 62-80.
The public school system; Eton; Oxford; university and college.

403   "New Novels", *BM* 128 (Sep 1880), 378-404.
Important preamble on the value of novels. Rev. of *Second
Thoughts*, by Rhoda Broughton; *Mary Anerley*, by R.D. Blackmore;
Poet and Peer, by Hamilton Aidé; *Troublesome Daughters*, by L.B.
Walford; *A Modern Greek Heroine*, anonymous (in fact by H.
Cresswell); *The Egoist*, by George Meredith.

404   "Autobiographies, no. I: Benvenuto Cellini", *BM* 129 (Jan
1881), 1-30.

405   "Autobiographies, no. II: Lord Herbert of Cherbury", *BM* 129
(Mar 1881), 385-410.

406   "Autobiographies, no. III: Margaret, Duchess of Newcastle",
BM 129 (May 1881), 617-39.

407   "Autobiographies, no. IV: Edward Gibbon", *BM* 130 (Aug 1881),
229-47.

408   "Autobiographies, no. V: Carlo Goldoni", *BM* 130 (Oct 1881),
516-41.

Each autobiography summarised, and the author characterised. The value of autobiography discussed.

409 "A Few French Novels", *BM* 130 (Dec 1881), 703-23.
Rev. of *Numa Roumestan* and *Le Petit Chose*, by Alphonse Daudet; *Monsieur le Ministre*, by Jules Claretie; *Perdue*, by Henry Greville; *Séduction*, by Hector Malot.

410 "Recent Novels", *BM* 131 (Mar 1882), 365-91.
Rev. of *John Inglesant: a Romance*, by J.H. Shorthouse; *The Portrait of a Lady*, by Henry James; *Beggar my Neighbour*, by E.D. Gerard; *Christowell: a Dartmoor Tale*, by R.D. Blackmore.

411 "*Democracy*", *BM* 131 (May 1882), 577-92.
Rev. of *Democracy*, an American novel (by Henry Adams).

412 "Autobiographies, no VI: In the Time of the Commonwealth", *BM* 132 (Jul 1882), 79-101.
Lucy Hutchinson and Alice Thornton.

413 "American Literature in England", *BM* 133 (Jan 1883), 136-61.
The novels of W.D. Howells; American magazines, esp. *The Century*; Henry James; American jingoism.

414 "Autobiographies, no. VII: Madame Roland", *BM* 133 (Apr 1883), 485-511.
The French Revolution.

415 "James Ferguson, the 'Astronomer'", *BM* 134 (Aug 1883), 244-63.
James Ferguson, a Banffshire peasant boy; his career and his scientific books. Self-made men.

416 "An Italian Official under Napoleon", *BM* 134 (Sep 1883), 379-93.
The autobiography of Cesare Balbo, a Piedmontese.

417 "The Story of a Little War", *BM* 134 (Oct 1883), 486-507.
Rev. of *Letters and Notes written during the Disturbances in the Highlands known as the "Devil" Country of Viti Levu, Fiji*, privately printed 1876.

418 "The Sons of the Prophets: Two Representatives of the Catholic Faith", *BM* 135 (Apr 1884), 529-53.
Rev. of *Memoir of James Robert Hope Scott*, by R. Ormsby; *The Life of Frederick Denison Maurice*.

419 "The Duke of Albany", *BM* 135 (May 1884), 700-2.
Obituary for Prince Leopold, son of the Queen.

420 "Venice", *BM* 136 (Jul 1884), 87-105.
Description of the city, and rev. of *Life on the Lagoons*, by Horatio F. Brown, and *La Vita Privata in Venezia: Vecchie Storie*, by Signor Molmenti.

421 "Three Young Novelists", *BM* 136 (Sep 1884), 296-316.
Rev. of *Mr Isaacs*, *Dr Claudius*, *To Leeward*, *A Roman Singer*, by

Howard Marion Crawford; *Vice Versa* and *The Giant's Robe*, by F. Anstey; *Called Back* and *Bound Together*, by J.F. Fargus (Hugh Conway).

422 "An Artist's Autobiography", *BM* 136 (Nov 1884), 614-31.
Rev. of *Thoughts on Art, and Autobiographical Memoirs of Giovanni Dupré*, translated by E.M. Peruzzi.

423 "London in May", *BM* 137 (May 1885), 684-705.
The weather, the parks, the art galleries, the theatres.

424 "General Gordon", *BM* 138 (Aug 1885), 247-72.
Biography, and rev. of *The Journals of Major-General C.G. Gordon at Khartoum ...*, Introduction and Notes by A. Egmont Hake.

425 "A Scotch Physician", *BM* 138 (Nov 1885), 669-90.
Rev. of *The Life of Sir Robert Christison, Bart, ... Professor of Materia Medica in the University of Edinburgh ...*, edited by his Sons.

426 "London in January", *BM* 139 (Feb 1886), 245-66.
The exhibitions, the theatres, the weather.

427 "Scotch Local History", *BM* 139 (Mar 1886), 375-97.
Rev. of *Records of Argyll: Legends, Traditions and Recollections of Argyllshire Highlanders ...*, by Lord Archibald Campbell, with Etchings by Charles Laurie; *Culross and Tullieallan ...*, by David Beveridge; *Aberdeen and Inchcolm, being Historical Notices of the parish and Monastery*, by Rev. W. Ross LLD; *Reminiscences of Yarrow*, by James Russell DD.

428 "The Late Principal Tulloch", *BM* 139 (Mar 1886), 414.
Brief obituary.

429 "Principal Tulloch", *BM* 139 (Apr 1886), 415-41.
Biography and character study. Signed "M.O.W. Oliphant".

430 "Novels", *BM* 140 (Dec 1886), 776-98.
Rev. of *The Children of Gibeon*, by Walter Besant; *The Princess Cassamassima*, by Henry James; *Sir Percival*, by J.H. Shorthouse; *A Bachelor's Blunder*, by W.E. Norris.
NB: The full title of the article includes the titles of the novels.

431 "In Maga's Library: The Old Saloon" 1, *BM* 141 (Jan 1887), 126-53.
Rev. of *Locksley Hall Sixty Years After*, by Alfred Tennyson; *Life of Shelley*, by Professor (Edward) Dowden, *The Life and Work of the Seventh Earl of Shaftesbury*, by Edwin Hodder; *Reminiscences and Opinions*, by F.H. Doyle; *Sketches from my Life*, by Admiral Robert Pacha; *Sententia Artis, First Principles of Art*, by Harry Quilter; *The New Amphion* (an anthology published for Edinburgh University Union); *The Struggle of the Bulgarians for National Independence*, translated from the German; *England's Case Against Home Rule*, by A.V. Dicey.

432 "The Old Saloon" 2, *BM* 141 (Feb 1887), 291-315.
Rev. of *Democracy, and other Addresses*, by James Russell Lowell;

Humorous Masterpieces from American Literature, arranged by
Edward T. Mason; *The Madonna of the Tubs*, by Elizabeth Stuart
Phelps; *Books and Bookmen, The End of Phaeacia*, and *The Mark of
Cain*, by Andrew Lang; *She: a History of Adventure*, by H. Rider
Haggard; *History of the University of Oxford*, by Maxwell Lyte;
Maitland of Lethington, and the Scotland of Mary Stuart, by John
Skelton; *The Dictionary of National Biography* (volume 9,
including Carlyle), edited by Leslie Stephen; *The History of
India under Queen Victoria*, by L.J. Trotter.

433   "The Old Saloon" 3, *BM* 141 (Mar 1887), 416-57.
Rev. of *Parleyings with Certain People of Importance*, by Robert
Browning; *The Service of Man*, by J. Cotter Morison; *Some Verdicts
of History Reviewed*, by William Stebbing; *A Journal of the Reign
of Queen Victoria from 1852 to 1860*; by the late Charles C.F.
Greville; *A Look Around Literature*, by Robert Buchanan; *The Life
of Agnes Strickland*, by her Sister; *Court and Private Life in the
Time of Queen Charlotte, being the Journals of Mrs Papendiek,
Bedchamber-woman to her Majesty*; *Eighty-Five Years of Irish
History - 1800-1885*, by William Joseph O'Neill Daunt.

434   "The Old Saloon" 4, *BM* 141 (Apr 1887), 552-72.
Rev. of *James Fraser, Second Bishop of Manchester*, by Thomas
Hughes; *Randolph Caldecott: his Early Art Career*; by Henry
Blackburn; *The Merry Men*, by Robert Louis Stevenson; *High Life,
or, Towers of Silence* ..., by Mrs Main (a mountaineering book);
Hurrish: a Study, by Emily Lawless; *Industrial Ireland*, by Robert
Dennis.

435   "The Old Saloon" 5, *BM* 141 (May 1887), 683-710.
"French Contemporary Novelists". Rev. of *Noir et Rose*, by Georges
Ohnet; *La Bête*, by Victor Cherbuliez; *Zyte*, by Hector Malot;
L'Affaire Froideville: Moeurs d'employés, by André Theuriot;
André Cornélis, by Paul Bourget; *Le Cavalier Miserey, 21e
Chasseurs*, by Abel Hermant; also a collection of short stories by
A. Halévy, and *Frankley*, by Madame Henry Grenville.

436   "The Rev W. Lucas Collins", *BM* 141 (May 1887), 734-6.
Obituary for a contributor to *Blackwood's Magazine*.

437   "The Old Saloon" 6, *BM* 141 (Jun 1887), 737-61.
"The Literature of the Last Fifty Years". Poets, historians,
philosophers and scientists, novelists, John Ruskin, journalism.

438   "The Old Saloon" 7, *BM* 142 (Jul 1887), 99-123.
(With Alexander Allardyce.)
Rev. of *Charles Reade: Dramatist, Novelist, Journalist*, by
Charles J. Reade and Rev. Compton Reade; *Anne Gilchrist: her Life
and Writings*, by Herbert H. Gilchrist; *Life of Rosina, Lady
Lytton: a Vindication*, by Louisa Devry; *Memoirs of the Margravine
of Baireuth*, translated and edited by HRH Princess Christian of
Schleswig Holstein; *A Lost Epic; and other Poems*, by William
Canton; *Letters from a Mourning City* (Naples, Autumn 1884), by
Axel Munthe, translated ... by Maude Valerie White; *Corres-
pondence between Goethe and Carlyle*, edited by Charles Eliot
Norton.

439 "The Old Saloon" 8, *BM* 142 (Aug 1887), 235-63.
(With Alexander Allardyce and R.K. Douglas.)
Rev. of *Lectures and Essays*, by Sir Stafford Henry Northcote; *The Pleasures of Life*, by Sir John Lubbock; *Italian Sketches*, by Janet Ross; *Arcady: for Better or Worse*, by A. Jessop DD; *Samuel Taylor Coleridge*, by Alois Brandl, University of Prague, translated by Lady Eastlake; *The Great Silver River: Notes of a Residence in Buenos Ayres in 1860 and 1881*, by Sir Horace Rumbold; St Petersburg and London, 1852-1864, *Reminiscences of Count Charles Frederick Vizthum von Eckstaed; Juvenilia, being a Second Series of Essays on Sundry Aesthetical Questions*, by Vernon Lee; *Allan Quatermain*, by H. Rider Haggard; *Sabina Zembra*, by William Black.

440 "The Old Saloon" 9, *BM* 142 (Nov 1887), 698-714.
Rev. of *A Collection of Letters of W.M. Thackeray, 1847-1855; Hortus Inclusus ...*, by John Ruskin; *Underwoods*, by Robert Louis Stevenson; *A Hundred Days in Europe*, by Oliver Wendell Holmes.

441 "The Old Saloon" 10, *BM* 143 (Jan 1888), 104-27.
Rev. of *The Life and Letters of Charles Darwin*, by his son Francis Darwin; *Personal Reminiscences of Sir Frederick Pollock; What I Remember*, by T. Adolphus Trollope; *My Autobiography and Reminiscences*, by W. Powell Frith RA.

442 "The Pictures of the Year", *BM* 143 (Jun 1888), 813-26.
The Royal Academy, The Grosvenor Gallery, The New Gallery.

443 "The Old Saloon" 11, *BM* 143 (Jun 1888), 831-26.
(With Alexander Allardyce.)
Rev. of *The Correspondence of Henry Taylor*, edited by Edward Dowden; *Partial Portraits*, by Henry James; *Papers of Professor Fleeming Jenkin*, with a Memoir by Robert Louis Stevenson; *On and Off the Stage*, by Mr and Mrs Bancroft; *The Lone White Mountain; or, a Journey in Manchuria*, by H.E.M. James; *Society in Rome under the Caesars*, by W.R. Inge MA.

444 "The Old Saloon" 12, *BM* 144 (Sep 1888), 419-43.
"French Novels". Rev. of *Trente Ans de Paris*, by Alphonse Daudet; *L'Immortel: Moeurs Parisiennes*, by Alphonse Daudet; *Conscience*, by Hector Malot; *Amour d'Automne*, by André Theuriet; *Folies d'Amour*, by Madame Hector Malot; *L'Unisson*, by George Duruy; *Pierre et Jean*, by Guy de Maupassant.

445 "The Old Saloon" 13, *BM* 144 (Dec 1888), 874-99.
(With Alexander Allardyce.)
Rev. of *The Life of the Right Honourable Stratford Canning ...*, by Stanley Lane-Poole; *Correspondence of Daniel O'Connell, the Liberator*, edited by W.J. Fitzpatrick, 2 vols; *Three Generations of Englishwomen*, by Janet Ross.

446 "The Emperor Frederick", *BM* 145 (Jan 1889), 109-19.
Rev. of *Frederick: Crown Prince and Emperor*, by Rennell Rodd; *The Emperor's Diary of the Austro-German War, 1866, and the Franco-German war, 1870-1871, to which is added Prince Bismarck's Rejoinder*, edited by Henry W. Lucy.

447 "Laurence Oliphant", *BM* 145 (Feb 1889), 280-96.
Obituary and biography, with personal memories. Signed M.O.W.O.

448   "The Old Saloon" 14, *BM* 145 (Mar 1889), 421-36.
(With Alexander Allardyce.)
Rev. of *HRH the Prince of Wales's Principal Public Speeches and
Addresses 1863-88*; *Letters on Literature*, by Andrew Lang; *The
Career of Major George Broadfoot, CB, in Afghanistan and the
Punjaub*, by Major W. Broadfoot; *Thomas Poole and his Friends*, by
Mrs Henry Sandford; *In Vinculis*, by Wilfrid Scawen Blunt.

449   "The Old Saloon" 15, *BM* 145 (Apr 1889), 561-72.
Rev. of *The Correspondence of John Lothrop Motley*, edited by G.W.
Curtis; *Leaves from an Egyptian Notebook*, by Isaac Taylor, Canon
of York.

450   "On the Riviera", *BM* 145 (May 1889), 676-88.
A travelogue; towns on the Riviera; an Italian invasion.

451   "The Old Saloon" 16, *BM* 145 (Jun 1889), 809-34.
Rev. of *The Two Chiefs of Dunboy; or, An Irish Romance of the
Last Century*, by J.A. Froude; *Greifenstein*, by F. Marion
Crawford; *A London Life*, by Henry James; *Plain Frances Mowbray,
and other Stories*, by Emily Lawless; *Elizabeth and other
Sketches*, by the author of *Miss Molly*.

452   "The Old Saloon" 17, *BM* 146 (Aug 1889), 254-75.
Edinburgh in the holiday season. Rev. of *The Wrong Box*, by Robert
Louis Stevenson and Lloyd Osbourne; *Ideala: a Study from Life* (by
Sarah Grand); *A Window in Thrums*, by J.M. Barrie; *Margaret
Maliphant*; by Mrs Comyns Carr; *French and English*, by F.G.
Hamerton; *The Ascent of Man*, by Mathilde Blind; *Clothed with the
Sun, being the Book of the Illuminations of Anna (Bonus)
Kingsford*, edited by Edward Maitland.

453   "The Old Saloon" 18, *BM* 146 (Nov 1889), 696-723.
(With Alexander Allardyce.)
Rev. of *The Master of Ballantrae: A Winter's Tale*, by Robert
Louis Stevenson; *An Irish Cousin*, by Geilles Herring (Edith
Somerville) and Martin Ross; *Marooned*, by W. Clark Russell; *The
Romance of Jenny Harlowe; and Sketches of Maritime Life*, by W.
Clark Russell; *The Friend of Man; and his Friends the Poets*, by
Frances P. Cobbe; *Mary Howitt: an Autobiography*, edited by her
Daughter; *Angling Songs*, by Thomas Todd Stoddart, with a Memoir
by Anna M. Stoddart.

454   "The Old Saloon" 19, *BM* 146 (Dec 1889), 857-78.
Edinburgh as an art centre. Rev. of *Art in Scotland: its Origin
and Progress*, by Robert Brydall; *A Memoir of Edward Askew Sothern
("Lord Dundreary")*, by T. Edgar Pemberton; *Fanny Burney and her
Friends*, by J.B. Seeley; *Louisa M. Alcott: her Life, Letters and
Journals*, by Ednah B. Cheney; *Further Recollections of Mr Thomas
Adolphus Trollope*; *The Pariah*, by F. Anstey.

455   "The Old Saloon" 20, *BM* 147 (Jan 1890), 131-51.
A preamble about "greetings and reminiscences". Rev. of *Asolando:
Fancies and Facts*, by Robert Browning; *Demeter, and other Poems*,
by Alfred Tennyson; *Appreciations: with an Essay on Style*, by
Walter Pater; *Falling in Love; and other Essays*, by Grant Allen;
Our Home in Aveyron, by G. Christopher Davies and Mrs Broughall.

456   "The Old Saloon" 21, *BM* 147 (Mar 1890), 408-28.
Rev. of *The Life of Harriet Beecher Stowe*; *Reuben Sachs* and *A London Plane Tree* etc, by Amy Levy; *The New Prince Fortunatus*, by William Black; *Kit and Kitty*, by R.D. Blackmore; *Claire Brandon*, by Frederick Marshall; *The Bull i'th' Thorn*, by Paul Cushing.

457   "Lord Lamington", *BM* 147 (Mar 1890), 449-50.
Obituary for a contributor to *Blackwood's Magazine*.

458   "The Holy Land", *BM* 148 (Jul 1890), 1-18.
Description of a journey with her son.

459   "The Old Saloon" 22, *BM* 150 (Aug 1891), 273-98.
Rev. of *Archbishop Campbell Tait, Archbishop of Canterbury*, by Randall T. Davidson ..., and William Benham ...; *Life and Letters of Robert Browning*, by Mrs Sutherland Orr; *Richard Redgrave CB, RA: a Memoir Compiled from his Diary*.

460   "The Old Saloon" 23, *BM* 150 (Nov 1891), 712-35.
Rev. of *Annals of my Early Life 1806-1846*, by Charles Wordsworth DD, Bishop of St. Andrews; *The Divorce of Catherine of Aragon*, by J.A. Froude; *Life's Handicap: Being Stories of Mine Own People*, by Rudyard Kipling.

461   "The Old Saloon - Lady Travellers" 24, *BM* 151 (Feb 1892), 299-318.
Rev. of *My Canadian Journal 1872-1878*, by the Marchioness of Dufferin and Ava; *My Three Years in Manipur*, by Ethel St.Clair Grimwood; *Journeys in Persia and Kurdistan*, by Mrs Bishop (Isabella L. Bird); *Two Happy Years in Ceylon*, by Mrs C.F. Gordon Cumming.

462   "The Duke of Clarence", *BM* 151 (Feb 1892), 326-8.
Obituary.

463   "The City of St. Andrews", *BM* 151 (Mar 1892), 370-7.
Rev. of *Twenty-five Years of St. Andrews*, by the author of *The Recreations of a Country Parson* (A.K.H. Boyd).

464   "The Old Saloon" 25, *BM* 151 (Mar 1892), 455-74.
Preamble on *Jane Eyre* and other literary sensations. Rev. of *The History of David Grieve*, by Mrs Humphry Ward; *Tess of the D'Urbervilles*, by Thomas Hardy.

465   "The Old Saloon" 26, *BM* 152 (Oct 1892), 574-96.
Rev. of *The Wrecker*, by Robert Louis Stevenson and Lloyd Osbourne; *The Naulahka: a Story of East and West*, by Rudyard Kipling and Wolcott Balestier; *Grania: the Story of an Island*, by Emily Lawless.

466   "Tennyson", *BM* 152 (Nov 1892), 748-66.
Obituary; survey of Tennyson's career and reputation.

467   "The Old Saloon" 27, *BM* 152 (Dec 1892), 852-73.
Rev. of *Records of Tennyson, Ruskin and Browning*, by Anne Thackeray Ritchie; *A Selection from the Letters of Geraldine Jewsbury to Jane Welsh Carlyle*, edited by Mrs Alexander Ireland; *Twenty-five Years of St. Andrews* (the second volume), by Rev.

A.K.H. Boyd; *Across France in a Caravan ...*, by the Author of *A Day of my Life at Eton*; *The Three Fates*, by F. Marion Crawford; *Lord Wastwater*, by Sidney Bolton.

468 "Marriage Bells", *BM* 154 (Jul 1893), 155-8.
The wedding of the Duke of York. Signed M.O.W.O.

469 "The Letters of Sir Walter Scott", *BM* 155 (Jan 1894), 15-26.
Rev. of *The Familiar Letters of Sir Walter Scott, from the Originals at Abbotsford and Elsewhere*.

470 "Dean Stanley", *BM* 155 (Feb 1894), 190-209.
Rev. of *The Life and Correspondence of Arthur Penryn Stanley, late Dean of Westminster*, by Rowland E. Prothero MA.

471 "The Looker-on" 1, *BM* 156 (Aug 1894), 285-308.
A rambling discursive essay on literature, the theatre, art, contemporary events etc.

472 "An Eton Master", *BM* 156 (Nov 1894), 693-9.
Obituary for Rev. Edward Hale.

473 "The Looker-on" 2, *BM* 157 (Jan 1895), 148-70.
Number 2; cf 471. Includes rev. of *The Yellow Book* 5.

474 "The Fancies of a Believer", *BM* 157 (Feb 1895), 237-55.
Speculations on Death, God, the Afterlife, mourning.

475 "Men and Women", *BM* 157 (Apr 1895), 620-50.
Preamble on portrait-painting and the art of biography. Rev. of *Life and Correspondence of W. Buckland, DD, FRS*, by his daughter, Mrs Gordon; *The Life of Richard Owen*, by his Grandson; *The Life and Letters of Dean Church*, edited by Mary C. Church; *John Addington Symonds: a Biography*, by Horatio F. Brown; *The Life and Letters of Maria Edgworth*, edited by Augustus J.C. Hare; *Mrs Henry Wood, a Memoir*, by her son Charles W. Wood; *The Recollections of the Very Rev. G.D. Boyle, Dean of Salisbury*.

476 "John Stuart Blackie", *BM* 157 (Apr 1895), 662-4.
Obituary for Professor Blackie of Edinburgh.

477 "The Looker-on" 3, *BM* 157 (Jun 1895), 902-29.
Number 3; cf 471. Includes a review of novels by S.R. Crockett.

478 "The Looker-on" 4, *BM* 158 (Dec 1895), 905-27.
Number 4; cf 471. Includes reviews of books by R.L. Stevenson and H.G. Wells.

479 "The Anti-Marriage League", *BM* 159 (Jan 1896), 135-49.
Rev. of *Jude the Obscure*, by Thomas Hardy; *The Woman who Did*, by Grant Allen. Signed M.O.W.O.

480 "The Looker-on" 5, *BM* 159 (Jun 1896), 901-26.
Number 5; cf 471. Includes reviews of poems by Christina Rossetti and Cecil Frances Alexander, and *Sir Walter Scott's Love Story*, by Adam Scott.

481 "The Looker-on" 6, *BM* 160 (Oct 1896), 481-507.

Number 6 and last; cf 471. Includes reviews of *The Amazing Marriage*, by George Meredith, and *Fellow Travellers* (short stories), by Graham Travers.

482   "The Verdict of Old Age", *BM* 160 (Oct 1896), 555-71.
Rev. of *The Philosophy of Belief*, by the Duke of Argyll; *Studies Subsidiary to Butler's Works*, by the Right Hon. W.E. Gladstone. Discussion of religious faith and of Purgatory. Signed M.O.W.O.

483   "John Gibson Lockhart", *BM* 160 (Nov 1896), 607-25.
Rev. of *The Life and Letters of John Gibson Lockhart*, by Andrew Lang.

484   "A Raid Among Books", *BM* 160 (Dec 1896), 822-46.
Rev. of *The Life and Correspondence of William Connor Magee, Archbishop of York, Bishop of Peterborough*, by John Cotter Macdonnell DD; *Letters of Frederic Lord Blachford, Under-Secretary of State for the Colonies 1860-1871*, edited by George Eden Marindin; *The Story of My Life*, by Augustus J.C. Hare; *The Carissima*, by Lucas Malet; *A Child of the Jago*, by Arthur Morrison; *A Book of Scoundrels*, by Charles Whibley; *The Second Series of Table-Talk of Shirley*, by John Skelton.

485   "Recent Books - French and English", *BM* 161 (Apr 1897), 455-84.
Rev. of *En Route*, by J.K. Huysmans; *L'Orme du Mail*, by Anatole France; *The Centenary Burns*, by W.E. Henley and T.F. Henderson; *The Land of the Dollar"*, by G.W. Steevens; *Pickle, the Spy*, by Andrew Lang; *Trooper Peter Halket of Mashonaland*, by Olive Schreiner; *Margaret Ogilvy*, by J.M. Barrie; *The Wise and the Wayward*, by G.S. Street.

486   "'Tis Sixty Years Since", *BM* 161 (May 1897), 599-624.
Memories of 1837; the sixty years of Victoria's reign.

487   "Siena", *BM* 164 (Jul 1898), 23-39.
Description of the town and its history. MOWO named as author. (Published posthumously.)

Chambers's Encyclopaedia

Revised ed. (3rd?), 10 vols, 1888-92.
Some articles attributed to authors in prefaces.

488   "Cowper, William", *CE* 3 (1889), 534-6.
Including bibliography.

489   "Irving, Edward", *CE* 6 (1890), 226.
Revised by MOWO. Including bibliography.

490   "Oliphant, Laurence", *CE* 7 (1891), 598.
Revised by MOWO? In the preface she is credited with revision of
articles, but no specific article is named.

491   "Oliphant, Margaret", *CE* 7 (1891), 598.
Perhaps revised in some details by MOWO. She could not have
written the article itself.

492   "Montalembert, Charles Forbes René de", *CE* 8 (1891), 281-2.
Revised by MOWO?

493   "Sheridan, Richard Brinsley", *CE* 9 (1892), 392-3.
Including bibliography.

494   "Tulloch, John", *CE* 10 (1892), 320.
Revised by MOWO?

495   "Venice", *CE* 10 (1892), 451-3.
Revised by MOWO?

496   "Windsor", *CE* 10 (1892), 682-3.
Revised by MOWO?

The Contemporary Review

497   "Mrs Carlyle", *CR* 43 (May 1883), 609-28.
Rev. of the *Letters* of Jane Welsh Carlyle in three vols. Analysis
of the Carlyle marriage.

498   "The Ethics of Biography", *CR* 44 (Jul. 1883), 76-93.
Analysis of the best approach to biography; the need for balance
and perspective. See Introduction, section VI.

499   "Victor Hugo", *CR* 48 (Jul. 1885), 10-32.
Obituary; study of Hugo's plays, poems and novels.

The Cornhill Magazine

500   "Assistant Masters", *CM* 33 (Mar. 1876), 288-99.
The growth of professional pride and concern for status among
schoolmasters. The recent dismissal from Eton of a master (i.e.
Oscar Browning). The power of headmasters.

501   "Giacomo Leopardi", *CM* 34 (Sep. 1876), 341-57.
Leopardi against the background of the Italy in his time; survey
of his poetry etc. Cf 250, 310.

The Dictionary of National Biography

502 "Oliphant, Francis Wilson", *DNB* 42 (1895), 129-30.
MOWO's husband, 1818-59. MOWO probably collaborated with her son
F.R. Oliphant in writing this article.

The Edinburgh Review

503 Rev. of *The Subjection of Women* etc, *ER* 130 (Oct. 1869),
572-602.
Rev. of *The Subjection of Women*, by John Stuart Mill; and *Women's
Work and Women's Culture, a Series of Essays*, edited by Josephine
G. Butler.

504 "The Epic of Arthur", *ER* 131 (Apr. 1870), 502-39.
Rev. of *Holy Grail* and *The Idylls of the King*, by Alfred
Tennyson. Also Malory's *Morte d'Arthur*, edited by T. Wright in 3
vols.

505 "Mr Browning's *Balaustion*", *ER* 135 (Jan. 1872), 221-49.
Rev. of *Balaustion's Adventure: including a Transcript from
Euripides*, by Robert Browning.

506 "The Correspondence of M. de Balzac", *ER* 148 (Oct. 1878),
528-58.
Rev. of *Correspondence de H. de Balzac 1819-1850*; *Balzac, sa Vie
et ses Oeuvres*, par Madame L. Surville, née de Balzac; *Balzac
chez lui*, par Léon Gozlan. Balzac's life and novels.

507 "The Life and Letters of George Eliot", *ER* 161 (Apr. 1885),
514-53.
Rev. of *George Eliot's Life Related in her Letters and Journals*,
arranged and edited by her husband J.W. Cross.

508 "Life and Letters of Mrs Craven", *ER* 181 (Apr. 1895), 315-
45.
Rev. of *A Memoir of Mrs Augustus Craven* (Pauline de la Ferron-
ays), by Maria Catherine Bishop, 2 vols.

The English Illustrated Magazine

509 "Heidelberg", *EIM* 2 (Oct. 1884), 39-47.
A description of the town.

510 "Edinburgh", *EIM* 8 (Oct. 1890), 48-57.
With illustrations by George Reid, RSA. A description of the
city, quite distinct from *Royal Edinburgh*, to be published in
Dec. 1890. (Cf "Margaret of Scotland", *EIM* 7, item 168, which
became the first part of *Royal Edinburgh*.)

The Forum (New York)

511 "Success in Fiction", *Forum* 7 (May 1889), 314-22.

A commissioned article. Discusses the value of novels, and the art of writing them.

Fraser's Magazine

512 "The Grievances of Women", *FM* 101 (n.s. 21) (May 1880), 698-710.
MOWO's most forceful expression of the radical point of view.

Good Words

513 "Anthony Trollope", *GW* 24 (Feb. 1883), 142-4.
Obituary.

514 "San Remo", *GW* 34 (Feb. 1893), 124-30.
Description of the city.

515 "The Queen", *GW* 38 (Jun. 1897), 380-6.
Diamond Jubilee article.

Macmillan's Magazine

516 "Clerical Life in Scotland", *MM* 8 (Jul. 1863), 208-19.
Rev. of *Memoir of the Life of the Rev. Robert Story, late Minister of Rosneath, Dumbartonshire*, by Robert Henry Story; *Life of the Rev. James Robertson DD, FRSE*, by the Rev. A.H. Charteris MA, Minister of New Abbey. (Attributed to MOWO by the *Wellesley Directory*.)

517 "Florence", *MM* 29 (Jan. 1874), 206-10.
Partly a rev. of *Walks in Florence*, by Susan and Joanna Horner. Not certainly by MOWO. The *Wellesley Directory* thinks not.

518 "Thomas Carlyle", *MM* 43 (Apr. 1881), 482-96.
Rev. of *Reminiscences*, by Thomas Carlyle, edited by James Anthony Froude, 2 vols., published posthumously. Many personal memories. Signed M.O.W.O.

518a "Carlyle's Last Days" (editorial title), an extract from 518, was published in *Harper's Weekly*, NY 25 (30 Apr. 1881), 290.

519 "Mrs Craik", *MM* 57 (Dec. 1887), 81-5.
Obituary, with personal memories.

The New Review

520 "A Noble Lady", *NR* 14 (Mar, 1896), 241-7.
Obituary for Lady Cloncurry, with personal memories.

St.James's Budget

See under *St.James's Gazette*.

St.James's Gazette

521 "A Fireside Commentary" 1, 11 Jan. 1888, 5-6. Rpt in *St.James's Budget* (hereafter *SJB*), 14 Jan. 1888, 9.
Memories of campaigning for the repeal of the Corn Laws. Signed

"A Dowager". (See Introduction, section IX.)

522 "A Fireside Commentary" 2, 21 Jan. 1888, 5-6. Rpt in *SJB*, 28 Jan. 1888, 11-12.
Changing attitudes to Roman Catholicism. Signed "A Dowager".

523 "A Fireside Commentary" 3, 30 Jan. 1888, 5-6. Rpt in *SJB*, 4 Feb. 1888. 9-10.
"About Working Women." Unsigned, as are all subsequent articles.

524 "A Fireside Commentary" 4, 6 Feb. 1888, 5-6. Rpt in *SJB*, 11 Feb. 1888, 9-10.
"On the Home-Work of Poor Women."

525 "A Fireside Commentary" 5, 10 Feb. 1888, 5-6. Rpt in *SJB*, 18 Feb. 1888, 9-10.
"Of the Gentilities; and of Certain Great Princes."

526 "A Fireside Commentary" 6, 17 Feb. 1888, 5-6. Rpt in *SJB*, 25 Feb. 1888, 9-11.
"M. Renan and his Life to Come: Magnanimous Heathenism."

527 "A Fireside Commentary" 7, 27 Feb. 1888, 5-6. Rpt in *SJB*, 3 Mar. 1888.
"Marriage on so much a Year - Clubs - Failures and their Compensations."

528 "A Fireside Commentary" 8, 5 Mar. 1888, 5-6. Rpt in *SJB*, 10 Mar. 1888, 9-10.
On English class-consciousness.

529 "A Fireside Commentary" 9, 12 Mar. 1888, 6-7. Rpt in *SJB*, 17 Mar. 1888, 13-14.
"Sabbath Breaking - the Clergy and the 'Smart' People."

530 "A Fireside Commentary" 10, 16 Mar. 1888, 5-6. Rpt in *SJB*, 24 Mar. 1888, 11-12.
"The Old Emperor and the New - Emperors of the Last Half-Century - The Illustrated Papers."

531 "A Fireside Commentary" 11, 24 Mar. 1888, 6. Rpt in *SJB*, 31 Mar. 1888, 9-10.
"Funerals - Men of Genius and their Wives - Mr Leslie Stephen's View."

532 "A Fireside Commentary" 12, 4 Apr. 1888, 5-6. Rpt in *SJB*, 7 Apr. 1888, 9-10.
"The Villa Palmieri - 'The Falcon' - Farewell Speeches: 'I wonder you will Still be Talking'."

533 "A Fireside Commentary" 13, 14 Apr. 1888, 6. Rpt in *SJB*, 21 Apr. 1888, 11.
"A Great Historical Scene - The Teuton and the Tartar - History on the Stage."

534 "A Fireside Commentary" 14, 23 Apr. 1888, 5-6. Rpt in *SJB*, 28 Apr. 1888, 10-11.
"High School Girls - The Power of Teaching - The Schooling of

Experience."

535 "A Fireside Commentary" 15, 28 Apr. 1888, 5-6. Rpt in *SJB*, 5
May 1888, 11-12.
"Berlin - The Persistency of Slander - A Robust Family - Monarchs
and Statesmen."

536 "A Fireside Commentary" 16, 5 May 1888, 5-6. Rpt in *SJB*, 12
May 1888, 9.
"Monsignor Persico - The New Taxes - Real Sufferers."

537 "A Fireside Commentary" 17, 9 May 1888, 5-6. Rpt in *SJB*, 12
May 1888, 9-10.
"Matthew Arnold - Westminster and St. Paul's - Decoration."

538 "A Fireside Commentary" 18, 16 May 1888, 6-7. Rpt in *SJB*, 19
May 1888, 8-9.
"Private Views - Burlington House - Portraits of Women."

539 "A Forthcoming Book and its Author", 22 May 1888, 5-6. Rpt
in *SJB*, 26 May, 9-10.
A summary of the career of Laurence Oliphant, leading to his
forthcoming book (unnamed; it is *Scientific Religion*). Unsigned,
but undoubtedly by MOWO, for reasons stated in section IX of the
Introduction.

540 "A Fireside Commentary" 19, 28 May 1888, 6. Rpt in *SJB*, 2
Jun. 1888, 9-10.
"The Spring - The Fireside Superseded - The Factory Girl and the
Lady."

541 "A Fireside Commentary" 20, 31 May 1888, 5-6. Rpt in *SJB*, 2
Jun. 1888, 10.
"Emigration and Immigration - The People's Palace - Admission
2d."

542 "A Fireside Commentary" 21, 8 Jun. 1888, 5-6. Rpt in *SJB*, 16
Jun. 1888, 11-12.
"Cold Weather - The Sweaters Again - A School for Dressmaking."

****

Articles signed "M"

543 "Taking Offence", 15 Jun. 1888, 6. Rpt in *SJB*, 23 Jun. 1888,
12-13.

544 "Heroes: Mortality and Immortality", 20 Jun. 1888, 6. Rpt in
SJB, 23 Jun. 1888, 12.

545 "The Baby Next Door", 25 Jun. 1888, 6-7. Rpt in *SJB*, 30 Jun.
1888, 14-15.

546 "The Fallible and the Infallible", 29 Jun. 1888, 5-6. Not
reprinted in *SJB*.

547 "The End of the Mourning", 5 Jul. 1888, 5-6. Rpt in *SJB*, 7
Jul. 1888, 8.

The mourning for the German Emperor.

548   "A Fine Day", 9 Jul. 1888,, 5-6. Rpt in *SJB*, 14 Jul. 1888, 10.

549   "Fantastic Politics: Patriotism and Pay", 18 Jul. 1888, 5-6. Rpt in *SJB*, 21 Jul. 1888, 10-11.

550   "Facts - and Fiction", 20 Jul. 1888, 6-7. Rpt in *SJB*, 28 Jul. 1888, 10.

551   "Silly Women", 25 Jul. 1888, 6. Rpt in *SJB*, 28 Jul. 1888, 12.

552   "Silly Men", 28 Jul. 1888, 5-6. Rpt in *SJB*, 4 Aug. 1888, 12-13.

553   "Incorporated Authors", 2 Aug. 1888, 6-7. Rpt in *SJB*, 4 Aug. 1888, 9-10.
A proposed trades union of authors.

554   "Publishers - Not Incorporated", 15 Aug. 1888, 6-7. Rpt in *SJB*, 18 Aug. 1888, 11-12.
A response to correspondence following the previous article.

555   "Authors and Publishers", 24 Aug. 1888, 6. Not reprinted in *SJB*.
A further response to correspondence, including a letter by Walter Besant, *SJG* 10 Aug. 1888, 5, and another by "Old Hand", *SJG* 22 Aug. 1888, 5-6.

St. Nicholas (New York)

"Windsor Castle", in six chapters:

556   Chapter I: "The Order of the Garter", *SN* 3 (Mar. 1876), 292-8.

557   Chapter II: "The Captive Prince", *SN* 3 (May 1876), 430-5.
James I of Scotland.

558   Chapter III: "The Baby King", *SN* 3 (Jul. 1876), 553-8.
Henry VI.

559   Chapter IV: "The Tudors", *SN* 3 (Aug. 1876), 626-31.

560   Chapter V: "The Stuarts", *SN* 3 (Sep. 1876), 689-96.

561   Chapter VI: "Queen Victoria", *SN* 3 (Oct. 1876), 759-66.

The Spectator

562   "The Rights of Women", 7 Mar. 1874, 301-2.
A Letter to the Editor, signed "M".

563   "The Study of History at Eton", 29 Jan. 1876, 142.

A Letter to the Editor, signed "An Eton Parent"; on the dismissal of Oscar Browning. Cf 500.

564 *"Memorials of a Quiet Life"*, 8 Jul. 1876, 866-7.
Rev. of *Memorials of a Quiet Life*, vol. IV, by Augustus Hare. Cf 355.

565 "The Christian Doctrine of Sin", 12 Aug. 1876, 1013-4.
Rev. of *The Croall Lectures 1876: The Christian Doctrine of Sin*, by John Tulloch.

[In the absence of documentation for the period December 1877 to October 1880, it is suggested that the three following book reviews may be by MOWO.]

566 "Venice", 19 Jan. 1878, 90-1.
Rev. of *Venise, Histoires, Arts, Industrie, La Ville, La Vie*, par Charles Yriarte. Cf 420 and 613, reviews by MOWO of books on Venice.

567 *"A Modern Greek Heroine"*, 11 Sep. 1880, 1163.
Rev. of *A Modern Greek Heroine*, anonymous novel (by H. Cresswell). Cf 403, which includes a review of the same book.

568 "The Standard Scotch Dictionary", 2 Oct. 1880, 1258.
Rev. of *An Etymological Dictionary of the Scottish Language*, new ed., by John Jamieson. (Dubious attribution, in view of MOWO's love of Scotland.)

[Documentation resumes in November 1880.]

569 "Ideal Men and Women", 8 Jan. 1881, 48.
A Letter to the Editor, signed with a pseudonym, protesting at an announcement by the periodical *The Day of Rest* that she was to contribute to it, as stated in an article in *The Spectator*, 1 Jan. 1881, 12-14.

570 *"Post Mortem"*, 13 Aug. 1881, 1053-4.
Rev. of *Post Mortem* (by Arthur Montagu Brookfield), a novel about the Next World.

571 "Mrs Oliphant and Bishop Wilberforce" (editorial title), 6 Jan. 1883, 13-14.
A Letter to the Editor protesting against unjust and inaccurate comments by Wilberforce on MOWO's *Life of Edward Irving*; a response to a review of a biography of Wilberforce, *Spectator* 30 Dec. 1882, 1685-6. Letter signed "M.O.W. Oliphant".

572 *"Life on the Lagoons"*, 21 Jun. 1884, 823-4.
Rev. of *Life on the Lagoons*, by Horatio F. Brown, 823-4. Cf 420 and 566.

573 "Are Women a 'Represented Class'?" (editorial title), 1 Nov. 1884, 1437.
A Letter to the Editor, signed "M", with two other suffragist letters, by Frances Power Cobbe and Anna M. Haslam.

574 *"Hurrish"*, 30 Jan. 1886, 147-8.

Rev. of *Hurrish, a Study*, by Emily Lawless.

575   "Principal Tulloch", 20 Feb. 1886, 250-1. ("Topics of the Day")
Obituary; cf 428 and 429.

576   "*The Story of the Nations: Ireland*", 14 Jan. 1888, 60-1.
Rev. of *Ireland*, by Emily Lawless.

577   "Maitland of Lethington", 6 Oct. 1888, 1363-4.
Rev. of *Maitland of Lethington: the Scotland of Mary Stuart*, by John Skelton. Cf 432.

578   "A Commentary from my Chair" 1, 7 Dec. 1889, 804-5. ("Correspondence")
The first of a series of discursive essays.

579   "A Commentary from an Easy Chair" 2, 14 Dec. 1889, 842-3.
The New Journalism etc.

580   "A Commentary from an Easy Chair" 3, 21 Dec. 1889, 881-2.
The funeral of Browning etc.

581   "A Commentary from an Easy Chair" 4, 28 Dec. 1889, 921-2.
Christmas etc.

582   "A Commentary in an Easy Chair" 5, 4 Jan. 1890, 13-14.
Mr Bradlaugh etc.

583   "A Commentary in an Easy Chair" 6, 11 Jan. 1890, 49-50.
Fashionable illnesses etc.

584   "A Commentary in an Easy Chair" 7, 18 Jan. 1890, 84-5.
Candour in fiction etc.

585   "A Commentary in an Easy Chair" 8, 25 Jan. 1890, 116-17.
The increase in sympathy for women etc.

586   "A Commentary in an Easy Chair" 9, 1 Feb. 1890, 164-5.
Plagiarism and the reworking of books by other writers; a reference to Hector Malot, cf 444.

587   "A Commentary in an Easy Chair" 10, 8 Feb. 1890, 199-200.
The growth of democracy - and of interest in royalty.

588   "A Commentary in an Easy Chair" 11, 15 Feb. 1890, 233-4.
Strikes etc.

589   "A Commentary in an Easy Chair" 12, 1 Mar. 1890, 302-3.
The prickliness of Scotsmen.

590   "A Commentary in an Easy Chair" 13, 8 Mar. 1890, 336-7.
Working-class speakers etc.

591   "A Commentary in an Easy Chair" 14, 15 Mar. 1890, 371-2.
The secret of successful old age etc.

592   "A Commentary in an Easy Chair" 15, 29 Mar. 1890, 438-9.

Education etc.

593   "A Commentary in an Easy Chair" 16, 3 May 1890, 620-1.
The House of Lords.

594   "A Commentary in an Easy Chair" 17, 5 Jul. 1890, 11-12.
Self-advertisement by letters to the press.

595   "A Commentary in an Easy Chair" 18, 12 Jul. 1890, 49-50.
Meaning in music and art.

596   "A Commentary in an Easy Chair" 19, 19 Jul. 1890, 81-3.
The inadequacy of pensions for widows of writers etc,

597   "A Commentary in an Easy Chair" 20, 26 Jul. 1890, 113-14.
Holiday travel.

598   "A Commentary in an Easy Chair" 21, 2 Aug. 1890, 146-7.
Renewal of the theme of 595.

599   "A Commentary in an Easy Chair" 22, 9 Aug. 1890, 177-8.
The start of the holidays; Rudyard Kipling etc.

600   "A Commentary in an Easy Chair" 23, 16 Aug. 1890, 210-11.
Oxford and Cambridge men as missionaries in the slums.

601   "A Commentary in an Easy Chair" 24, 23 Aug. 1890, 242-3.
The danger of social anarchy.

602   "A Commentary in an Easy Chair" 25, 30 Aug. 1890, 274-5.
Garden parties etc.

603   "A Commentary in an Easy Chair" 26, 6 Sep. 1890,307-8.
Dullness; domestic servants etc.

604   "A Commentary in an Easy Chair" 27, 13 Sep. 1890, 339-40.
The drinking fountain in Stratford-on-Avon etc.

605   "A Commentary in an Easy Chair" 28, 20 Sep. 1890, 374-5.
The skilled labourer.

606   "A Commentary in an Easy Chair" 29, 4 Oct. 1890, 438-9.
The same subject continued.

607   "A Commentary in an Easy Chair" 30, 11 Oct. 1890, 473-4.
The writing of love stories.

608   "A Commentary in an Easy Chair" 31, 18 Oct. 1890, 520-1.
The problem of poverty.

609   "A Commentary in an Easy Chair" 32, 1 Nov. 1890, 593-4.
The need to improve rural conditions etc.

610   "A Commentary in an Easy Chair" 33, 8 Nov. 1890, 644-5.
The bond between Britain and America; Irish nationalists etc.

611   "*Aunt Anne*", 6 Aug. 1892, 195-6.
Rev. of *Aunt Anne*, by Mrs W.K. Clifford.

612 "The Apology of Age to Youth" (editorial title), 24 Dec.
1892, 923.
A Letter to the Editor, signed "An Old Lady". First of a sequence
on the generation gap.

613 "Venice", 24 Jun. 1893, 827-9.
Rev. of *Venice - an Historical Sketch of the Republic*, by Horatio
F. Brown; cf 420, also 565 and 571. (Possibly by F.R. Oliphant,
MOWO's son.)

614 "Prayers for the Dead", 15 Dec. 1894, 847.
A Letter to the Editor,signed "M". On death, the Next World and
God's forgiveness.

615 "The Seen and the Unseen", 1 Feb. 1896, 166.
A Letter to the Editor, signed "M". A response to R.H. Hutton's
review of "The Library Window", *The Spectator* 25 Jan. 1896, 130-
1.

616 "*The Land of the Dollar*", 13 Feb. 1897, 240-1.
Rev. of *The Land of the Dollar*, by G.W. Steevens; cf 485.

Wit and Wisdom

617 "Advice to our Young Women Readers" ("From Noted Authors")
(editorial title), 9 Apr. 1892, 370.
MOWO contributes one short letter to this symposium, in response
to a request for "wise counsel and advice" from some young American women.

II Contributions to Books by other Authors

618 *Life and Remains of Robert Lee, D.D.*, by Robert Henry Story,
With an Introductory Chapter by Mrs Oliphant, Author of *The Life
of Edward Irving* etc., 2 vols. (London: Hurst and Blackett,
1870.) (In fact published late 1869.)
Introduction by MOWO in vol. 1, xi-xxiv.

619 *The Art of Swimming in the Eton Style*, by "Sergeant Leahy",
Champion Swimmer of the Red Sea, 1849-50; and at Present Teacher
of Swimming at Eton College. With a Preface by Mrs Oliphant ...
Edited by Two Etonians. (London: Macmillan & Co; Nottingham,
Shepherd Bros, Angel Row, 1875.)
Preface by MOWO, i-ii.

620 *Memoirs of the Life of Anna Jameson*, by her Niece Gerardine
Macpherson. (London: Longmans, Green and Co., 1878.)
Postscript to the Preface, by MOWO, xiii-xvii. The book was also
edited for the press by MOWO.

C Poems and Plays

621 "The Christian Knight's Vigil, a Chant, Addressed to a Young Minister on the Eve of his Ordination", in *The English Presbyterian Messenger* n.s. 2 (Dec 1850), 564. Signed M.O.W.
In honour of her brother's ordination as a Presbyterian minister.

622 "The Shadow on the Way", in *Blackwood's Magazine* 73 (Jun 1853), 730-1. Signed M.W.O.

623 "From India", in *BM* 82 (Oct 1857), 505-6. Signed M.O.W.O.

624 "The Nation's Prayer", in *BM* 91 (Jan 1862), 136.
In memory of the Prince Consort.

625 "In the Garden", in *BM* 94 (Aug 1863), 244-5. Signed M.O.W.O.

626 "Amen! - in the Cathedral of St. Andrews", in *BM* 94 (Oct 1863), 497-8. Signed M.O.W.O.

627 "Day and Night", in *BM* 97 (Jan 1865), 89-91. Signed M.O.W.O.

628 "The Innermost Room", in *BM* 101 (Mar 1867), 338-40. Signed M.O.W.O.

629 *An Elderly Lover*, privately printed, 1885, a one-act play. 52 pp. Anonymous, but presumably by MOWO. Copies at NLS among Oliphant papers.

630 "Alfred Tennyson", in *The Spectator*, 15 Oct 1892, 528. Signed M.O.W.O.
The second of two obituary poems, the first being by T. Herbert Warren.

631 "A Farewell", in *The Spectator*, 2 Mar 1895, 294-5. Signed M.O.W.O.
In memory of E.S. Pigott, died 23 Feb 1895.
[Pigott was the Censor of Plays. See Jay ed., *Autobiography*, 142.]

632 "22nd June 1897", in *BM* 161 (Jun 1897), 887-8.
For the Queen's Jubilee.
Also reprinted in *A&L*, 435-6.

633 "On the Edge of the world I lie, I lie", published in 1899 in *A&L*, 438. (Written in 1897.)

D Manuscripts

Great Britain

Information on some libraries with minor Oliphant holdings comes mainly from David C. Sutton ed., *Location Register of English Literary Manuscripts and Letters, Eighteenth and Nineteenth Centuries*, 2 vols (London, The British Library, 1995). Where information comes only from this book the abbreviation Sutton is used. For some libraries the information in Sutton has been amended and extended. Many manuscripts are omitted from Sutton, and are included here; where a library has not been visited it may be that that library has more Oliphant MSS than are listed below. In many instances suggestions of dates and of names of correspondents are my own.

Included in this section are, not only letters and manuscripts by MOWO, but also some letters written to her, and a few written about her, and letters by her immediate family. Thus it is possible to make the section as useful to biographers and scholars as possible.

634 Berkshire Record Office, Reading

D/EBY F48, p. 126. Letter, n.d. (1874?), to Lady (Mary Anne) Barker.

635 Birmingham Reference Library

Birmingham City Archives, MS 135. Includes one letter, n.d. (possibly of the 1870s), to Mr Newman, probably of the firm Hurst and Blackett; and one letter, n.d., to Mr Macmillan (not further identifiable).

636 The Bodleian Library, Oxford

MS Autogr b4, p. 53a. Letter, n.d. (1867 or 1868), to Mr (George) Simpson of Blackwood and Sons.
MS Autogr b11, no 1239. Letter, n.d. (between 1865 and 1871) to Mr (?Stone, ?Storm, ?Story).
MS Autogr c25, fols 177-78. Letter, n.d. (1887?, 1888?), to Dr Coghill.
MS Autogr d33, fol 114. Letter, n.d., to Mr (Henry or John or Stephen) Hawtrey.
MS. Eng.lett.e.200, fols 71-74. Two letters, n.d.[1890, and 1890?], to Madame [Linda] Villari of Florence. Also, fols 75-77, letter, n.d. [1890?] of Madge Oliphant Wilson to Madame Villari, with attached note by Madame Villari.
MS. Eng. misc. d.179, fols 206-12. Three letters, n.d. [1894, 1895], to Sir Sidney Lee; and a brief biographical note on MOWO's sons C.F. and F.R. Oliphant.
MS. Eng. misc. f 395/1, fol 170. Memorandum, 1885, of an agreement between MOWO and Mr W.F. Tillotson of Bolton.

637 Bolton Central Library, Bolton, Lancashire (Sutton)

Archives ZBEN/4/1,69. Letter, 1891, to Messrs Tillotson and Son.

Archives ZBEN/4/6. Letter, n.d. to Mr Tillotson.

638 **The British Library, Department of Manuscripts, London**

Add MS 42576, f. 300. Letter, 1894, to Mr J. Bryce.
Add MS 46359A (Knightly MSS vol IVA), f. 155. Letter, n.d.
(1880) to woman unnamed, relation or friend of Sir Rainald
Knightly.
Add MS 46616, ff 26-40. Nine letters, 1851-52, to Richard
Bentley, publisher.
Add MS 46641, ff 131, 136, 145, 171, 173, 175, 176, 215,
216, 318, 323, 335. Copies of letters, 1851-53, from Richard
Bentley to MOWO, and one to Francis Wilson Oliphant.
Add MS 54919. Letters, 1858-95 and n.d., to the publishers
Macmillan and Co. Also signed agreements and receipts.
Add MS 60865, ff 85-6, 101-06, 140. Five letters, 1881,
1886?, and n.d., to Lord and Lady Carnarvon, and a copy of
an answer by Lord Carnarvon to one of these letters.
RP631. Photocopy of the MS of "Mr Thackeray and his Novels".
(See item 257 above.)
RP1314. Includes photocopies of eighteen letters, n.d.
(1852-60), one of them fragmentary, to Francis Bennoch, and
one to Mrs Bennoch; a second copy of the first page of one
letter. Also included a letter, n.d. (after 1865), to Mr
(Alexander?) Strahan.
RP3282 (XXXV). Photocopy of letter, 1894, to Miss Murray
Smith.

639 **The British Library, Oriental and India Office Collections,
London**

MSS. Eur. F.234/26, pt. II, no 59. Letter, n.d. [1883], to
[Sir Mountstuart Elphinstone] Grant Duff.

640 **The Brotherton Library, Leeds** (Sutton)

Brotherton Collection. In Gosse Correspondence. Letter,
1883, to Edmund Gosse.
Brotherton Collection. In an autograph album, p.22. Letter,
n.d. to an unknown correspondent.

641 **Cambridge University Library**

Add 7349/15/143, 144 Two letters, n.d., and n.d. (1882?),
to Sir James [Fitzjames] Stephen. (It may be that the first
letter is to another member of Sir James's family, possibly
his son James Kenneth Stephen.)
Add 7649/102. Letter, n.d. (1879?), to man unnamed (contributor to the Foreign Classics for English Readers series,
probably Walter Besant).
Add. 7633.5/109-10 and 7/42. Three letters, n.d. [1880,
1887, 1890], to A.W. Kinglake. Also, 7/41, letter, 1890,
from Cyril Oliphant to Kinglake.
Add. 9854/112. Letter, n.d. [1893], to Mrs Wynne (unidentified).

642 **Cheshire Record Office, Chester** (Sutton)

Delves Broughton Archive, Box M. Two letters, 1881, to Rhoda Broughton.

643 **Dorset County Museum, Dorchester**

Thomas Hardy Memorial Collection. Letter, n.d. (1882), to Thomas Hardy.

644 **Edinburgh University Library**

DC.4.101-3 (Irving). Letter, 1860, to Rev J. Matheson, Ecclefechan.

645 **Eton College Library, Eton**

Ritchie 6. Includes thirteen letters, [1875-96], to Anne Isabella Thackeray, later Anne Thackeray Ritchie. Also the MS of MOWO's poem "On the edge of the world I lie, I lie" (item 633), in the handwriting of Janet Mary Oliphant. Also two letters, 1897 and n.d., by Janet Mary Oliphant to Anne Ritchie, and one, 1897, by W.R. Valentine, MOWO's nephew by marriage.

646 **Fitzwilliam Museum Library, Cambridge**

Ashcombe Collection V. 39. Letter, n.d. [1874] to (?) Donald Macleod of *Good Words.*
Henderson, Literary and Scientific Celebrities, Vol 1. 57. Letter, n.d., to an editor of an unnamed periodical.

647 **Girton College Library, Cambridge**

BRP IX:141. Letter, n.d.[1878], to Madame Belloc (Bessie Rayner Parkes).

648 **John Rylands University Library, Manchester**

Letters to the firm Tillotson and Sons of Bolton, included in the Tillotson Papers:
Loose with typed transcript: Letter, n.d. (1882? 1883?).
Included in a large album of letters:
Item 69: Letter, 1891;
Item 94: Envelope of letters, inc letter, n.d. (between 1884 and 1888); and letter, n.d. (1891?).

649 **Leeds District Archives** (Sutton)

Ingilby Records 3608 (Novelists). Letter to [Mrs?] Sellar.

650 **Lincoln Central Library** (Sutton)

Tennyson Research Centre 4055-4058, 4990. Five letters, 1884-1892 and n.d., to Hallam Tennyson.

651 **The Mitchell Library, Glasgow** (Sutton)

891104. Five letters, n.d., to Mr Wright.

652 **The National Library of Scotland, Edinburgh**

A The Blackwood MSS

MS 3925 ff 162-5. Two letters to Mr (John) Blackwood, n.d. (1874? and 1876).
MSS 4099, 4103, 4106, 4111, 4112, 4119, 4126, 4133, 4141, 4152, 4163, 4166, 4169, 4172, 4731, 4184, 4191, 4202, 4213, 4225, 4238, 4251, 4266, 4280, 4295, 4309, 4323, 4337, 4349, 4360, 4364, 4366, 4380, 4396, 4410, 4413, 4424, 4437, 4449, 4462, 4476, 4490, 4497, 4507, 4511, 4523, 4540, 4558, 4560, 4578, 4592, 4605, 4621, 4635, 4636, 4643, 4650, 4664, 4725.
Letters, 1851-97 and n.d., from and to MOWO, also concerning her; receipts etc.
MS 4856. MS of *Margaret Maitland*, chs 1-3.
MSS 4857-8. MS of *Zaidee*, Books 1, 2, 3 chs 1-22.
MS 4859. MS of *The Quiet Heart*, chs 9-37.
MS 4860. MSS of the articles "Bulwer" (item 258), "Theology: The Broad Church" (item 261), "Macaulay" second part (item 271), and "Siena" (item 487); and MS fragments of additions to *Annals of a Publishing House*.
MS 4937. Letter, 1868, concerning MOWO. Also includes letters concerned with the Blackwood *Annals*.
MS 4939. MS of *Annals of a Publishing House*, chs 1-22. Differs from final version.

B Other Letters and MSS

MS 581, no 529. Letter, n.d. (1854), to Mrs [Catherine E.] Moir.
MS 666, ff 176-7, 210-11. Letters, 1868 and n.d. (1872). to Thomas Carlyle.
MS 741, no 128. Letter, n.d., to Dr (Norman or Donald) Macleod.
MS 966, f 276. Letter, n.d., to Mr Mattali (?).
MS 1774, ff 206-7, 214, 304-5, 306-7, 308, 310-11. Letters, 1861 and n.d. (all between 1860 and 1863), to Jane Welsh Carlyle.
MS 1778, f 82-3. Letter, n.d. (1875) to David Masson.
MS 2636, ff 193, 267. Letters, n.d. (1886 or 1888), to Professor John Stuart Blackie.
MS 7171, item 93. MS of a page of the review of *The Reign of Queen Anne* (item 400), pasted into a scrapbook.
MS 7175, ff 55-6, 57-8, 59-60. Letters, n.d. (1880s), to Sir Henry Craik.
MS 7178, no 112. Letter, n.d. (1860?), "Dear Grandmamma".
MS 9752, ff 40-1. Letter, n.d. (c. 1870), to an unnamed actress.
MS 9754, ff 126-33. Letters, n.d. (1860s), to a Miss Scott of Hampstead;
ff 134-5. "The Vigil of All Souls", a poem.
MS 9828, ff 34-9. Three letters, n.d. (1874?, 1884?, 1884?), to Mr William Isbister and Dr (Donald) Macleod.
MS 10256, f 38v. Signature of MOWO pasted into an autograph book, with biographical note.
MS 10994, f 94. Letter, n.d. (between 1861 and 1863), to Miss Macfie.
MS 23183, ff 198-203. (In the Smith, Elder Archives.)

Letters, n.d. (1892, 1869?, 1873?), to Mr (George) Smith.
MSS 30023-30050. Correspondence, 1871-84 and n.d., between
MOWO and William Blackwood and Sons.
MS 30485. Letters, 1857-79, to Isabella Blackwood.
MS 30721. "Doing evil that good may come", seven chapters of
the draft of a novel; chapters X-XLIII of *The Story of
Valentine and his Brother*; MSS, 1894 and n.d., of articles
"Thomas Chalmers" and "An Ultra-montane Idyll" intended for
Blackwood's Magazine. (Sutton)
MS 30968, ff 51-62. Six letters, n.d. (1863, 1863, 1863,
          1866, 1876, 1876), to Mrs Blackwood.
          ff 63-72a. Letters and a Christmas card, 1884,
          1885, 1885, 1886, 1886, 1887, to Bessie (Black-
          wood).
          ff 73-4. Letter, 1890, to the Blackwoods.
          ff 75-80, 82-3. Four letters, 1897, by Janet Mary
          (Denny) Oliphant, about MOWO's last hours.
          f 81. Annotated title page of *William Blackwood
          and his Sons* (*Annals of a Publishing House*).
          ff 84-7. Telegrams about MOWO's death.
          f 88. Solicitor's letter about MOWO's will.
          ff 89-97. Letters, n.d. from MOWO to Bessie
          (Blackwood) and/or Emma (Blackwood).
          ff 98-103. Three letters, n.d. (one 1868), from
          MOWO to Mr (John or William) Blackwood.
          f 104. Envelope previously containing the letters
          to Mrs Blackwood, "returned from Mrs Coghill, Feb
          1st 1899".
MS 30973. Revised MS of *Annals of a Publishing House.*

C Recent acquisitions donated by the heirs of MOWO

MS 23193. Letters, 1852-78 and n.d., to MOWO from John and
William Blackwood.
MS 23194. Correspondence, 1862-92 and n.d., with various
people, including some of her relations; letter from Jane
Welsh Carlyle, ff. 131-33, and two letters, 1876, from A.W.
Kinglake, ff. 178-81; receipted bill, 1890, of MOWO for an
overseas tour with Thomas Cook Ltd.
MS 23195. Correspondence, 1870-90 and n.d., with her sons
Cyril Francis (Tiddy) and Francis Romano (Cecco).
MS 23196. Letters, 1878-97 and n.d., to her nieces Madge,
later Mrs William R.F. Valentine, and Janet Mary (Denny)
Oliphant.
MS 23197. Letters, 1889-93, of her nieces.
MS 23198. Letters, 1894-7 and n.d., of her nieces.
MS 23199. Letters, 1878-90, of Madge to Denny.
MS 23200. Letters, 1891-3, of Madge to Denny.
MS 23201. Letters, 1894, of Madge to Denny.
MS 23202. Letters, 1895-7 and n.d., of Madge to Denny.
MS 23203. Letters to Madge and Denny from various correspon-
dents.
MS 23204. Miscellaneous letters and papers, 1822-69, 1893
and n.d., to Francis Wilson Oliphant, and of and concerning
various members of MOWO's family.
MS 23205. MSS of *A Child's History of Scotland*, chs 9-22;
and of part of "The Life and Death of Jeanne d'Arc the Maid
of France" (*Jeanne d'Arc Her Life and Death*, 1896).

MSS 23206-7. MSS of Francis Romano Oliphant.
MS 23208. Corrected typescript of a tale by F.R. Oliphant.
MS 23209. Letters, ?1878-1897 and n.d., to her sons, her nephew Frank Wilson, and her nieces, to William Blackwood, Francis W. Cornish, Anne Lady Ritchie and R.H. Story and others.
MS 23210. Letters, 1848-97 and n.d., from various correspondents, including members of MOWO's family.
MS 23211. Miscellaneous correspondence and papers, 1754-1921 and n.d.: letters of various friends and contemporaries of MOWO; letters to Janet M. Oliphant; memorandum of agreement with Henry Colburn 1849; death certificate of MOWO; photographs and other depictions of MOWO and her family; extracts in Janet M. Oliphant's hand of MOWO's *Autobiography*; press-cuttings containing reviews of MOWO's books and obituary notices; MS of James M. Barrie's preface to *A Widow's Tale and other Stories* (1898); papers of Francis Wilson Oliphant; sketches by Francis Tarver; papers concerning Thomas Oliphant, wright, Anstruther (1754, 1762, n.d.); miscellaneous papers, including, ff 153-6, a poem "Valedictory Address to the Very Revd the Dean of Windsor".
MS 23212. Bank pass-book of MOWO with Messrs Cocks, Biddulph and Co., London, 1877-9.
MS 23213. Diary of MOWO, 1883.
MS 23214. Diary of MOWO, 1887.
MS 23215. Diary of MOWO, 1888.
MS 23216. Diary of MOWO, 1896.
MS 23217. MS of *Jerusalem, Its History and Hope*.
MSS 23218-19. MS of the *Autobiography*, along with additions on separate sheets, and press cuttings.

D Other recent acquisitions, uncatalogued

Acc 5772. Letter, n.d. (1870), to "Little Nelly" (Miss Clifford, MOWO's neighbour at Windsor).
Acc 7384. MS of "Recent Books - French and English" (item 485), and part of corrected proofs of "The Looker-on", dated March 1897, but not used. (It would have been no. 7. Cf items 471, 473, 477, 478, 480, 481.)
Acc 7385. MS of "The Looker-on", as in Acc 7384.
Acc 7828. Letter, n.d. (1885 or 1886), to Mr (Andrew) Lang.
Acc 8201. Three letters: n.d. (1860?), to Geraldine Jewsbury; n.d. (c. 1893), to a woman unknown; n.d. (c. 1895?) to Mr Housemann.
Acc 8807. Three letters, n.d. (1877, 1877, 187-), to Mr Isbister, publisher of *Good Words*.
Acc 9047. Letter, n.d. (1889?, 1892/3?), to man unnamed.
Acc 9357. Five letters, n.d. (1884, 1884, 1886, 1890, 1877/78), to Walter Besant.
Acc 9811. Four letters: n.d. (1879-1880s), to Sister (?) Frances; n.d., (1876?, 1877?), to a "Mrs Oliphant" (of St. Andrews?); n.d. (1852/3/4?), to Mrs Johnstone; n.d. (1879), to Mrs Price.
Acc 9856 no 1. Letter from Margaret Wilson (MOWO before her marriage) to D.M. Moir. (Sutton)
Acc 10329. Letter, n.d. (before 1879?), to Mr (John?) Blackwood.
Acc 11119 Letter, n.d. (1867?), to Mrs Armitage

(unidentified).
And on deposit:

Dep.341/101, no 46. Letter, n.d., to unknown correspondent. (Sutton)

653 The National Library of Wales, Aberystwyth (Sutton)

Dolaucothi Correspondence, nos 4727-14515, letters by Geraldine Jewsbury. Includes one, 1879, probably to MOWO.

654 Reading University Library

Longman Archive II, 72/235. Letter, n.d. (1895?) to Mr (James) Payn.

655 Royal Institution of Cornwall, Truro (Sutton)

Courtney Library. Enys Collection 1040. Letter, 1890, to [?John Addington] Symonds.

656 Scottish Record Office, Edinburgh (Sutton)

GD205/Box 46/Portfolio 17. Includes one letter, 1883, to Mr Skelton.
RH4/29. Two letters, n.d., to Mr Dean. Microfilm copies.

657 Shakespeare Centre Record Office, Stratford-upon-Avon

DR495 (Autograph book). Includes one letter, n.d.[between 1866 and 1872], to Mr Hale [Rev. Edward Hale of Eton College].

658 Torquay Museum, Devonshire (Sutton)

HP.N-O. Letter, n.d., to Mr Brookfield.

659 Trinity College Library, Cambridge

Cullum P148[1]. Letter, n.d. [1884], to Mrs Bronson. Houghton 18[221-224]. Four letters, n.d. [1879], to Lord Houghton, with a printed article on Thomas Carlyle. Also, 18[225], a letter from Lord Salisbury to Lord Houghton referring to MOWO's son Cyril.

660 City of Westminster Archives Centre, London

Included in the Barkly Papers. Acc. 618/138. Letter, n.d., to Mr [Robert] Harrison at the London Library.

United States of America

(Information from the librarians of the respective libraries.)

661 Henry E. Huntington Library, San Marino, California

CB 647-648. Two letters, n.d. (c. 1880 - c. 1890), to Frances Power Cobbe.

HM 1839. Letter, n.d. (c. 1890), to unnamed correspondent.
HM 6255. MS, n.d., of "Queen Victoria; a character sketch",
6 pp. Not in MOWO's handwriting. The date 1911 appears,
the date when the text was bound. (Evidently unrelated to
Queen Victoria of 1880, items 97 and 98. Perhaps an
unpublished article; or a contribution to an as yet
unidentified American periodical.)
HM 15357. Letters to MOWO, n.d. (c. 1886), from Lady Anne
Isabella (Thackeray) Ritchie.
HM 35050. Letter, n.d., to Lady Frances (Campbell) Balfour.
HM 35873. Letter, n.d., to Gladys Mulock Holman Hunt.
HM 44073. MS of "An Anxious Moment", with autograph
corrections, 11 pp. (This is the story included in the *New
Amphion* volume in 1886, item 694 in VFRG XI, 1986.)
PIGOTT COLLECTION, Box 2. Includes seven letters by MOWO,
n.d.[1891 etc], to Edward Smyth Pigott.

662 **Houghton Library, Harvard University, Cambridge, Mass.**

Autograph File. Includes letter, n.d.(1880s?), to [Thomas
Bailey] Aldrich, and letter, n.d., to [Charlotte Mary]
Yonge.
bMS Am 1429 (3337-3353). Seventeen letters, n.d.[1884-7], to
Thomas Bailey Aldrich.
bMS Am 1745 (169). Letter, 1896, to Sarah Orne Jewett.
bMS Am 2010 (107). Letter, n.d., to unknown correspondent.
bMS Am 2016 (24). Letter, n.d., to James Thomas Fields.
MS Eng 1186. MS of *A Rose in June*, 110 pp.

663 **University of Iowa Libraries, Iowa City**

In Special Collections.
MsL 046st. Letter, n.d. (after 1865), to Mr (Alexander?)
Strahan. (The original of the photocopy included in RP1314
at the British Library.)
MsL 046 15 Feb. Letter, n.d., to unknown correspondent.
MsL 046 6 July. Letter, n.d., to unknown correspondent.
MsL 046 b. Eighteen letters, n.d. (1852-60), to Francis
Bennoch. (The originals of the photocopies included in
RP1314 at the British Library.)
MsL H174 AC. Includes one letter, n.d., from Mrs S.C. Hall
to Mrs Oliphant.

664 **Princeton University Library, Princeton, NJ**

Donald and Robert M. Dodge Collection of Mary Mapes Dodge
(C0113), Box 2, Folder 50. Two letters, n.d.(1875?.1876?),
by MOWO to Mary Mapes Dodge. (One letter dated 1884 in Jay,
Oliphant (see Introduction, n. 3), 320, n. 135.)
General Manuscripts [Misc.] (C0140), Box OA-OL, Folder: Oli-
phant, Mrs (Margaret), 1828-1897, Subfolder 2. One letter,
n.d., by MOWO to Mrs Fitzgerald.
General Manuscripts [Misc.] (C0140), Box OA-OM, Folder: Oli-
phant, Mrs (Margaret), 1828-1897, Subfolder 1. One letter,
1888, by MOWO to unknown correspondent.
General Manuscripts [Misc.] (C0140), Box PAU-PAZ, Folder:
Payn, James, 1830-1898, Subfolder 3. One letter, n.d., by

MOWO to James Payn.
Robert H. Taylor Library, Robert H. Taylor Collection
(RTCO1), Box: File Cabinet, Folder: Procter, Anne Benson
Skepper. One letter, n.d., about MOWO by Anne Procter to "Mr
Archdale".
Robert H. Taylor Library, Robert H. Taylor Collection
(RTCO1), Box: Reade Letterbook, Folder: Leaves 39, 74, 78.
Three letters, n.d., by MOWO to Charles Reade.
Robert H. Taylor Library, Robert H. Taylor Collection
(RTCO1), Box: Trollope, Anthony: LETTERS TO. Three letters,
n.d., one a fragment, by MOWO to Rose Trollope.
ST. NICHOLAS Correspondence of Mary Mapes Dodge (C0029),
Folder 36. One letter, n.d.(1875?, 1876?), by MOWO to Mary
Mapes Dodge.
William Isbister Collection (C0065), Box 3: O - S, Folder O.
Fifty letters, [1879] - n.d., by MOWO to William Isbister.
Sir John Maxwell Papers (C0583), Series IV, Additional
Papers, Box 31, Folder 34. One letter, n.d., by MOWO to "Mr
Collins" (Wilkie Collins? Rev. W. Lucas Collins?).
Archives of Charles Scribner's Sons (C0101), Series: Author
Files I, Box 108, Folder O Misc. Five letters, 1873, by MOWO
to the firm of Charles Scribner's Sons.
Also a photograph of MOWO, n.d., included in General Manu-
scripts [Bound] (C0199), Series H, Box: Hutton, Laurence,
1843-1904, Folder: Collection of Photograph Albums, Vol 6.

APPENDIX

Foreign Classics for English Readers

This is a list of the eighteen volumes in the series, *Foreign Classics for English Readers*, edited by Mrs Oliphant, published by Blackwood. It is worth listing these books in an appendix, since Mrs Oliphant may no doubt have had some influence upon the books, especially the one by her son Cyril Francis Oliphant, which she personally revised. The names of authors are not taken from title pages, but from biographical sources and the British Library catalogues.

Dante, by MOWO, 1877. (See above, items 84-9.)
Voltaire, by General Sir Edward Bruce Hamley, 1877.
Pascal, by Principal John Tulloch, 1878.
Petrarch, by Henry Reeve, 1878.
Goethe, by Abraham Hayward, 1878.
Molière, by MOWO and Francis Tarver, 1879. (See above, items 92-6.)
Montaigne, by W. Lucas Collins, 1879.
Rabelais, by Walter Besant, 1879.
Calderon, by Elizabeth Julia Hasell, 1879
Saint Simon, by Clifton Wilbraham Collins, 1880.
Cervantes, by MOWO, 1880. (See above, items 106-9.)
Corneille and Racine, by Henry Merivale Trollope, 1881.
Madame de Sevigné, by Anne Thackeray, 1881.
La Fontaine and other French Fabulists, by W. Lucas Collins, 1882.
Schiller, by James Sime, 1882.
Tasso, by Elizabeth Julia Hasell, 1882.
Rousseau, by Henry Grey Graham, 1882.
Alfred de Musset, by Cyril Francis Oliphant, 1890.

******

In 1890 a book on Leopardi by MOWO was announced as "In the press". It did not appear.

Addenda and Corrigenda

ADDENDA 3 TO MARGARET OLIPHANT'S FICTION

The item numbers in this section refer, not to the present volume, but to the earlier bibliography of Margaret Oliphant's fiction, Victorian Fiction Research Guide XI, 1986. Listed are all additions since Addenda 2 (1990) to VFRG XI, including new publications.

I Novels

The House on the Moor

98   [1912 ed.] The publisher is Hurst and Blackett, not Chapman and Hall.

Innocent

239a   "New and cheaper edition". 1 vol. Sampson Low, 1888.

In Trust

365a   Serialized by the title of *Left in Trust* in *The New York Tribune*, in weekly instalments from 6 Mar., 1881 to 31 Jul., 1881, mostly "from advance sheets", always either p. 3 or p. 4. Cf item 366.

II Stories of the Seen and Unseen

"The Secret Chamber"

611a   Reprinted in *The Lifted Veil, the Book of Fantastic Literature by Women, 1800 - World War II*, ed. A. Susan Williams (London: Xanadu Publications Ltd., 1992), 226-54.

A Beleaguered City

621   [1910 ed.] Title simply *A Beleaguered City*, omitting the elaboration of the earlier editions.

III Shorter Fiction, Collected and Uncollected

664a   "A Winter Journey", published in *Blackwood's Magazine* 85, Apr. 1859, 429-49.
A fictionalised travelogue.
(Item 664a, Addenda 2, "Three Days in the Highlands", should be renumbered 664b.)

669a   "A Hidden Treasure", published in *The Argosy* 1 (January, 1866), 149-55.

"That Little Cutty"

691a   Reprinted from Home in *The New York Tribune*, 28 Aug., 1881, p. 3.

**

691b   "The Covenanter's Daughter", serialized in *The Youth's Companion* 57 (Boston, Mass), in eight weekly instalments, 6 Mar 1884 to 24 Apr 1884, 85-6, 97-8, 105-6, 117-18, 129-30, 141-2, 153-4, 165-6.
A fictionalised version of the story of the Scottish heroine Grizel Hume.

691c   "Elinor", serialized in *Sunday Talk* n.s. 1 (Glasgow), in seven instalments, Jun. to Dec. 1884, 67-71, 99-103, 131-35, 164-67, 195-99, 227-31, 263-66.

"Queen Eleanor and Fair Rosamond"

693a   French translation, serialized in *Le Correspondant* (Paris) 161-2 (n.s. 125-6), 25 Dec. 1890, 1078-93, and 10 Jan. 1891, 113-40. ("La Villa des Ormes", translated by O. Bignon; partially an adaptation.)

"A Chance Encounter"

701a   Reprinted in *Harper's Bazaar* (NY), 15 Dec., 1891, 974-5. (Item 701a in VFRG XI should be renumbered 701b.)

704a   ## "A Story of a Wedding Tour"

Included in *Nineteenth-century Stories by Women, An Anthology*, ed. Glennis Stephenson (Peterborough, Ontario: Broadview Literary Texts, 1993), 402-27, with portrait, notes, endnote and bibliography.

V Autobiography and Letters

727a   American ed. NY: International Association of Newspapers and Authors, 1901. (Information from D.J. Trela.)

730   Edition of Autobiography direct from manuscript. *The Autobiography of Mrs Oliphant*, edited with Introduction and Notes, by Elisabeth Jay. Oxford: OUP, 1990 (Nov.).